Everyone Loves Jenny Colgan

She is very, very funny."
—*Express*

"A delicious comedy."
—*Red*

"Fast-paced, funny, poignant and well-observed."
—*Daily Mail*

"Had us eating up every page."
—*Cosmopolitan*

"A smart, funny story laced with irresistible charm."
—*Closer*

"Chick-lit with an ethical kick."
—*Mirror*

"A quirky tale of love, work and the meaning of life."
—*Company*

THE GOOD,
THE BAD,
AND THE
DUMPED

Also by Jenny Colgan

THE GOOD,
THE BAD,
AND THE
DUMPED

A Novel

Jenny Colgan

WM

WILLIAM MORROW

An Imprint of HarperCollinsPublishers

THE GOOD, THE BAD, AND THE DUMPED. Copyright © 2010 by Jenny Colgan. All rights reserved. Printed in the United States of America. No part of this book may be used or reproduced in any manner whatsoever without written permission except in the case of brief quotations embodied in critical articles and reviews. For information, address HarperCollins Publishers, 195 Broadway, New York, NY 10007.

HarperCollins books may be purchased for educational, business, or sales promotional use. For information, please email the Special Markets Department at SPsales@harpercollins.com.

Originally published as *The Good, the Bad, and the Dumped* in the United Kingdom in 2010 by Sphere.

FIRST U.S. EDITION

Designed by Diahann Sturge

Library of Congress Cataloging-in-Publication Data has been applied for.

ISBN 978-0-06-286960-9

21 22 23 24 25   LSC   10 9 8 7 6 5 4 3 2 1

To my darling, darling girl. Thank you so much for coming; we're so glad you could make it.

Acknowledgments

Special thanks on this to my editor Jo Dickinson. I love working with you. Thanks and lots of love. Huge thanks also to Rebecca Saunders. Also Ali Gunn, agent provocateur; Emma Stonex for the copy-edit, Manpreet Grewal, Rose Tremlett, Hannah Torjussen and Tamsin Kitson; David Shelley, Ursula Mackenzie, Frances Doyle and all the brilliant team at Little, Brown.

Thanks also to my friends, even though we are usually somewhere else; to the board and as always, to my best Mr. B and the three wee Bs.

THE GOOD,
THE BAD,
AND THE
DUMPED

Chapter One

Posy is wishing she'd checked the weather forecast,
    even if they are a bit useless.
Comment, Matt: There's no such thing as bad weather,
    just bad clothing.
Comment, Posy: Well, you would know.

Posy Fairweather wasn't quite sure why she was at the top of a mountain.

Mountains weren't exactly her thing—they hadn't been here in ages—even though it was very beautiful up here, she supposed, the clouds shifting, sending patterns onto the fields and sheep. They really hadn't done anything like this for yonks. Probably because she moaned too much about the weather. She turned to look at Matt in the clear light. He looked slightly effortful, his face pinker than the walk warranted.

Suddenly she had a flash of clairvoyance, and knew exactly what he was about to do. And her stomach lurched.

"What a view," he said, looking nervous. "Are we right at the top?"

"Not yet," she said, smiling, feeling her throat constrict as she said it. She would just make sure. "Is it *really* important that we make it all the way to the top?"

"Uh." Matt looked conflicted. Obviously it didn't, not really, if they were just looking for somewhere to have a picnic. But Posy suspected that, today, the small things like whether they were really at the top might actually matter.

"Come on, let's just go," she said, and he scrambled up the scree behind her gratefully.

The view, from beside the little pile of rocks, wasn't much different, although with no more rock above them and nothing left to climb, she felt closer to the clouds than ever. The sky was a freshly washed blue. Posy watched as Matt tried to look innocent, although he was clearly waiting for another pair of walkers, in blue cagoules, to move away from the summit. Her heart pounded.

Finally they did and, jiggling slightly, he turned to face her. The dark bristle on his unshaven face suited him, she thought, made his jawline taut and his cheekbones more evident. He grinned at her, more awkwardly than he had since the first moment they'd met.

"Posy," he said, swallowing.

And Posy found herself thinking, stupidly: I wonder how your face should look when you're being proposed to. Happy? Obviously. Surprised? Sexily surprised? How would that work? Maybe pretend you're getting an Oscar. No, hang on, don't pretend it's *anything*, this is one of the most amazing experiences of your life that you're meant to remember forever! But then, the last thing you want to think of is whether or not you were making a pig's face. Or even thinking about your face at all, instead of love, and the future, and the wonderfulness of it all! Why didn't she put more lipstick on? What if he wasn't about to propose and she'd got it all wrong? Maybe he was going to chuck her. But on top of a mountain? Who would do that? Maybe he was going to chuck her *off* the mountain?

"Uh, Posy, are you all right? You look like you're about to be sick."

Posy managed to hold it together. Vomiting was definitely *not* the look she was after. No. There was a long moment of silence, and in the distance a bird circled the sun. Posy turned to look at it, giving what she felt was a nice polite long stare. And sure enough, when she turned round again, Matt was very awkwardly perched on one knee. Suddenly, she didn't have to worry about her face, because she could feel her heart leap straight into her mouth, and an uncontrollable grin start to stretch into her cheeks.

"Matthew Farmer!" she said, in a surprised tone.

Matt returned the grin, somewhat lopsidedly.

"You should know," he said. "This is profoundly uncomfortable. I have pebbles sticking into me and, I think, some poo."

"I shall remember these words until my dying day," said Posy. Matt went pink.

"Sorry," he said. "Hang on. I meant to be . . . Right. Hang on. I have it."

Posy nodded expectantly.

Matt held up a blue box and popped it open. The noon-time sun caught the glint of the diamond inside, and it winked across the hilltops like a signal beam.

"Posy. *If it's not love . . .*" He took a deep breath.

Posy caught her breath. Then, just to be equal, she knelt down too, in the sheep poo and small rocks on the ground. He proffered her the box.

"Do you mean it?"

"More than anything, Posy. More than anything."

They stared into each other's eyes; Matt's blue and clear, Posy's so dark they were almost black, with a thick fringe of lash.

From nowhere, she felt a little stab of something that felt suspiciously like panic. Matt and her . . . they were so different. Such an unlikely match, everyone said.

But on the other hand, they were here. Now. After everything that had happened. After every morning she'd woken up feeling she could never be happy again . . . here, finally, was the moment she'd dreamed of for such a long time. Not always with the same man, it had to be said. But still.

She burst out, "Oh yes! Ooh yes! I love you!"

Matt's face split into a grin.

"But not *too* much of The Smiths at the wedding, all right?"

They both jumped up and dusted themselves down, so they could embrace more easily.

"Some."

"No!"

"I'm going to invite Morrissey."

"You are not. He'll bring the mood down."

They kissed again, laughing. Posy felt light-headed and giddy, as if she were outside her own body, watching herself.

"Can you get a signal up here? Can we phone everyone?"

"Put the ring on first."

"Ooh, yes." Posy extended her finger. "Did you get it fitted?"

"No," admitted Matt. "I just said that my girlfriend has really gigantic shovel-like man hands."

"You *didnt*?" said Posy, whose large hands and feet were the bane of her life.

"I did too," said Matt, as the ring slid perfectly onto the fourth finger of her left hand. "They thought I was buying it for a chap. The jeweler kept trying to intimate that it was quite all right, gay weddings were legal and everything. It was really embarrassing."

He looked at her. "Do you like it?"

It was a perfect solitaire, with two smaller cut diamonds on either side, on a platinum band.

"I love it," said Posy, truthfully.

"You didn't want to shop for it?"

"Matt. Ssh." She looked at him. "You chose it. Which means it's exactly right. Now can we call everyone?"

"*Not* your sister. You'll be on for two hours and I want lunch and champagne and lots of nice things!"

"*Can't* promise," said Posy. Then she paused. "Did you say . . . champagne?"

Posy is !!!!!!!!!
Comment: Like.
Matt Farmer likes this.

So Posy had to wait till they'd got down the mountain and celebrated rather loudly in a pub (she'd thought people would have been more excited, but it turned out that loads of couples got engaged on the peak every year, they even kept a special bottle of champagne in the fridge just for the purpose). But this didn't dent her amazing feeling—that she had caught a cloud from the mountaintop and surfed it down.

Later, post an afternoon sojourn at their bed-and-breakfast (Posy felt obscurely weird having sex in a B&B, after all it was someone else's house and someone else's bed. And in the afternoon, too! Their landlady had been full of congratulatory winks, but oddly that didn't seem to make things any easier):

"Ooh, marital relations," Matt said. "I could get used to this."

"Well, you're going to have to," said Posy, then wondered if reminding Matt he was only going to get to sleep with one woman for the rest of his life wasn't a bit mean.

"Good," said Matt, smiling at her, and she reached up to meet him. "I'm very, very happy. I was bricking it a bit though."

"Why?" said Posy, genuinely surprised. "Didn't you think I would say yes?"

Matt shrugged. "Well, I don't know, do I? Women, you're funny things."

Posy bit her lip. It wasn't like he didn't know she had a past.

"But you know I love you, don't you?"

"Yeah, course I do," said Matt.

"Well then, why were you nervous?"

"No reason. I just . . . you know, sometimes you're a bit private . . ."

Posy sat up and put her arms around her legs. "You say that like it's a bad thing."

"It's not a bad thing. But, you know. Sometimes I think there's a part of you locked away that I can't get to—I don't mind so much. A woman should be a bit of a mystery. But it makes you . . . unpredictable."

"I'm the least mysterious person ever! You're the one that spends six hours boiling up their Oyster card to get the magnetic bit out and stick it to a wand so you can magically open the tube barriers. *That* is mysterious."

"You're right," said Matt. "Forget I said it. Shall we go out for a super slap-up engagement feast? And tell the waiters and everything? We must be able to get freebies *somewhere*—what's the point in having a big life event if people don't buy you drinks?"

Chapter Two

Posy is cheerfully shagged out.
Comment, Fleur: XXX hoho missus.

When they got home on Sunday, it was inevitable that Posy would head straight to Fleur's, and Matt didn't try to prevent it.

They were lying on Fleur's sofa-cum-bed-cum-dinner table. Fleur liked to think that her flat was Bohemian—i.e.. it had lots of things hanging from it—but really it was just a very small tip with some windchimes in it. Being a freelance herbal therapist (Fleur didn't like to pin herself down to what types of therapy she actually liked to do) didn't pay that well. Fleur said the satisfaction of helping people was obvious enough, although Posy noticed that Fleur did sigh a little and talk about wills when in the houses of her more elderly clients.

Still, Fleur had got the looks in the family—long wavy curls (Posy sometimes wondered if people with long Bohemian curls got into Bohemian jobs because of their hair or if the hair came later), and a beautiful bee-stung cupid's bow of a mouth, which made men go all funny and fail to listen to what

8

she was saying. Which, when she went through her period of wasp venom healing, was probably just as well.

Posy was pretty-ish in a slightly determined way, with dark hair and shrewd, dark eyes. It wasn't, after all, that bad to be the "smart" one, but just occasionally she'd like to borrow Fleur's head—just to walk into a party, for example, or a room where she didn't know anyone.

"So he said I was mysterious," Posy was saying, slurping the last of her Frappuccino.

"You? Mysterious? Does he or does he not remember how many times you've sent him out to buy your Tampax because you've forgotten it?"

"Yeah, I know, but . . . well . . ."

"I think he's just pretending to himself that that's the case, so that he doesn't think he's marrying someone who's really straight up and not that interesting and works in insurance."

"In insurance *marketing*," said Posy, although she didn't know why she still bothered to attempt to convince her sister that that was an interesting take on insurance. Or herself. "Do you really think?"

Fleur ignored this. "How was Mum?" she said. She shook her Frappuccino. "I wonder if you could read the ice cubes in these? Like, reading tea leaves but for today?"

"Might be money in it," said Posy.

"I'm not interested in money," said Fleur. "I'm interested in divination and helping people. If they want to recompense me royally for that, who am I to dissuade them?"

"And until then, you'll just keep borrowing from your sister," said Posy.

Fleur sniffed grandly, as if this was too trivial to bother with.

"Have you told Mum yet?"

Posy sighed. "What do you think?"

Posy and Fleur's mother was a psychotherapist. She was constantly exhorting them to tell her about their childhood. Because of her extreme nosiness and occasional experimental techniques (such as starting each day when they were younger with dream dissection, as a result of which Posy and Fleur pretended to dream about nice friendly butterflies and rainbows for about four years apiece), the girls elected to tell her as little as possible about their lives.

Posy screwed up her eyes and pretended to take off imaginary glasses.

"It seems to me that the loss of a father figure at a young age has led to trust issues with the masculine species, compounded by a particularly difficult break-up in the subject's late twenties, thus leading me to conclude that . . ."

Fleur continued, ". . . her desperate hunt for commitment from any source has led her to accept a life of rape-filled slavery from a human male masquerading as a P.E. teacher."

"OK, that's enough," said Posy, throwing a cushion at her head. "And he's a *personal trainer.*"

"These feelings of inadequacy and social pressure as she approaches her middle thirties . . ."

Posy kicked her firmly on the leg. The girls had mostly grown out of their belief, as know-it-all teenagers, that their mother's clients, some of whom came for years to the rambling clinic at the top of the house, were just losers, and their mother should inform them of this fact. But a certain distrust of their mother, who was frequently so deep in her clients' problems she would forget to put supper on the table, who believed doing housework was a sign of slavery and/or anxiety, and who clearly loved them but only in quite an abstract fashion, ran deep.

"Want to know what I really love about Matt?" she asked her sister suddenly.

"I don't know ... it's that you want to be taken care of combined with a horror of your biological clock running out? A horror of getting your heart broken again? A fear of being alone at thirty-two and possessing a deeply conventional nature?"

"He is *uncomplicated*. Jeez. I'm off to phone Leah. You're turning into Mum, by the way. The imitation is absolutely spot-on."

Fifteen minutes after the phone call, Leah turned up on the doorstep bearing a bottle of gift-wrapped champagne and four editions of bridal magazines.

"EEEEK!" she shrieked, the second Posy opened the door.

"*That's* more like it," said Posy, gratefully accepting her best friend's hug.

"EEEEK!" said Leah again. "You're getting married!"

"I know!"

"Did you buy all those magazines?" said Fleur. "Wow, that was quick."

"Uh, no, I had them lying around," said Leah, trying to look nonchalant at this fact. Fleur rolled her eyes.

"Fleur, you are not too old for me to send you out of the room," said Posy.

"This is *my* flat!" said Fleur, looking stung. She had always been the younger sister when Posy and Leah were dressing up and going out, and had never quite got over her feelings of resentment.

"Let me see, let me see!" clamored Leah, going for Posy's hand.

"Oh," she said.

"What do you mean, 'Oh'? I love it," said Posy.

"I know, I just wondered if he'd let you choose it." She turned to Fleur. "I'm going to have emerald-cut rose diamonds on a rose-gold band."

Fleur heaved a sigh. "*I'm going to have blah blah blah*, waste of head space. I'm going to make tea. Do you want some?"

"Is it still that stuff that tastes of toe jam?" said Posy.

"I roll my own tea. What's wrong with that?"

"No, thank you," said Leah and Posy simultaneously.

"Well, *I* love it," said Posy determinedly, gazing at her ring.

"Posy," said Fleur maddeningly from the corner of the room, kettle in hand. "How does Leah know what kind of ring she wants when she hasn't got a boyfriend?"

"Shut up, Fleur," Posy said.

Leah stretched out. "Are you the happiest girl in the world?"

Posy smiled. "I suppose."

"What do you mean, *you suppose*? Aren't you delirious? Don't you keep bursting into song, like Amy Adams?"

"Yeah," said Fleur from her corner. "'The Drugs Don't Work.'"

"SHUT UP, FLEUR."

"No, I'm really chuffed, I really am," Posy said. "Honestly. It just took me a bit by surprise, that's all."

"I really thought Robert was going to propose," said Leah. "I walked really slowly past jewelry shops and everything."

"You went out with Robert for *two weeks*," Posy said, trying to keep the surprise out of her voice. She knew Leah was pretty keen on finding a man, but she'd never suspected the depths of it.

"Yes, but I just thought he might be The One. I thought we might get caught up in a whirlwind and he might fly me to Vegas and just whisk me off. It could happen."

"It could happen," Posy agreed. "To *crazy* people. You didn't mention this to him?"

"No!" exclaimed Leah. "Well. Maybe I just said it one night *for a joke*."

"We're over thirty! How could that be a joke?" Something dawned on her. "I always wondered why you two broke up so quickly."

"Well, he wasn't ready for a commitment," said Leah sulkily.

"After eight days." Posy shook her head. "Fleur, stop boiling that kettle. Instead, I think we need booze."

"Anyway," said Leah, "I've highlighted some really lovely venues in here but there's a few I wouldn't want you to use because I'd like them."

"Lots of booze," Posy said.

Several hours later they were all lying on the floor of the bedsit. *Dirty Dancing* was playing on the DVD. Posy didn't think it was the first time it had been on. Leah had a pair of black tights tied round her arm in memoriam.

"*You*," Leah was saying loudly, "are the luckiest girl in the *world*."

Posy stared at the cracks in the ceiling. Was that one spider's web or two?

"Course I'm not," she said. "People get engaged every day."

That wasn't the right answer. There was a loud sniff. Posy felt terrible.

"Come on, Leah, that's not what I mean."

But it was too late. She'd started sobbing.

"What is it?"

"Everyone's going to get married! Except me! And I'll be left behind and then I'll have to have a donor baby only it will turn out to be sperm donated by a prisoner and it will grow up and hate me and turn evil and do mass murder and I'll be in all the papers."

Posy propped herself up on one arm.

"You've really thought this through, haven't you?"

"I've kind of been married," said Fleur.

"You have not!"

"I have! I got married to that drummer I met at Glastonbury. A tree married us. In a field. It was gorgeous."

"I am not lending you the money to go to Glastonbury any more."

"I wonder where he is," mused Fleur. "I think he wanted us to have a threesome with that tree."

"See! What's wrong with me?" sniffed Leah.

Posy sat up. "Nothing is wrong with you."

Posy meant this sincerely. Leah had been her best friend since she'd been cutting out wedding gown dress-up doll patterns in Miss Wheeler's Year Four. "Look at you! You're supercool. You have a great flat and a really great job."

Leah did PR for a fashion company. Not much money in it, but she always got to go to cool things *and* she got free clothes. Frankly, sometimes Posy thought the clothes were a bit odd—today she was wearing gigantic parachute pants and a silver Star Trek T-shirt—but she did love it.

"So it's just going to take you a bit longer."

Leah rested her chin on one hand.

"It's not fair. You work for the most boring company on earth and all you do is meet hot men in suits and ties all day long and get to slip off and have sex in the toilets with them."

"That was *one* time Matt came over and—"

"Meanwhile I, who have a fabulous job lots of people would kill for, spend all day with really *really* thin women deliberately not eating lunch, and gay men complaining about how fat everyone is these days. Next to nine-foot-tall sixteen-year-old Croatian girls. It's *totally* not fair. And I haven't got long!"

Fleur looked up to where she was mimicking Baby's dance moves on the screen, but using her fingers. "What about men who come up to you on the street and in bars and give you flowers and stuff?"

Posy and Leah both rolled their eyes at her.

"We don't look that available," Posy said.

"Or that *hot*," said Fleur quietly.

"Well, whatever," said Leah. "It's still not fair. Especially when you're not really cut out for marriage."

"What?" Posy said. Suddenly she didn't feel quite so drunk.

"Well, you know. To Matt. You're just not that fussed."

"That's not true!" Posy said. "I'm . . . *quite* fussed."

"Oh, I understand. After everything that happened before with—"

"Don't say his name," said Fleur.

Leah rolled her eyes. "OK. Lord Voldemort."

Posy tutted. "You can say his name."

"I can," said Leah. "Can you?"

Posy could see what they were driving at. She could. One moment she was whirling in shock, recovering from the love of her life, her heart ripped out, stamped on, rolled in the dust and ground into the floor. The next she was dating big bluff handsome Matt, straightforward, plain speaking, and not particularly exceptional in any way. She understood that it looked weird to them. She did. But she just didn't . . . she didn't feel like talking about it. It was three years ago, it was all in the past. She hardly gave . . . *him* . . . she hardly gave him a second thought these days. Hardly at all.

Leah was still talking.

"And of course," she was saying, "with your dad and everything."

"Bollocks. It's nothing to do with my dad." Posy sat up. "Hang on. How come we're meant to be celebrating my engagement and we're all lying on the floor nearly in tears?"

"I'm fine," said Fleur. "Except that Leah's right about everything."

"Shut up!"

Chapter Three

Posy is not opening her eyes just yet.

"How was it?" said Matt. He'd brought bagels in bed and a very large coffee to soothe Posy's aching head.

"Yeah, great," said Posy crossly.

"Really?"

"No, it was terrible. I need to change my best friend and my sister. But apart from that, fine."

Matt sat on the edge of the bed. They were kind of over the stage now of Posy wanting to put lipstick on before he saw her, but she kept her post-wine breath away from him in any case.

"Why?" he said. "Aren't they happy for you?"

"Yes, of course they are," Posy said reassuringly. "They're wildly jealous."

"Even Fleur?"

"Apart from Fleur."

"So, just the scary one."

"Leah isn't scary! She's just fashionable."

"She looks like an emaciated crow."

"That was just her emaciated crow period. Now she's much more . . ."

"Japanese vampire."

"She just wants to meet a nice guy and settle down."

"Then she should stop dressing like she's in the mood to suck blood. It's not rocket science. You're going to be late for work."

"I don't want to go to work. Can't I stop working now and just stay at home and float about in a floral pinny and you can support us both?"

For a second Posy saw a momentary stab of panic cross his face.

"I'm kidding. Kidding!"

"Oh, OK. Yeah, I knew that."

"So what are you up to today?"

"I was going to think about talking to my backer."

Matt looked a little awkward. He'd been thinking about setting up his own practice for a while—he had plenty of clients—but was nervous about leaving his imposing boss, and a little unsure as to whether he wanted to be self-employed. Posy thought he'd be absolutely fantastic: he was so calm and well-organized. She couldn't understand why he didn't think that too. He had a nice down-to-earth sensibility that she thought would see him well, and was naturally cautious; he already worried about the mortgage more than they needed to.

Posy was absolutely, definitely going to stop buying coffee in a paper cup to keep her hands warm while she got to her office opposite Victoria Station. It was ridiculously expensive, she told herself, they had a perfectly good coffee maker at home from which she could easily fill up a flask, and it was just so self-indulgent, like, "I am so special and precious I must have an overpriced cup of froth every day to make me feel fulfilled."

But of course she still did it. Commuter's compensation.

As she left the station, head down, clutching her hands around it to keep them warm and deeply regretting her sore head and scratchy tongue, she heard a voice say her name.

"Posy?"

Posy glanced up. It could be a bit of a problem, having to cross a major London terminal twice a day. Statistically, everyone you've ever met in your life is going to pass through there sooner or later. Posy tried not to sound unsurprised when someone remarked on what an amazing coincidence it was to run into her when 300,000 people pass through every week.

Sure enough, her heart sank. It would always, always be on the days when she was feeling really cruddy and a bit grubby, when she wasn't quite sure she'd rubbed the last bits of the previous night's mascara from under her eyes. The glamorous ones. And this girl—what was her name again? Anyway, she was certainly glamorous. Posy reminded herself that brides-to-be were meant to be on diets, not chowing down gigantic full-fat lattes. Under her sleeve, Posy found her thumb rubbing up against her new, unfamiliar-feeling ring. It felt comforting, like a magical talisman. Sasha. That was it.

"Oh. Hello, Sasha," Posy said, smiling as nicely as she could. Which wasn't very, and wasn't fair under the circumstances—it wasn't Sasha's fault that she was five-foot-ten, all of it legs and lips and long glossy hair. It wasn't her fault that she was a friend of Adam, after all, and that when they broke up she had naturally taken his side. It wasn't even her fault that throughout their six-month relationship she had treated Posy as some kind of temporary distraction, unworthy of attention, because, as it turned out, that's exactly what she was.

None of this useful, mature, grown-up reflection, however, made Posy's first instinct—to shout, "Go away, ho!" and run for her life—any less strong. But she swallowed it down.

"Hello!" Sasha gushed, as if they were great friends. "How *are* you? It's been ages."

Well, yes, it had. Nine years. She looked the same as ever—no, she didn't, she looked more expensive. She worked in the City so had probably stashed away some cash in the big meltdown. Posy was surprised she'd remembered her name. Then she realized she hadn't actually said it, and probably didn't.

"I'm engaged!" Posy announced, before she could help herself. Instantly she cringed. It sounded like the most crass naff thing ever.

Sasha's eyes didn't widen. "Oh, lovely, how gorgeous. Can I see the ring?"

Posy showed her and she glanced it over quickly, as if just checking it wasn't too big or anything.

"*Lovely*. So who is he?"

"You don't know him," Posy said. "But he's great."

"Of course he is!" She patted Posy on the arm, as if she'd been defensive, which she had been. They stood there another second.

"So . . ." Posy said finally. Sasha seemed to be waiting for her to ask. "How's Adam?"

Sasha's voice took on a serious tone. "Oh, same as ever, you know Adam."

"Cars, money, booze . . ."

"Yes, well, it starts to look less appealing at his age." Sasha eyed her closely. "It's a shame he didn't end up with someone like you, you know."

"No, it's not!" Posy said scornfully. The sting of it came back to her again. Adam, his eyes slightly red-rimmed from late nights and long days staring at the bank's computers; his pure white collar skew-whiff and his expensive suit rumpled. How funny to be thinking of Adam, after a weekend when it should be all about Matt.

It's just, babe—Adam always called her babe. Sometimes Posy wondered if maybe remembering her name was too much trouble—*I just can't be tied down, you know? With everything that's going on? It's not you, babe, I'm just . . .*

Now Posy was older, she did understand what he was saying. He was too young to get tied down. Somehow Posy thought he might always be too young to get tied down; inside he would forever be a twenty-three-year-old with a Ferrari and a cool job who simply could not believe his luck.

She smiled at the memory. "He's such a doof. Say hi from me."

"Will do," said Sasha. Posy wondered if she'd ever married that gorgeous Syrian derivatives expert she used to see.

"Well, nice to talk," Posy said, and watched as Sasha moved elegantly—she always moved elegantly—toward the cab rank.

How strange, she mused, arriving at the reception of her office. Just as I get engaged, I suddenly have to think about Adam, who really hasn't crossed my mind in years. Posy remembered how glamorous and fun he'd been, with his mad car, glamorous friends, late nights, and endless yabbering about money.

And it had been fun—and money was important. But the young guys who make it and move it about . . . they seemed to be a law and a world unto themselves. One into which Posy didn't quite fit.

Deep in thought, she muttered a hello to the receptionist and clicked her ID pass through the doors to get to the lift.

"Hold it!" shouted a voice as she went to press floor nine. "Hello, Posy! You are absolutely miles away. What happened to you, dream of marshmallows and wake up eating your pillow?" Gavin smiled.

Posy liked her Australian boss. He had thinning hair, a big squishy paunch, and an unutterable disdain for insurance and practically anyone who bothered to take it out. "If it's going to hit you, it's going to hit you," he was fond of saying. "Five thousand lousy dollars aren't going to make you feel much better. And we're going to dispute the hell out of it anyway and send the investigators in. You should probably just go to Primark and get new stuff and not bother us." It was hard to know how he'd got into a service industry really. He had the delicate sensitivities of a hungry goat.

"So, what's up?"

Posy mentally shook herself, then showed him her ring. "Matt and I got engaged."

Gavin rolled his eyes. "Another one bites the dust."

"What do you mean?"

"Oh, nothing . . . marriage is great. If you like, you know. Fatness. And doing the same stuff all the time but finding new ways to bicker about it. And writing a book of resentment."

"What's a book of resentment?"

Gavin gave a twisted smile. "Oh, you'll find out." He was

going through a very nasty divorce, and it did occasionally leak out into the office.

Gavin pulled himself together as the lift pinged at their floor. "But, you know, congratulations. Statistically, you know, it's slightly better than fifty-fifty. How old are you again?"

"Thirty-two."

"Oh," he said. "Well, OK, it's about fifty-fifty. That's great!"

"That's the least convincing pronunciation of "That's great" I've ever heard," Posy said.

Fortunately at reception there were some of her friends in marketing, who all squealed in delight. They liked Matt (most people did) and liked weddings and, apart from Margie, who said it made her nails look a bit square—but that was Margie, and had been since . . . well, she wasn't thinking about him now—they liked her ring too. Margie was in her late thirties, with frizzy hair, magnificent breasts always hidden in a cardigan, no waist, and a deep-seated grudge against a world that did not have enough handsome men for dumpy women who had four cats.

Posy had been at the firm for five years. She now headed up the marketing team and although she knew it was fashionable to hate your job, she rather liked hers. She liked her officemates, and her boss. Sometimes she felt she ought to move a bit more, round out her CV, but then again, it wasn't like there was much out there, and she was respected where she was. Her mother thought she was woefully unambitious, but Posy felt safe and competent and couldn't understand her mother's disappointment.

They turned it into an excuse to go to Pizza Express for lunch to celebrate and Posy told the whole story of the proposal and everyone oohed and aahed, except Margie, who sniffed and looked bored, and all in all it felt much more satisfactory than when she'd told supposedly her two closest people in the world. She started to perk up.

It was great. It was fine. Any doubts she had . . . anything Leah had said . . . it was only pre-wedding nerves. Wasn't it? Wasn't it?

Chapter Four

"What's up with you?" said Matt as Posy turned and twisted on the bed.

They had bought the flat together in an area of south London that was profoundly tipped to be up and coming. Soon. At any point. In the next four decades or so. They were on the seventh floor of a tower block, their neighbors a mix of original residents and young people trying to buy their first home. The sitting room was tiny, their bedroom only really big enough for them and a bed and ten pairs of Matt's gigantic trainers, but it was theirs, it was affordable, and when the clouds cleared, and if you stood on tiptoe, you could see Big Ben.

"Nothing," Posy said, taking the opportunity of knowing Matt was definitely awake to ripple over in the bed.

Posy knew it wasn't fair to inflict her insomnia on Matt. He had a big day—physical training was hard work, he was always knackered and needed his energy for the morning. It had seemed such a ridiculous job when she met him. Everyone she knew went into the office in the morning, and ever since she'd moved to London she'd rather enjoyed that: the commuter coffee, the flow of the masses of people from trains and buses and tubes, enjoyed feeling part of the engine of work. But here was someone who got up at five a.m., who disappeared to distant parks with rich wives and American bankers, who often went to bed at eleven in the morning for a nap, who was always hungry and ate whatever she put in front of him, sometimes followed by four scrambled eggs and three bananas.

He was always trying to get her into doing more exercise, which of course she resisted furiously, although she couldn't deny she loved its effects on him; his smooth muscles and flat stomach. She knew her friends and family thought he was a bit of arm candy, not really a brain box, and didn't take him seriously. But they were wrong, weren't they? she thought to herself. OK, so he wasn't a poetic, serious type like . . . Still her brain refused to let her think of the name. OK, he was more straightforward. But that was a good thing.

What was wrong with her? Everything was going so right. Maybe she was just excited. Posy turned over and glanced at his profile in the bed. He was gorgeous, much better-looking than her. When pressed he would confess that he thought she was "cute." Nobody ever thought Fleur was cute. They thought she was gorgeous and deserved having poetry written for her.

Anyway. She wasn't thinking about Fleur. She was thinking about how she was the luckiest girl in the world. Yes. She was. She had a fantastic man by her side who wanted to spend his life with her. What a spoiled witch to even have to think twice about it. After her checkered love life . . . There had been Chris, of course, her university boyfriend. She was sure they were friends on Facebook somewhere and she remembered him fondly. Unlike Adam, who she'd been reminded of today. Oh Adam, he was such a wanker. Although . . .

She wished she'd got a bit more information from Sasha. About where Adam was, at least; what he was doing. She hadn't wanted to ask, it would have made her seem such a saddo. All these years on. But it was natural, wasn't it?

She twisted her ring fiercely in the dark. No. No, it wasn't. Oh God.

"*Stop wriggling*," said Matt fiercely. "Or you are going *under the bed*, I'm up in three hours."

Posy wants to go back to bed but do night properly
   this time.

"Are you on Facebook again?"

"No," said Posy, hurriedly switching her applications round. Trust Margie not just to notice that she was on Facebook, but bellow it out to the entire office.

"I really think they should take it off the system, don't you?" said Margie. "It's not really fair on the rest of us when we're trying to work hard."

Posy didn't want to add that Margie's idea of working hard seemed to involve walking round the office with a file under her arm and a coffee cup in her hand, sniffing out other people's chocolate biscuits.

"Hmm," she said, but the second Margie left, she flicked it back on again; something had caught her eye. She felt terrible, like she had a hangover, even though she hadn't been drinking—it was just lack of sleep. She glanced at the page again, an odd pang of guilt assailing her. Nonetheless, it couldn't be denied.

Coincidence be damned. She gets engaged, then runs into a friend of Adam's, and now this. The universe *wants* her to look up her exes. It must do.

Because there in black-and-white it was, next to an indecipherable photograph:

Chris is cold.

Funny, she'd hardly even noticed Chris friending her. Maybe in the heady early days when you got four friend requests a day. It was surprising he was even on there, he had always been such a Luddite. And suddenly, just a day after she'd run into someone connected to Adam, here he was. In fact . . . She checked the time. It was posted last night. So on the *same day* she'd had to think of Adam, Chris had popped up in her consciousness too. If she were Fleur, she would definitely *definitely* take this as a sign. She wasn't, of course, she reminded herself. No way. If she were Fleur she'd have a ribbon-covered net over her bed that she thought could catch dreams.

Anyway, she hadn't seen hide nor hair of him in years, years . . . Posy realized that she'd always have liked to have thought of herself as someone who stayed casually and politely in touch with all her exes. Hmm. Big Chris.

Posy took herself out to lunch. Strangely, when she'd first come back to London she didn't like doing this, thinking it made her look single and alone. But now, of course, she had her ring. Her protector. She ordered a mozzarella panini (Matt would have sniffed very loudly had he seen it), and remembered. Big Chris. He'd been on the next landing to her in Freshers' Week. A big bear of a chap, with shaggy, sandy-colored hair and broad shoulders, they'd noticed each other in the ref, at the freshers' party, at the student paper—until it started to get embarrassing that they hadn't been introduced. He didn't seem to know the cluster of girls Posy had met straight off. And when they'd been drawing up their list of uni "hunks," he'd been straight on it. But Posy thought, also, that there was something different about him. He wasn't just a good-looking lunkhead; there was something else, and not just the fact that he stood head and shoulders above everybody else.

"Hey," she'd said finally.

"Hey," he'd said. "What?"

"What do you mean, "What"? It's Freshers' Week, isn't it? When we're meant to be making friends and talking to people and stuff?"

"Oh," he said. "Was that it?"

After that there was a pause. Posy just assumed he was weird, and didn't think about him again, throwing herself with gusto into every club she could find. Then, three days later, he came up and sat next to her in the breakfast canteen.

"Hey," he said.

"What?"

"Nothing! I thought that's what we were doing."

"Well, you are, but then you have to introduce yourself and stuff. Have you actually met a human person before?"

His accent was nice; Liverpudlian. He sighed. "I just . . . I mean, are you about to tell me how many A-levels you got?"

"It might have been on my list as a topic for discussion, yes."

"And ask me what I'm studying?"

"It's just small talk. It doesn't mean anything! It's just a way of saying hello."

"OK," he said. Then he proceeded to plow silently through an enormous bowl of porridge.

After four days of this, Posy could take it no longer. "What do you want to talk about then?"

Chris had shrugged. "I don't know. Do you like animals?"

Posy was taken aback. She'd expected him to say quantum physics, or poetry—she'd met a lot of people who'd arrived at university determined to make a splash as serious grown-up intellectuals who disdained small talk, and had assumed he was just one of them. But now she wasn't so sure.

"To eat or to look at?"

"Whichever."

"Well, I like bears," said Posy slowly, not entirely sure where this was going. "Polar bears mostly. Hey, what do polar bears eat for lunch?"

"I don't know—a Happy Seal?"

Posy grinned. "A brr-GRR!"

That was the first time she ever saw him smile. He had lovely teeth.

"Yeah," he said. "Polar bears are cool. I like the way they're almost perfectly camouflaged except for their enormous eyes. Seals must think they get attacked by small lumps of coal."

"Brown bears are funny too," said Posy. "When, you know, they're in the circus. Wearing hats and driving small cars."

"I don't think you're allowed to do that to bears anymore," said Chris.

"Oh no," said Posy. "Quite right too. I didn't mean it wasn't viciously cruel, you know . . ."

"When they nail the hat to the bear's head?"

"Yeah, kind of."

He'd smiled. "Want to go for lunch?"

"Don't we already go for breakfast every day?" said Posy.

"Yes, but there are a lot of animals in the world. We've barely scratched the surface."

And, to her complete surprise, that had been that. He was, bar a few adolescent fumbles, Posy's first real, proper boyfriend. Incredibly sweet, good-looking in a shaggy, large kind of a way, unusual and intense, Posy had simply never met anyone like him before. All around her at university her new friends were experimenting with boys and drinking, but she was quite happy to spend her time with Chris. He wasn't like anyone else and he didn't give two figs for them either. Compared with her desperate nervousness, trying to bounce between her mother and her father (and his new wife Marian, a brittle blonde who talked a lot and bought Fleur and her sweets like they were nine years old, which Jonquil immediately threw in the bin), he was like a slightly distracted professor. It was quite sexy.

All his clothes were covered in holes. He was studying Civil Engineering, and could often be found in pubs absent-mindedly building physically unlikely bridges out of matches and cigarette papers. He didn't give the tiniest rat's fart what anyone thought of him and bowed to no social graces whatsoever. Oddly, this only seemed to make him more popular. This was hard for Posy to understand—she'd spent most of her life trying not to stick out too far, as much as one could with a mother who liked to use her as a psychiatric test case: "*POSY! This skeleton who lives under your bed—would you say he was very threatening, quite threatening or actively terrifying? Maybe I should use you at a conference.*"

Chris, though, stuck out a mile, being at least five inches and twenty kilos larger than anyone else, with holes in his shoes the rain came in and a pencil usually stuck in his hair.

Two weeks later, she lost her virginity to him on a narrow bed in their halls of residence, the metal frame banging against the small sink, the comforting fuggy smell of him—wool, a slightly bovine warmth, beer, and rolled up cigarettes—something she would take with her till her dying day.

"Hey, what did you think?" she'd whispered afterward. "Was it your first time too?"

"Uh, no," he said. "Well, at least I don't think so."

"What do you mean, you don't *think* so?"

"You may find this hard to believe, but I think it can be difficult to tell." Chris snuffled a bit.

"Are you . . . are you *embarrassed*?"

"No! Are you?"

In truth, Posy had spent quite a lot of the experience thinking, Oh my God! I'm having sex! This is what I'm doing! Right now! Oh my God! and resisting a strong urge to giggle at the sheer ridiculousness of it all.

"Uh, yes," she admitted finally. "I am a bit embarrassed."

"By me? Are you embarrassed by me?"

"*No*," said Posy, snuggling into his cozy hairy chest. "You are very very sexy. It's more the concept than anything else."

Chris thought about it. "God, you're right. Can we be honest with each other?"

"Uh, dunno." Now it was Posy's turn to feel weird.

"Oh, OK."

"Well, *what*? What is it?"

"It doesn't matter. You're beautiful, you know?"

He ran his hand over her smooth tummy and round hips. At

the time Posy thought he was just being polite. Only now, at thirty-two and definitely feeling her normally easy-to-manage figure start to deteriorate—always a problem when you liked to cook—could she fully appreciate how lovely her young body must indeed have been. She wished she'd appreciated it at the time instead of fretting a lot and wearing dungarees.

"Yeah yeah yeah."

They kissed, so they wouldn't have to face up to the truth that neither of them knew at the time that it could, and would, get a lot better. Posy could feel the raw stubble grazes on her chin.

"Shall we try again?"

She smiled. "Do you think we need the practice?"

"Couldn't hurt."

It did hurt a bit, actually, but Posy was so pleased to finally get her wings, she didn't really care.

It was odd being a couple at university. While all around them their friends were getting drunk, throwing up, having unfortunate one-night stands, and missing lectures, they found a house together and cooked up cheap veggie lasagne. They became a port of call for friends in trouble, broke, upset. They were like an old married couple, more than one person remarked to them. This irritated Posy. They weren't anything like a married couple, thank you very much. They sat up late, discussing the universe. They got drunk at gigs and voted in college elections. They were a fixture, and perfectly happy about it, thank you.

As Fleur pointed out loudly and repeatedly when she visited, you didn't need to have a PhD in Psychology to watch Posy, cooking up bean stew and chili, fussing around Chris like a mother hen, to guess what she was up to.

Their little terraced house, with its ethnic cloths on the walls and tables littered with Rizla papers, was cozy and frequently crowded. It was a home. Posy didn't mind the fact that people treated them like Mum and Dad, didn't even mind getting frequent cups of tea for the evening Chris had his engineering chums round and they sat in a circle and talked load-bearing parabolas and rolled joints. She even liked the fact that she didn't understand what they were talking about—her own degree in Marketing seemed a lot more banal by comparison. OK, she wished some of his friends would change their socks more often, but that was all part of the experience, wasn't it? As well as living off bean casserole. OK, Chris and his mates were smoking more and more dope, which she could do without—they got messy and smelly and very hungry and she found it too boring to join in—but apart from that life seemed to be turning out quite well so far. Calm. Posy felt she'd negotiated the shift from home to university rather well.

Not everyone saw it like that. Her mother tutted a lot and, while polite to Chris, clearly showed that she felt Posy should be experimenting with drugs and boys and not getting steady B averages.

"You're young for such a short time, darling," she'd sigh, seeing Posy come up the path to their house in Hampstead in the holidays in her dungarees, hand in hand with Chris and carrying ingredients for supper. "You have such a long time to be middle-aged and settled and boring."

"I am standing right here, Mrs. F," said Chris amiably.

"Chris. You are a lovely man, OK? I just don't want my daughter to miss out on all that life has to offer."

"Like boffing every guy at uni?" said Posy disagreeably.

"Really, I never talk to my mother about stuff like this," said Chris.

"You should! You should always strive to communicate in life," said Jonquil.

"Yeah, OK," said Chris.

"No, don't," said Posy. "Your way's much better."

In fact, Posy felt a little awkward at Chris's house. His mother was a lovely, nervy, inexplicably short woman, who was constantly trying to feed them or make sure they were all right. Posy was uncomfortable with the way Chris would throw his washing at her—in Posy's house, she and Fleur had been doing their own washing since their ninth birthdays—then go off to discuss some new development in engineering with his dad, who had worked in mining construction until they closed the pits. She would hang around their small beige Formica kitchen, decorated with hay sheafs, making small talk about cooking while Chris's rude little sister came and stared at her from the gap in the dining room door, listening intently to her unfamiliar southern accent.

"Families should share everything!" Jonquil would announce grandly, in Hampstead, while leaving the girls some money to order a take-away as she popped out to a psychiatric society fundraiser. Back in Warrington, Chris's family all sat round their little brown table, with its omnipresent ketchup bottle, every night. It had seemed obvious to Posy at the time which way was right and which was wrong.

At the time.

To celebrate the beginning of Third Year, they decided to have a big party. Posy was quite excited about getting dressed up for once, sometimes she felt she'd spent her entire university career living in Chris's holey sweaters. They invited everyone from their courses, Chris even adding a lecturer or two. He was that kind of person, Posy thought affectionately. Didn't distinguish between people. Didn't have narrow prejudices. Liked people on their own merits. She stirred a large, somewhat indiscriminate punch, and wondered how many people would come.

All of them, as it turned out. Their little house was overrun. Fortunately—and perhaps a first in the history of student housing—Chris had good relationships with their neighbors, having helped Mrs. Chadha change her fuses, so they weren't causing a nuisance as the ice in the bath tipped over and started dripping through the thin floorboards, and red wine started to collect in rivulets and puddles from spilled glasses placed on wobbly fireplaces.

One room was unofficially, clearly, the dope smokers' room, and Posy's heart sank as she watched Chris disappear into it. The gentlest and most charming of men, smoking dope turned him into an incredibly slow-moving bore, and could take a long time. It meant him crawling into bed at seven in the morning, telling her about some deep sea ocean facts he'd just discovered and asking if she'd make pancakes for him and his seventeen friends. She much preferred the sharp, energetic hit of alcohol, then dancing for hours. Dope made her sleepy and tired.

"Chris!" she said as she saw him head in.

He lifted his shoulders slowly—it would have been imperceptible to another observer—in a manner which, to Posy, looked suspiciously like huffiness.

"What?" he said.

"Nothing!" She was never ever going to become a nag, for

sure. "I was just going to say . . . well, see you in the morning, I guess!"

He frowned. "What do you mean?"

"Nothing. I mean, you're off to smoke dope, I'll go have a party."

"This is a party."

"It is," she said. "I like the bit when you get into a really slow argument about the Middle East."

Around them the house was steadily filling up with people—no one ever felt the need to knock. Plastic polythene bags filled with cheap cider clinked against each other, and Posy could already smell the toaster being pressed into action.

Chris's brow furrowed.

"Sorry, Posy, have you got a problem? Should I be at the door, having guests' names called out by a butler?"

Now it was Posy's turn to feel disgruntled. "No! But it might be nice to say hello to your friends."

"Well, my friends I see every day, and most of them are in here." He indicated the room. "And everyone coming in the door is probably some Third Year corporate-bound nob I don't even know, so does it really matter, Pose?"

"No," she said.

"Come here." He enfolded her in his familiar bear-like embrace. "You really are my lovely middle-class girlie, aren't you? Are you sure you wouldn't rather have formal seating for twelve?"

"Shut up, ketchup boy."

"Having ketchup on your dinner table is actually a sign of staying close to your roots, doncha know."

"Yeah yeah yeah," said Posy, kissing him.

"Ugh, you two are so in love it's sickening," said Carla, in the same tutorial group as Posy, lurching past with her arm round an enormous rugby player. "Look at these two, Fugs."

Posy wasn't entirely sure what Carla was doing there. She had worn full makeup and highlights every single day of university and spent a lot of time bemoaning how provincial she thought the town was—she never went to the student bars and unions and spent a lot of time in London, afterward recounting at length tedious stories about nightclubs. But it had seemed rude not to ask her along really. Posy was amazed she had come. She must be really desperate for a boyfriend.

"FUUUG!" said Fugs.

"He's not much of a talker," said Carla apologetically. "All the good ones are taken."

"She couldn't possibly mean you," Posy told Chris.

"Not a bone idle old doper like me, no. Absolutely not."

"FUUUG!" said Fugs. "Where are the kegs?"

"Kegs?" said Posy to Carla.

"He thinks he's in an American frat house," said Carla. "They all do. It's quite embarrassing."

Sure enough, there was a roar from downstairs. Posy poked her head round the door to see the entire rugby team turning up, waving a keg over their heads.

"Uni is definitely changing," said Posy. "Oy! Watch the bookshelves!"

Posy really noticed it that evening. Until then, they'd been drifting along, not really talking about the future, happy to spend their evenings deep in discussion, at cheap gigs or down the student union taking advantage of the cheap alcohol.

Now, however, she could sense something in the air. The feeling that life was about to get serious. Some, like the rugger buggers, were coping with it by pretending it would never happen, and immersing themselves in partying and fun. But others, she could see, had spent their summers doing internships at banks and large companies. It sounded gruesome to her, and Chris had never mentioned the future at all. She'd always assumed she'd go back to her mother's and look for something interesting to do, or that she and Chris would rent a little flat somewhere and do . . . well, something, she supposed. Now everyone was scurrying about with application forms and new, suspiciously smart haircuts.

Here came a group now. She went downstairs to say hello. More people she knew from her Marketing course. They looked smart and organized, and instead of two liter bottles of cider had bottles of wine and were making remarks about the glasses.

"Hi," said Posy, suddenly feeling a little under-dressed in her ethnic smock with the little mirrors embroidered into the hem.

"Hiya, Posy," one of the girls said cheerily, even though it was the first time she'd been in Posy's house and she had an expression on her face that said she found it wanting. Posy glanced at the group. They had with them a boy she'd never seen before and didn't think was even at the university. He must be a friend from out of town. He was even wearing a suit! Maybe a townie. Surely not, the townies hated the students.

"Hi," she said to him. "Welcome."

The boy looked at her. He was taking in her hippie dress, she knew, and her bare feet. He didn't look impressed. She found herself getting irritated. She didn't care how casual this was, he was still a guest in her house.

"What's the matter?" she found herself saying. "Not your scene?"

The boy shrugged in his suit. He was handsome, she supposed, if you liked that kind of thing.

"Adam!" screeched Carla, diving down the stairs behind Posy. "You came!"

"Urgh," said Fugs from up the stairs, but it looked obvious that his time had passed.

Carla rushed up to the boy, who looked unimpressed by the commotion.

"Posy, this is Adam," gushed Carla, grabbing his suit by the elbow.

"Hi," said Posy again, unenthusiastically.

"Hi," said Adam, equally unenthusiastically.

"Have you got any clean wineglasses?" asked Carla, faux-naively.

"Yes," said Posy. "Just go past the wine cellar and take a left at the art gallery. Or you can use a toothpaste mug like everyone else."

Adam smiled for the first time.

"Thanks for inviting me."

"I invited you," squawked Carla.

"But it's your house, right? That's why you're not wearing any shoes."

"Well, it was good of you to get off early from your court appearance to join us," said Posy, surprised she was so riled.

"Oh, sorry about the suit . . . I had an interview."

"For prison?"

"For the Bank of England, actually."

Posy tried to raise her eyebrows to show she wasn't impressed, but she was, a little.

"Adam's doing Economics," said Carla possessively. "He's going to get a first."

"Are you at our university?" said Posy.

Adam smiled derisively and Posy decided to dislike him again. "Uh, no. I'm at LSE."

He said this as if she would automatically know where that was. Annoyingly, Posy did. It was the London School of Economics, open only to the very bright.

"That's the London School—"

"Yeah, I know, thanks, Carla. So how long have you two been an item?"

"Oh, no, Adam is a friend of my brother's . . . he had to come up here for an interview."

"For a London bank?"

"They have a recruiting center up here."

"You *are* a dedicated career hound."

"Well, it won't be sophisticated parties like this one forever."

He was definitely sparring with her.

"So," he went on, "what are you going to do? Take a couple of gap years . . . bum around India . . . start doing something arty and low-paid in London, staying at Daddy's?"

Well, it would be Mummy's, but Posy was annoyed to admit that in essence he was probably right.

"I don't know why everyone thinks it's so uncool to want to make a living," he said. "As opposed to what, exactly?"

"Enjoying your youth? Not becoming an office drone?"

"I fully intend to enjoy my youth," said Adam. "But not at anyone else's expense."

Posy raised her eyebrows. "Well, enjoy the party."

Carla grabbed Adam's hand and they fought their way into the kitchen, and that was that. Later on, she saw them vanish home together without saying goodbye. Carla's push-up bra was obviously working.

Posy didn't expect to see Adam again, but somehow his annoying voice had gotten into her head. It said things like, Why don't you fill in this application form? and made her want to attend milk-round presentations. Chris couldn't understand it at all.

"Why would you want to go and work for a bunch of pricks, surrounded by pricks, for some pointless prick thing?"

"Because I do *Marketing*," Posy would say. "It's what I *do*."

Chris sighed, staring out of the terraced window into the cold wet street beyond.

"What are you going to do anyway?"

Chris shrugged. "I don't know. Maybe travel for a bit, maybe do a postgrad."

Posy shivered. Their last heating bill had been a shocker—too many friends coming round and switching up the radiators while they sat up all night—so they were on an economy drive.

"That means we'd be poor for years and years," she found herself saying, conscious that she sounded a bit like Meg in *Little Women*.

Chris looked up from his book. "Is that very important to you, pickle? Money and so on?"

"No!" said Posy quickly. "I just . . . I guess I just want to do something with my life." If she'd thought it through a bit more, she might have said that she wanted to be normal, to live a normal life. She was excited about going into the world, half terrified too, but she did want to take her place among professional people, with ordered lives.

"With . . ." He leafed through one of her application forms disdainfully. "Equal opportunities policies?"

It turned out that he wasn't joking, and that was perhaps the first serious disagreement they'd ever had. Everything that for their last two years had felt like fun, like playing at grown ups—going shopping, having dinner parties, sharing house keys and secrets and laundry—all of that suddenly seemed like exactly what it was: a rehearsal for the real, real life. And that life suddenly seemed to be approaching at appalling speed.

Finals, revision, interviews . . . As usual, Chris worked his way through his work quietly and stoically, as if nothing were happening. He was going to do well, it was clear. Posy, on the other hand, couldn't settle: moving carrels in the library, jumping from reading list to reading list and pestering tutors. It didn't help that her mother was making polite inquiries as to her future plans—"I raised you to be an independent woman. Have you thought about social work?"—and Fleur had enrolled on a homeopathy course which seemed to involve going to beautiful spring meadows to pick wildflowers, then pouring water into tiny bottles, then partying like rock stars for weeks at a time, with extra credit given if you managed to sell any of your concoctions at an international music festival.

Their futures were anything but resolved. By the time spring limped around, Posy found herself filled with dread. She and Chris seemed to be speaking less and less around the house, the long, late-night parties had stopped and they tiptoed round each other politely. Chris often studied well into the night, coming to bed too late for them to think about making love. The elephant in the room never went away. What now? What next? For each other, as individuals making their way in the world, but as a couple too. As a home.

"I'm never going to pass this paper!" Posy groaned a week later, sitting at the table by the window.

"Well, you should have studied earlier in the year then," said Chris infuriatingly, who was reading a book in the armchair. "You can't drink tea for three years then panic at the last minute."

"Well, why didn't you mention that to me before?"

"I dunno, I suppose I thought you had a secret plan that would render this unnecessary. But obviously not."

"I'm going to throw this book at your head."

"Then you really will be in trouble. They're sixty quid each, those things."

Then, silence. Posy looked at his shaggy hair and his bowed head, frowning in concentration over some difficult political text he was reading for fun. It was then, somehow, with the warm motes of summer light dancing through the small, dirty terraced windows, reflecting off the mismatched mugs and the fringed tablecloth, off the wall with all the photos of their friends stuck up with Blu-Tack; the fireplace, shrouded in beer mats and funny gold candlesticks; the moth-eaten sofa with the throw over it, it was then that she knew. She looked around it, took it in, this life she had tried on. She had outgrown it just as surely as she'd outgrown keeping milk on the windowsill, Mark Owen, and spray perfume deodorant.

She couldn't think over the last three years and feel, like her mother did, that it was a waste. She couldn't think like that. But she knew she had to move, she needed certainty and stability in her life and she needed to know if she was going to be alone or not when she did it.

She put the book down.

"Chris," she said. He raised his head, and she looked directly and without rancor into his light brown eyes for the first time in a long time.

"If I left . . . went away . . . would you come with me?"

He didn't try and brush it off or joke around. He knew exactly what she meant.

"To London? To live at your mum's? Or in a cupboard somewhere?"

Posy shrugged. "Well, you haven't come up with any other ideas."

"I have been thinking, actually."

Posy's heart sank. Chris was thinking all the time, of course he was. The difference was, he normally shared the things he was thinking with her. This was now.

"Yes?"

"Well, I thought I might go do some proper work for a bit. Stop fannying around with books. Go work on a farm, maybe. Some honest toil."

"Getting back to your roots?"

He smiled shyly. "Well, something like that. I do feel I've been a bit mollycoddled away . . ."

"By me?"

"I didn't mean that. I mean, by this life in general." His voice tailed away. He did mean by her, she could tell.

"Your mum and dad are over the moon you're at university."

"Of course they are. I just want to . . . you know. Take my own year out, if you like. I want a proper job, Posy. A man's job. Just to . . . just to know that I can."

There was a long pause. Posy felt a great lump grow in the back of her throat. She could hardly speak or get the words out.

"Could I . . . could I come?"

There was an even longer silence, as Posy watched the tiny dust particles float in the rays of the soft sun.

"Of course," said Chris. "If that's what you want."

They limped on. Chris didn't even want to go to the university ball after finals—he thought the whole idea of dressing up in tuxes and pretending to be posh was totally ridiculous. Posy couldn't see the problem with getting dressed up for just one night, and decided to go with her single girl-friends. She was pleasantly surprised to find just how many people were happy to talk to her and dance with her, along with expressing surprise at seeing her out and about without being half of a couple. As she looked around, she wondered if she should have got out more during her three years, met more interesting people. She was surprised at how many faces she didn't recognize. Had she and Chris really been guilty of what her mother thought, being too insular and homey; not taking enough advantage of the opportunities? She thought too, as she saw everyone passing by in their borrowed finery, how grown up they all looked compared with the kids they must have been when they started. She was wearing a pale blue dress she'd found in a vintage shop, nipped in at the waist with a full skirt. It contrasted well with her eyes and she knew it suited her.

At midnight, as the toasts were made, she went out to the

balcony of the Corn Exchange, where the ball was held, and leaned against the columns, chilier now after the warm late-spring day but still with a hint of blossom in the air. Is this what it would be like, she wondered, facing the future alone?

Being without Chris . . . it would be like doing without one of her arms or legs. They were so used to one another. But did she need a crutch? She couldn't deny that the thought of heading up to Yorkshire to shear sheep filled her with horror, whereas the idea of heading to London with Carla and a bunch of her friends to start temping and finding something to do in the City—that sounded like fun. Carla thought they should all get a flat together, go out, be like that new *Sex and the City* show that had started on TV.

But shouldn't she love Chris enough, she thought, to want to do anything with him? To shear sheep, if that's what it took?

She took a long sip from her glass of wine and sighed.

"I didn't recognize you," came the voice behind her. At first Posy didn't realize it was directed at her, but she gradually became aware she was the only other person on the terrace—and she was cold.

"Hello?" she said, whipping round. It was Adam, from her party. He looked . . . well, there were no two ways about it. He was utterly gorgeous. Dark hair, long dark eyelashes over green eyes, high cheekbones. He was wearing a dinner jacket that clearly belonged to him and his tie was artlessly loosened. On purpose, Posy was sure, but the effect was still pretty devastating.

"I miss the mirrors on the skirt," he said. "And you're wearing shoes. Does it feel weird?"

"What are you doing here, at Cow College?" she asked him

snidely. She hadn't forgotten his rude comments from the last time they'd met. "Bit down at heel for high flyers like yourself, isn't it?"

"Carla sent me a ticket," he said. "Then her brother said if I made her sad he was going to duff me up."

"How charming."

"Aren't you cold?"

Posy ignored the obvious goose pimples appearing along her chest and arms.

"No!"

"Here, let me give you my jacket."

"No, thank you."

It was too late. Adam had already taken it off. Posy couldn't help notice how well-defined his muscles were, and how tight and flat his waist. She had always been used to the burly, soft bulk of Chris, had never really known anyone else. Suddenly the thought flashed through her mind of what it might be like to be with someone like Adam—lean, dangerous, smooth.

He was looking at her curiously, holding out his coat. Over his shoulder, in the chandeliered lights of the ballroom, Posy suddenly caught sight of Carla, stumbling around slightly drunkenly and obviously looking for Adam. She felt out of her depth, and a little sick, suddenly, and all she wanted to do was go home.

"No, thank you. I mean it. I have to go now."

Chapter Five

Chris is cold.
Comment, Posy: Why are you cold?
Chris: Because it is January.

Direct message:
Hey Chris, That's not a very helpful response.
Hey! How are you? I'm getting married!

Posy wasn't sure that worked very well. Maybe a bit bouncy and in your face. It sounded like she'd dashed off to write to him the second she'd got engaged. Which . . . OK, it had been a week. Hmm. She stuck to *Hey! How are you?* But it did remind her. There was someone else she needed to speak to.

"What are you so engrossed in?" Matt came up behind her and nuzzled her neck. She was hoping they'd go out to dinner tonight—she hadn't had the chance to get anything in—but already he had that yawny look he often got by six o'clock, plus he was wearing his favorite pair of old tracksuit trousers, which had been worn down practically smooth by devoted use. The fact that Matt wore nothing—nothing at all—but sports clothes had slightly confused her at first. He didn't own a tie, or an overcoat. Or an iron. Or a belt.

"What about when you have to look smart?" she'd asked him.

"Well, then I wear Shred Head," he said.

"That stuff that's all ripped up?"

"It's cool. It's surf stuff."

"So what if you had to . . . I don't know, meet the Queen?"

"Oh, the Queen likes me naked."

"I do too," Posy had said. "Still, though, your wardrobe . . ."

Matt had raised his eyebrows and Posy had dropped her point. It didn't matter.

Now she closed the computer guiltily. "Oh, just messing about on Facebook. Do you want to go out for supper?"

Matt winced. "I was helping Mindy McAndrew through army fitness at six-thirty a.m. Must we?"

Posy shook her head. "No, sweetie, of course not. What would you like?"

Matt squinted. "Can I have four eggs, two chicken breasts, some spinach, and a pint of milk?"

When she was fourteen, Posy had taught herself to cook. Her mother was horrified. It was the most rebellious move she could have made.

"Don't you realize how long women have been subjugated by the frying pan?" she had insisted. "There's nothing wrong with crackers and tinned soup."

Posy had ignored her, concentrating hard on a charity shop copy of Delia Smith. And slowly, surely, she had worked her way up, through omelettes to pies, lasagne, everything comforting and nice to come home to. Her mother usually skipped meals, but she and Fleur ate lamb chops, shepherd's pie, bolognese, and steak and kidney until they started to fill out and look a little less pinched (their mother called this "puppy fat"). She took the habit to university too, where she fed Chris up on a student diet of chili, beans, chick peas, and sidelined into cakes and pies. It was little wonder they were popular on campus.

Food was home. Matt's insistence on great pieces of lean protein—days of only fruit or huge steaks—she found slightly confusing and off-putting, as well as impossible to eat.

"When we're married," she found herself asking shyly as she followed him into the kitchen, "do you think we'll eat normally? As a family?"

Matt glanced at her over the juicer.

"This is normal, sweetie," he said. "For, you know, optimum bodily fitness. I wish you'd do it."

"If I ate nine eggs and a pint of milk a day you'd have to winch me out of the house," she said. "It's all right if you're doing nine hours of physical exercise. It's just a bit dull to cook, that's all."

"Darling, I'm not marrying you for your cooking."

"Yes, but you *should*! I worked really hard at it."

"OK, well, I'll make myself some chicken and you whip yourself up something delicious."

"No, thanks," said Posy.

"And also . . . my parents want to come down. Well, actually, they were wondering . . ."

"What?"

"If we were going to have an engagement party."

"Oh," said Posy.

"Are we?"

"I hadn't really thought about it."

"Too ashamed to show me off?"

"No! I was just thinking, though. I'll probably have to . . ."

"Tell your mum."

"Yes."

"Well, you're going to tell her at some stage, aren't you? We're not going to elope, are we?"

"Could we?"

"And break my nice, totally normal mother's heart?"

Posy sighed. It was telling her mother—and her father, she assumed. Her heart dropped. It was all so complicated. Plus it seemed a little odd. Not that she didn't love Matt, of course she did. But to announce it to the world, to put up with all the obvious questions about You Know Who and was she sure and was he really a P.E. teacher . . . She didn't really want a party, to be honest.

"OK, a party then," she said unenthusiastically.

Matt looked perturbed. "Is that the sound of you doubting a party?"

"No, it's just, it's a lot to organize, and I've got loads on at work—"

"You've got nothing on at work! Come on, I've met Gavin, you just sit about all day trying to get people to buy insurance then telling them you won't clean their carpets after they've had a big flood."

"That isn't . . . well . . ."

Matt picked up the phone. "Anyway. Don't worry about the party just now. There's one thing you *really* have to do."

"Don't make me."

"She'll find out."

"Maybe we could just pretend to be trendily living in sin . . . for, like, forever?"

"PHONE!"

"Uh, Mum?"

"Call me Jonquil, dear."

Jonquil sounded distracted.

"Is this a good time? I can call back later."

Still behind the juicer, Matt raised his eyebrows at Posy.

"No, dear, sorry. I'm just rescheduling the paranoid for after the passive-aggressive, but trying to do it in a way he doesn't feel picked on, and I have a paper I'm delivering to the NPS Women's Group, then I have that charity commission board I'm already *totally* late for . . ."

"I'll call you back," said Posy, flicking Matt the V.

"Aha! Found it!" said Jonquil. "Now, darling, how about lunch? Give me a chance to catch up on all your news."

It would do that, Posy thought. "OK," she said. "Tomorrow?"

Her mother laughed. "I think I can do Thursday."

"Thursday," said Posy.

"Thursday," said Matt. "And I'm going to speak to a mate about a party."

"Oh, you don't have to . . ."

But he'd already grabbed the phone off her to stop her hogging it.

Chapter Six

Posy is checking she has ironed her blouse for MOTHER
  INSPECTION.
Comment, Fleur: I bet you don't tell her.
Comment, Posy: Shut up, Fleur.
Comment, Matt: What Fleur said.

Posy had to admit, when they were out and about, it was quite
impressive to see her mother in action. Never the homemaker,
she was nonetheless a striking dresser and still looked slender
and chic in her sixties, her dark hair a carefully styled helmet,
with full makeup and a smart green suit on. She looked like she
meant business and always wore heels. Posy felt like her very
messy charge when they were out together. Funnily enough
Fleur was the one more interested in her appearance than Posy,
even if her style—Bohemian and relaxed—made their mother
comment that she looked like a life-avoiding woman-child.
Posy's lack of interest in clothes and makeup were dismissed as
hiding her psyche from the gaze of the world. A simple trip to
Topshop when they were teenagers, Posy sometimes thought,

would probably have been enough, but their mother didn't do high street fashion and insisted on dressing them like miniature adults until they got their own Saturday jobs.

Jonquil still caused heads to turn as she marched into the small Italian trattoria across the road from Posy's office.

"So," said her mother, after she'd brusquely told the very friendly waiter that she would have a seafood salad, thank you, no dressing, and Posy had ordered linguine *alla vongole*, garlic bread on the side and a glass of red wine, just to watch her mother's eyebrows raise. "To what do I owe this . . ." She gestured for the right word.

Posy figured the best thing was just to spit it out. How odd, she mused. When she thought of her friends' mothers, most of them were desperate to see their daughters married off; hungry for grandchildren with an appetite that bordered on the unseemly; trying not to go too far for fear of having their ears snapped off by their clever, liberated, late-settling offspring, but unable to hide their joy and relief on news of pregnancies, rings, churches, and everything else that suggested on some universal scale that the children they had raised had "passed."

Jonquil was not quite like that. In fact, from when she could remember, Posy had heard stories about the horrors and subjugation of marriage, not just Jonquil's, but every dreadful story she heard from the chamber of horrors that was her mother's consulting room in the attic. The wife beaters, the husband beaters. The emotional withholders, the compulsive confessors. The cleaners, the messers. The cheaters, the eaters, and the just plain miserable. All of them were picked apart as the family of three ate toasted cheese and tomato soup for supper, books propped in front of them. And the cause for half the misery? "Never, ever *ever* make your happiness reliant on another person," Jonquil would lecture fiercely to her patients and her daughters. "Never. If you live your lives truly, as truly rounded people, that's enough."

"Well," said Posy. "Matt and I . . ." She reflected later that many mothers would have leaped out of their chairs the second they'd heard the words "Matt and I."

"Yes?" prompted her mother impatiently.

"Well, he's asked me to marry him."

Her mother didn't say anything, just calmly raised her water glass.

"And what did you say?"

"Well, I said yes, of course." Posy looked up, hurt. "I do love him, Mum."

"Of course you do, darling," said her mother. "But must you *marry* him?"

Posy bit her lip. "No," she said, "I have a choice. That's what makes it romantic and special. I am choosing to marry him."

Her mother heaved a sigh. "Well, if you must."

Their food came. As the waiter laid it out in front of them, Posy tried to swallow back her rising anger.

"What do you mean, 'If I must'? I know your views on marriage, OK? I heard them every night for fifteen years. But can't you even pretend to be happy for me?"

Her mother blinked. "I gave you an honest reaction, darling. Would you expect anything less?"

"I mean . . . Matt's a really good man. Loads of women would be delighted to have him as a son-in-law. Loads of women would be really pleased to see their daughter happy."

Posy realized she was choking up, and didn't want to give

her mother the satisfaction. She took a long slug of the rough red wine and concentrated on her huge bowl of pasta.

Her mother put her hand across the table in a gesture of reconciliation. "Posy, I'm sorry. Darling. Of course I want you to be happy. It's just marriage seems such a complicated way of going about it—"

"Lots of people like being married. Not everyone's miserable like the sad acts you treat."

"I'll ignore that," said her mother. "But, yes, of course Matt is a lovely chap. Not the brightest . . ."

"Muuuum!"

"But are you sure . . . the two of you. I mean, are you *really* compatible? Everything he wears is elasticated."

"Just because he doesn't work in an office, everyone thinks he's a thicko."

"Not at all, darling, I think offices are wildly overrated. I just mean . . ."

"Well, spit it out."

"Well, it was terribly sudden after . . ."

Jonquil didn't say his name. Posy was pleased.

"I mean, it was quite soon, wasn't it?"

Posy nodded sullenly.

"And you haven't been together for that long now."

"Nearly three years."

"Yes, well, marriage is a little longer than three years, dear."

Posy bit her lip.

"He may be—he is—terribly handsome, but are you sure he's not just someone you rebounded on to? Who doesn't ask too many questions, or make life feel too complicated for you?" She went on. "I've always wanted to bring you up to soar, to see the world, to ask questions. Not to stay somewhere you don't want to be in case you get hurt again."

Posy was shocked. "It's not like that at all."

Jonquil raised an eyebrow, but Posy held her ground, even though, deep inside, what her mother had said had pierced her to the core. Was it true? Was it because none of her other relationships had gone right that she was clinging to this one, with an uncomplicated man?

"You're my eldest daughter, you know. I do love you heart and soul. And I know you, too." Her mother gazed at her with the sharp, critical eye Posy knew so well. "But if you think this will make you happy, and that you can make Matt happy, then of course, I'll be delighted."

"It will."

"Excellent. Waiter! Two glasses of champagne *por favor*! *Mia figlia se sposa!*"

The waiters rushed over, delighted and full of congratulations and pleasure. Jonquil was smiling graciously, Posy boiling inside.

"Mum! Stop showing off!"

"Jonquil, darling, Jonquil."

Matt was sorting out sports socks when she got home from work. He had about twenty pairs of white toweling socks. He liked to sort them out all together, matching them up with tiny similarities only he could see. Posy watched him as she opened the door. Was this his idea of a fun way to spend an evening?

"Hey!" she shouted cheerfully as she got in.

"Hey! How'd it go? Is she having me hunted down and shot?"

Posy rushed through the newly edited version she had put together in her head.

"No, she ordered champagne, actually. I was quite squiffed by the time I got back to the office, I even asked Margie who does her hair."

"A drunken monkey. For a bet," said Matt automatically. "Really? She was pleased?"

"Kind of. She asked if I was truly wife material."

"Who, Margie?"

"My mother, dumbo."

"Huh, well, she should know."

"Exactly."

Matt kissed the top of her head. "You're *my* wife material."

Posy smiled and pulled away.

But in the tiny galley kitchen of their minuscule one-bedroomed flat, all Posy could think about was the message she'd sent Chris earlier when she got back to the office:

How cold? And WHERE ARE YOU?

At three a.m., Posy's insomnia moved up a gear. The lunchtime champagne hadn't helped. Then it became horribly apparent that sleep, if it did come, wasn't going to be enough. She couldn't relax, there was no way around it: she was exhausted, grumpy, cross with herself, cross with her mother and every stupid thought that kept bouncing through her brain. She was even cross at Matt for . . . for nothing. For lying there so peacefully and sleeping so calmly. It was very irritating.

Posy could feel her brain shrinking through tiredness, her

limbs begging and pleading for rest. But her mind, her pesky dancing mind, wouldn't leave her the hell alone. Thinking things like, *Did you really imagine you would end up with a man who cares a lot about folding his socks?* and *The wedding is going to be full of people looking at you guys and thinking it won't last, because Posy isn't wife material and he's a jogging teacher* and *Why is Chris cold? What is Adam doing? And what about . . .*

Posy lay in the darkness, biting back the name she still couldn't bear to even think of.

All her exes, parading in a row—the significant ones, not the two-week fling with the bicycle courier with very taut calves, or the identical twin who was a bit creepy. But all of them. What were they doing? Had they got married to people much better than her?

Will they care that you're getting married? Will they be miserable? Will they wish it were them? Or did they know too, that you're not wife material? Did they know all along?

The voice couldn't be stilled by a pillow over the head. It couldn't be stilled by some quiet tears.

At half past four, Posy gave up the night for good and went and made herself a cup of tea to drink in the bath. She thought Matt might hear and get up and tell her to stop being so silly and make everything all right again.

He didn't.

At half past five, it struck her.

Posy is completely wide awake. Anyone there?
Comment: Like.
Comment, Chris: Hello?

On the whole, decisions taken at half past five in the morning are rarely good ones. They say things like, "Hell yeah, let's just go to that dodgy bar for another drink." Or, "Yes, why *don't* I stay over?" Or, "Let's just go to the airport right now."

Posy wasn't going to go to the airport right away, she thought, clutching her tea. But she'd decided. She had to know. Was this wrong or right? And who knew better than the ones who hadn't made it this far?

She had to see. She had to know if this was the right thing to do. Not just for her, but for the lovely, dear, sweet-hearted man lying completely oblivious in the next room. She didn't want to upset him, she just needed to know a few things . . . She needed to ask Chris. And Adam, if he could spare five minutes in his hectic schedule to remember who she was. Face to face, not Facebook to Facebook.

And then, of course, there was . . . No. She wasn't going to think about him just yet. Not when she couldn't even say his name.

Chapter Seven

Posy is drinking a lot of coffee. Really. A lot.
Comment: Like.
Comment, Matt: You know, coffee isn't very good
   for you.

She would tell Matt she was looking for wedding venues. That would work. That would definitely work. All men found wedding stuff unbelievably boring, didn't they? He'd be totally desperate to close his ears and just go "Lalalala!" She could get away with anything.

Posy sat at work suddenly feeling more excited than she had done for days. This was it! This was the right thing to do! She was going to grab the bull by the horns and do whatever it took to get rid of this tiny, silly, nagging voice in her ear that kept on telling her she was making a mistake. She was going to sort it out, get to the bottom of it, and then they could have a triumphant, wonderful wedding, something that didn't have people gossiping in the aisles like some she'd been to, or brides overspending horribly on cake and favors and nonsense for an obviously doomed relationship to try and convince themselves that it was all real. Because hers would be real. Because she'd know, for definite.

"What kind of wedding do you want?" Matt had asked her, just after he'd proposed. And now she finally knew. An honest one.

"You look *knackered*," said Fleur. "Letting yourself go already?"

Posy was regretting gathering Fleur and Leah to drink wine in the Slug and Lettuce and discuss her brilliant plan. Or, at least, a plan that had seemed brilliant at five o'clock that morning. Now, she wasn't so sure. She bought the first bottle of rosé.

"What's up?" said Leah. She was wearing a lime-green striped T-shirt, a vinyl miniskirt and Doc Marten boots. She looked extremely cool, if slightly about-to-kick-your-head-in. "I've had a hell of a day. Our new fake fur line isn't selling at all."

"That's because you left the heads on," Posy pointed out.

"It's *ironic*. They're not real heads."

"They look like real heads."

"Especially the blood," added Fleur, pouring out three huge glasses.

"People are stupid," grimaced Leah.

"How did your date go?" asked Posy.

Leah made a low growling noise. She'd been asked out by a journalist when she was talking up her clothes over the phone. Posy had thought this was a good sign; he must already be at least passingly familiar with the kind of stuff she was likely to roll up in.

Not so, it turned out. They'd headed for a noisy city center bar, where the journalist had attempted to get her as drunk as possible as quickly as possible during two-for-one cocktails, ignored everything she'd attempted to tell him about the direction of contemporary womenswear, and said, "Have you actually got any tits under that thing or is that fashion too?" (In his very weak defense, she was wearing a ruff.) She hadn't quite got up the courage to leave then, but one near-fatal-strength alcoholic margarita later he lurched forward off his bar stool and said, "God, I wish my wife were as skinny as you." Then he fell down.

"Oh," said Posy helpfully.

"I wouldn't mind," said Leah, "but that's actually the best date I've had this year. I'm chalking it up as a partial success."

"Are you seeing him again?"

"No! He's married."

Posy gave it a second.

"Maybe. It's a horrible drought out there at the moment. A horrible, horrible drought! Honestly, you have *no idea* how lucky you are to have found Matt! None! They should clone him so we can all have one! A nice, sweet fit guy who wants to marry you. You're the luckiest bitch in the whole world. It's totally unfair. Anyway, what did you want to see us for?"

"Ah," said Posy. "Well." She took a big slug of wine. "I've been thinking. About what Matt said and about what my mum's said . . ."

"Oh God, what has Mum said?" said Fleur. "Whatever it is, do the exact opposite immediately."

"She thinks I should get married for the right reasons," Posy said. In the harsh neon light of the bar, this wasn't coming across quite as she'd hoped.

"Fear? Desperation? Being thirty-two?" said Fleur.

"True love?" said Leah.

"Well, yes," said Posy, feeling a bit desperate. "But also companionship. A sharing of life goals; a match of equals."

"Well, that's no use to you, is it?" said Fleur. "Matt is like a championship athlete and you won't even take the stairs in John Lewis."

"Yes, and you read magazines and books and things and he reads *Uncover the Fighter Within*."

"And he applied for the SAS."

"And you like shopping and cocktails and parties and having a nice time and giggling and he likes riding a bike up a really fucking steep mountain."

"And you like to hide from your mother and he likes to go and see his ma and dad in Blackpool."

"And you love food and he eats those powder things that come in big tubs."

"And you used to go on marches and he isn't registered to vote."

"And he's got abs and you've got a supersized cupcake-y muffin-top thingy."

"And I like watching TV and DVDs and he likes running up cliffs," said Posy. "Hang on, why am I joining in with this? Forget about all that for a minute," she added, trying to get things back on track. "I was just thinking . . . do you remember Chris?"

Fleur widened her eyes. "That really boring old man you lived with at university?"

"He wasn't an *old man*," spluttered Posy. "He was my first love."

"He smelled old," said Fleur.

"That was his tobacco," said Posy, reminiscing. "He rolled his own."

Leah cast her eyes to heaven. "Oh, right, marry him. Didn't he wear, like, sacking and stuff? And only own one pair of shoes?"

"What about him?" said Fleur. "Has he died of old age?"

"OK, shut up, everyone," ordered Posy. "I just got a message from him, that's all. *And* I ran into a friend of Adam's at the station."

"Adam? Cocksucking hairy prick Adam?" said Leah.

"Well . . . yes. You forgot to add handsome."

Leah looked exasperated.

"Cocksucking hairy *handsome* prick Adam."

"So? Don't you think that's interesting?"

"So nothing!" said Leah. "You have *true love*. Stop mucking about!"

But Fleur was in rapture.

"It's a sign," she said. "These kinds of things are always a sign."

"It's a sign you have too much time on your hands when you should be planning your wedding," said Leah. "You need a month by month countdown."

"Well, actually I thought I might scout one in particular," said Posy. "What do you think about me getting married on a Scottish island?"

"Ooh, does it have a castle? That would be *so* romantic," said Leah. "*Now* you're thinking about it properly."

"Well, yes," said Posy. "But also . . . here's the thing. Chris lives there. So I thought I might just pop in and—"

"This," said Leah, "is the worst idea you have *ever* had."

"Can't you be more supportive?"

"I can!" said Fleur. Then she took on a concentrated look.

"Oh no, hang on, I've just thought about it and it turns out I can't. Sorry. This is a stupid idea. Maybe it isn't a sign after all."

Posy's face looked set. "Well, I need to." She looked at Leah. "It's all right for you. You've always had a mum and a dad who loved each other and looked out for you. You know what good relationships are meant to look like."

"That's why I've found them so easy to come by," muttered Leah into her wine.

"And you *know* how . . . Well, you know how I was after Thingy. I just want to make sure that Matt and I are doing the right thing."

"So you're working up to confronting Thingy?" said Fleur.

"I'm closing the door on my past," said Posy.

"It's a terrible terrible terrible idea," said Leah.

"Well, just as well I haven't booked the tickets then," said Posy.

Chapter Eight

The tiny little plane bumped off the airstrip in Aberdeen. Posy looked out of the window at the sunset—at four o'clock!—and wondered again at how strange it was here.

The oddest, the worst, thing had been lying to Matt. Ever since they'd met she'd made a pact with herself to be honest with him, because as far as she could tell, he had always, always been honest with her. So when she'd announced that she was going to Scotland to scout wedding venues, he'd looked a bit furrowed—"How are you Scottish? Via Poland?"—then offered to come with her. She'd had to swallow hard and lie again and say no, she wanted to narrow it down a bit before she got him involved. Well, she did want to have a look around while she was there, although frankly she was just hoping she could get their friends and family to come as far as London to get married, really; she certainly wouldn't risk insisting they marched to Scotland.

"Well, Madonna got married in the Highlands," Matt had said finally.

"Yeah, and look how that turned out."

The night before she left, still not sleeping, she'd lain on her side and stared at his profile, wanting to stroke it with her finger, although she didn't want to wake him. She felt as if she were cheating on him, somehow.

Leah agreed.

"Let me see, you're sneaking off without telling him to see your ex-boyfriend. I just can't see how it sounds good."

"How about . . . it's a journey to find myself?"

"Hmm."

"I just feel, Leah . . . Somehow it will make me feel ready for marriage."

"*I* am ready for marriage," sighed Leah. "*You* are an idiot."

God, Chris had been right, she'd thought, hanging around Aberdeen airport for the connection. It was absolutely bloody freezing, easily ten degrees colder than London. She'd brought a big coat, but even with that the wind was raw, blowing even through the small terminal, with its Scottie dogs and haggis for sale in the gift shop. Obviously she was crazy.

The second plane was even smaller, just a little cigar shape sitting on wheels. Posy hadn't been sure if she was going to fit inside or if she'd need to stand up on the wings. There was barely time to drink a cup of terrible coffee. Looking around, the flight was filled with men with beards and books on rare wildlife; a friendly American girl beside her was a geologist who enthused at length about Shetland's extraordinary strata.

The tiny shed that served as Lerwick airport didn't look like it had much extraordinary strata when the plane bumped down in the dark. It looked derelict and lonesome and flat—there wasn't a tree to be seen in the moonlight.

Dismounting, scarcely able to believe she was in the same country technically as bus lanes and tube overcrowding and the

Gherkin, Posy wondered if she'd recognize Chris when she saw him. After all, it had been more than ten years. People didn't change much in ten years . . . did they? Maybe they did. Maybe she couldn't see him through those eyes again, a naive college girl who'd never met anyone or been anywhere.

She hoped he wasn't an idiot. She hated to think of herself as giving up three years of her life on a jerk. That would make her worry about Matt, and her judgment, even more.

He was, it turned out, completely unmistakable. In fact, it couldn't be, but . . . was he still wearing the same old coat? No. It couldn't be.

Chris stood, broad, handsome, and messy as ever, his face completely masked in a beard, at the back of the sparse crowd. She saw him first and felt her face break into a smile. In fact, a few years were nothing after all. She raised her hand to attract his attention and he returned her smile, shyly, and lumbered over.

They stood a meter apart, looking at one another. Chris was shaking his head.

"What?"

"Well. This is mad."

"Why? We're two people who know each other, aren't we? Meeting up?"

"Well, yes, but . . ."

Posy's face cracked into a smile. "Yes. I know. It does feel a bit mad."

"I mean, it's so out of the blue."

Posy looked out at the dark and ominous sky. "Actually it was more like out of the very dark gray."

Chris shook his head again. "OK. You're doing a crazy girl thing. I'm just going to accept that."

"I think that would be best," said Posy.

"So, what . . . are we meant to hug, or kiss or what?" said Chris, eventually.

"You still haven't changed your position on the old small talk, have you?" said Posy, surprised to find she was nervous.

"No. It's a waste of time."

"OK. My flight was fine, thanks."

They stood uncomfortably. Then Chris said, "You look posh."

"It's Topshop."

"I don't know what that is."

Posy felt this conversation slightly slipping out of her grasp, which, as she was planning on asking him some pretty personal questions later on, wasn't exactly ideal.

"Chris," she said finally. "It's good to see you."

"It's good to see you, too Posy."

And they leaned together for a very awkward hug. The warm musky smell of him instantly transported her to a world of single beds, of joss sticks burning, of dirty carpeting and cold mornings.

"Hey you," she said.

He drove the world's most beat-up Land Rover through the gravel roads. Neither spoke very much. Posy was taking in the bare landscape, outlined by the large moon.

"There's no trees."

"Not much of anything up here," said Chris. "It's just a lump of volanic rock, really. Populated by Vikings."

"Are they all Vikings?"

"Pretty much. You'll hear it when they talk."

Posy frowned. "Why is it so cold?"

"Well, we're near Iceland, and—"

"No, I mean, why don't you have heating in the car and things?"

The back of the Land Rover was open and the wind whistled through. It was perishing.

"In the car?" said Chris, as if this was the first he'd thought of it. "What, in here? You think it's cold in here?"

"Never mind," said Posy.

Chris turned and looked at her. "Posy, it's nice to see you, and I will say it is really lovely to have visitors. Lots of people say they want to come visit but never do, but you weren't invited or anything and yet . . . here you are."

"Here I am," said Posy.

Posy looked out at the sea, just visible to her left then disappearing into blackness. It was so desolate, but wildly beautiful in a way.

"Would it make me sound mad if I said I'm on a bit of a quest?"

Chris's eyes gleamed in the darkness. "No! What kind of a quest?"

Too late, Posy remembered his latent fondness for *Dungeons and Dragons*.

"A kind of finding myself quest."

"Oh," said Chris, sounding disappointed.

"Sorry. Were you thinking spears and that kind of thing?"

"We have all sorts up here."

"Like fish?"

"Is it fish?"

"No . . ."

"Silence? That we have."

Posy felt stupid having to spell it out. "I'm . . . I'm visiting my ex-boyfriends."

Chris raised his eyebrows.

"To make sure there are no more unanswered questions in my life. To make sure I'm ready to make a lifelong commitment to someone. To tie up the loose ends."

"Ah," said Chris.

"Is that . . . does that sound too awful? Do you want to drop me off on the way?"

"There is no more way," said Chris, stopping the car. "We're here."

"Where?" said Posy.

They were on a tiny inlet. The sea was lapping close to their feet, but it was so dark now Posy could barely see it. Before them stretched a vast darkness. She could hear in the wind the clink and clutter of tethered boats. She shivered. Chris went round to the boot and pulled out a lantern.

"Is this the bit where you pull out the boat hook and tell me that you still know what I did last summer?" said Posy nervously.

Chris rolled his eyes. "Follow me," he said.

Carefully, and wishing she'd worn slightly more grippy boots, Posy picked her way along the wooden slats of the jetty, past small fishing boats, their paint peeling and worn. Chris couldn't mean –

"Do we need to take a boat to get to your house?" she asked. "Are the Shetlands not remote enough for you? Do you live on another island?"

"No!" laughed Chris. "No."

"Well then . . . Ohh," said Posy as it became clear.

73

She glanced up. The stars were terribly bright; they felt closer up here. Posy breathed in the air. It was clean, salty, and so sharp it caught the back of her throat. Beautiful, really. She glanced around. What would she have been like? What kind of a girl would she have been, if she'd come here? What would she have done all day? She glanced at Chris, carrying the lantern along the jetty. It seemed fitting somehow, like he was always meant to be carrying a lantern somewhere in the middle of nowhere. His reassuring old-fashioned-ness, his stolid sense of getting on with things . . . it suited him. But who would she have been?

"Uh, I'm not going to carry you," he said suddenly, turning back. The spell was broken.

"No, of course not!" Posy scuttled up the narrow wooden slats, the black oily water very close underneath her feet.

The little houseboat bobbed just ahead of them. It was a square thing, not particularly pretty, but the lights in the window looked cozy and warm. The boat was quite long, and Posy could just tell it was painted green. It was called *Brunella*.

"Oh, this is sweet," said Posy. Chris looked at her to see if she was being sarcastic. "I mean it!" she said. "It's a lot bigger than my flat, for starters."

"OK," said Chris. "Watch the side."

"I can't see a single thing."

Sighing, Chris put down the lantern and gave her his hand. The feel of it—large, warm, bear-like—brought back a sense memory of him so strong and intense that, in the dark and strangeness of the night, almost made her forget who she was, and where, and why.

"Hey," he said, as she jumped on board, feeling a little shaky. "Welcome."

"Casa Chris!" said Posy, in a wobbly voice. "Wow. I feel like I'm at the end of the world."

"Just the inhabited bits of it," said a not particularly friendly voice, as a low cabin door opened in front of them. "It is freezing binkety bollocks out there."

Posy blinked, the spell broken again. A large, comfortable silhouette opened the door widely.

"Are you Posy?"

Posy nodded.

"Hello. I'm Elspeth. Come in."

Inside, the little boat was actually quite cozy. A woodburning stove crackled away merrily in one corner. There was a table with cushion-strewn benches all round it, which formed the main part of the room. A few books were jammed up against the walls, and an enormous pair of Chris's boots took up some of the space on the floor. A little galley kitchen had a kettle boiling on the two-burner hob. The couple of doors at the end suggested a bedroom and a bathroom.

"Oh, this is lovely," said Posy, meaning it. It looked like the kind of place talking woodland animals would live, although she didn't want to mention that. She scooted up around the table.

"Are you hungry?" said Elspeth. "I have stew."

"That is exactly what I would like," said Posy. She glanced around again. There was no computer, no television. A Scrabble set was up in one corner of the galley. It was the travel set, small enough to fit its surroundings and with clinging corner tiles.

"This is *very* cozy," said Posy.

"Thank you," said Elspeth. She had very long strawberry blonde hair, was wearing no makeup, and had a comfortable figure. Posy could barely stop staring—this was it! The alternate her! This was how she would have been living. Elspeth was, she noticed, as far away from Posy as it was physically possible to be, pretty much. Posy found herself slightly wishing she would go away so she could talk to Chris. That must be one of the hazards of boat living. Very hard to go away.

Elspeth eyed Posy carefully. Posy supposed they must be the same age, but somehow Elspeth felt a lot more grown up.

"So, did you have a good trip?"

"Uh, yeah, I did, thanks."

Chris was busying himself with the kettle. Posy wondered if she'd missed her opportunity to ask for some wine. Probably. Weren't they all abstemious up here? And she didn't want to look fancy or uppity or just plain drunken.

"So, uh, Posy . . ." The tea was ready. Elspeth set it in front of her with quite a jolt. "To what do we owe this pleasure?" she asked, huffily.

Posy glanced over at Chris. It was him she'd come to talk to, not whoever this was. He looked faintly embarrassed. Posy bit her lip. Did this woman think she'd come to get Chris back? Surely not, that would be crazy. Although, tracking down an ex-boyfriend on Facebook; flying seven hundred miles to see him—maybe Elspeth had a point and her huffiness was, frankly, quite justified. But she wasn't here to get him back! And why hadn't Chris mentioned he had a girlfriend anyway? At least she assumed they were boyfriend and girlfriend; they couldn't possibly share a space this small without inserting bits of their bodies into each other at some point, surely, even by accident.

"Hi . . . sorry, Elspeth is it? Chris didn't mention you."

Elspeth raised her eyebrows at him. "Is that right?"

"Uhm, Posy and I never talk," he said quickly.

"Except on the *internet*," said Elspeth, as if she'd said, "Except on the devil's notepad."

"I need to use that for work," said Chris, a little wearily. Posy wondered how this relationship was going, exactly. Secret internet use? Mind you, even big islanders need to go online occasionally. "And to check the cricket," added Chris quietly.

"OK," said Elspeth. She put out three bowls and ladled something from a single pot. Posy leaned over and smelled something familiar. She glanced up at Chris.

"Is that . . . is that *bean casserole*? The *same one*?"

Chris shrugged. "I don't know."

"What's wrong with bean casserole?" asked Elspeth sniffily. Posy felt bad. Elspeth had hardly asked for Chris's ex-girlfriend to stomp into her houseboat and start making smart-alecky remarks.

"Nothing," she said. "I tried to teach your boyfriend to cook once. Not much stuck. It's lovely. Look, Elspeth, I'm sorry to land on your doorstep like this."

"Where are you staying?" said Elspeth.

Posy was taken aback. She'd kind of assumed Chris would be putting her up—of course, she hadn't known about Elspeth then. Or the whole boat thing. Research. She should have done some research.

"Uhm," she said. "Well . . ."

Maybe there wasn't actually anywhere to stay on the entire island. Maybe they'd let her lie down with her head near the stove.

"She can stay here," said Chris. "No?"

"Well, seeing as I only found out she was coming about two hours ago . . ."

Posy felt increasingly awkward. "I could . . ."

What could she do? Did they have Holiday Inns in Shetland? She wasn't sure. It was getting quite late in the day too. Plus her leaving meant that, well, she really would have to have a holiday here, which hadn't exactly been the original plan. And it would be a lot harder to corner Chris and talk to him about what she'd planned.

Elspeth heaved a sigh. "Well, I suppose she could stay."

Posy thought about her bag and suddenly remembered she had a trump card—hurrah! The duty-free! Plus it might help wash down the bean casserole. Her tastes had definitely moved on from university.

"Uhm, I have some . . ." She brought out a bottle of gin. "Just to say thanks for having me," she added.

"Did you bring tonic?" demanded Elspeth.

So far, pondered Posy, this wasn't going so well. She hadn't really considered the other halves. There were loads of stories, she supposed, about old boyfriends and girlfriends meeting up again through the internet, and, she guessed, look, here she was. And Chris would always have been with someone; he was just that type of chap. Hmm. Well, Adam wouldn't be with anyone. He had the concentration span of a gnat with ADD. As for . . . no. He wouldn't. He couldn't have. He couldn't have moved on so quickly. Like she had.

*

After a couple of gins and orange squash (the second being markedly better than the first), Posy had ascertained that they did, in fact, have a "spare" room. Well, in reality it was more like a little coffin space they had tucked under the far end of the boat, filled with their stuff, with a paper-thin wall separating it, their bedroom, and the chemical toilet. Every time Posy thought about having to use the chemical toilet, it made her so anxious she had to drink more gin.

Elspeth had relaxed a little, but was still forming a very distinct barrier between her guest and Chris; her ample form leaning across the table. She was explaining their life philosophy at some length to Posy, who was trying to be polite.

"Yes, we live a sustainable lifestyle here. We grow our own vegetables."

"Turnips, mostly," said Chris, looking slightly sad.

"And fix everything ourselves. Did you fly up here?"

"No," said Posy. "I canoed."

Elspeth looked sad. "See, just two flights here and that pretty much wrecks our carbon savings for a year."

"So you never leave the island?" said Posy.

Elspeth shook her head.

"Wow. It's like a colder version of *Lost*. What do you do, Chris?"

"Well, I do some farming management, and I work for island conservation."

"They want to build bridges here," said Elspeth, proudly. "Chris opposes them."

"But you're a civil engineer!" said Posy in surprise. "Building bridges is what you *do*."

Chris looked embarrassed. "Well, you know, bringing in more cars is bad for the environment," he mumbled.

"What environment?" said Posy. "You don't even have any trees!"

Elspeth sniffed loudly. "So what do you do, Posy? Sit on the *internet* all day, looking up people to visit?"

Posy shrugged. "I work in marketing."

Elspeth's face took on an expression of phony concern. "Och, that must be terrible! Stuck in an office all day in the middle of a big city?"

"It is awful," agreed Posy. "Just coffee and shopping in your lunch breaks, and nice and warm in the winter and free internet and stuff."

All of a sudden there was a large gurgling noise. For an instant, nobody spoke. Then Elspeth and Chris eyed one another.

"It's your turn," said Chris.

Elspeth heaved a sigh. "But we have company."

The gurgling noise came again.

"All the more reason . . ."

"All right, all right."

With bad grace, Elspeth raised herself heavily from the table and disappeared through one of the doors at the end of the cabin. She returned carrying a very large yellow container, which glugged ominously. Posy shrank back as Elspeth shrugged on a heavy coat and hauled the container outside.

At last she and Chris were alone. Posy looked up at him. He smiled ruefully.

"I don't think your girlfriend likes me very much," she offered.

"No," said Chris. "I slightly sprung it on her. There's not a lot of girls on the island . . . Elspeth probably feels a bit intimidated."

"By *me*?" said Posy. "She could gut me like a fish!"

"She could," agreed Chris. "But she's all right really, just feeling a bit threatened." He moved across the room and stoked the fire in the little stove.

"Should she?" he said, so quietly at first that Posy couldn't believe she'd heard it.

"What?" said Posy.

He turned to face her. "Well, why are you here?"

"You think I've come to get you back?" asked Posy.

"Well," said Chris, "I didn't think you were here to examine the local wildlife. And, you know, you're getting to that age where you want a baby . . . you're probably thinking, Oh yes, good old reliable Chris, he'll do."

Posy was so shocked, she couldn't speak. He thought she'd come all this way . . . and Elspeth thought she'd barged onto their barge to grab her man.

"But . . ." She wished suddenly she hadn't redone her lipstick in the car. This was not a lipsticky kind of place. And she'd thought she was dressing down in black trousers and a patterned top, but maybe she looked up here like some kind of terrifying vamp. No wonder Elspeth was shooting daggers at her. "That's not . . ."

Elspeth banged her way back into the room, carrying the now empty yellow plastic container. Posy didn't want to think about that too much. She immediately clocked the tension, and was glad she wasn't sitting too close to Chris. Nonetheless, there was a prolonged silence in the air.

"It's a good clear night outside," said Elspeth, clearing her throat. "Why don't youse two go take a walk or something? I'm sure you've got lots to catch up on."

Posy looked at Elspeth with some respect. She hadn't realized that she looked like she was on the old pull. It was ridiculous anyway, as if she could swan back into Chris's life, ten years on, click her fingers and make him follow her back to SW4. She wanted to convey this somehow to Elspeth, but the austere set of the latter's chin made this seem very unlikely.

"Sure," she said happily, wondering if her coat could take it.

"Give me a minute," said Chris, and he took out the same old Rizla tin he'd had since they were in digs. Posy eyed it in amazement. He proceeded to pull out papers and his little pouch of tobacco.

"You still smoke?" she said before she could help herself. Of course he did; that's why he still smelled the same. It wasn't even a smell she disliked.

"Hmm," he said. "Why, is it against the law in England now?"

"No," she said. "It's just . . . I'd kind of got used to people giving up."

"Well, maybe some things don't change," he said, eyeing her meaningfully.

It took Chris nineteen hours to roll his cigarette. Posy smiled hopefully at Elspeth, who took this as an excuse to turn her back and start boiling the kettle for the washing up.

"Can I help?"

"No," said Elspeth shortly. "There isn't room."

There wasn't.

Posy and Chris left in silence.

*

Outside the only sound was the wash of water lapping on the side of boats, and their masts, clattering to themselves under the stars. Posy was silent until they reached the end of the narrow pier, following Chris's lantern and seeing around her by the light of the huge high moon. He stumbled through some high grass over a dune and, feeling increasingly strange and lost, she followed. The air was still freezing, but at least the dunes behind them banked some wind.

They were standing on a long deserted moonlit beach, as desolate as anywhere Posy had ever seen. There were just no people about, nobody at all. Presumably the sea went on from here to—where? Norway? The North Pole? Greenland? The sense of miles and miles of empty space, stretching upwards to the frozen wastes, made her feel incredibly small, and a long long way from home.

Chris walked toward the dark lapping waves, stopping to pick up a handful of stones on the way. He paused, then started to skim them. Posy could hear the light *plip, plip* of every one. She buried her hands deep in the pockets of her borrowed coat and walked toward him.

"Sorry," she said.

"What for?" said Chris. "It was a long time ago."

"No, I mean, upsetting your girlfriend."

"She'll get over it."

"Do you ever think about us, Chris?"

Chris shrugged. "Not really."

"Oh."

"Well, what do you want me to say? Yes, you ruined my whole life? We went out, it was nice, we wanted different things, we broke up. Not exactly an uncommon story, is it?"

"No," said Posy.

"Plus, you wouldn't have liked it."

"Aha! You *have* thought about me."

"Well, I didn't erase your name from my memory, if that's what you mean."

"What would it have been like for me here?" she asked, softly.

"Uhm, well, you wouldn't have liked it," he repeated.

"You don't know that," said Posy, stung. "I might have learned to like it. Maybe I'm more adaptable than you think."

"Well, it's dark for four months a year," he said. "Then in the summer it's light all the time and you can't sleep and you think you're going slightly crazy."

"That sounds like fun and a novelty," said Posy stubbornly.

"The locals suspect you if you haven't lived here for forty-nine generations and have red hair."

"Suspect you of what? Stealing all the trees?"

"That's a good question. I'm still not sure."

"Well, that's the same anywhere."

Chris turned round suddenly.

"Posy? If you don't want my spunk, then why are you here? Are you trying to stick your lifestyle in my face? Is it some kind of competition and you're meant to have won or something?"

"No!" said Posy, truly taken aback. "No. I'm sorry. I just wanted to see . . . Well. Matt's asked me to marry him."

"Who's Matt?"

"He's this bloke . . . well, he's my boyfriend, I suppose."

"You don't sound too sure."

"No, no, I am. I mean, well, I'm not sure if I should be saying fiancé."

"And he's asked you to marry him?"

"Yes."

"And you said yes."

"Uh huh."

"He's your fiancé."

"Thanks, Doctor Literal."

"So why aren't you sure?"

Posy sighed. "Because I just think sometimes . . . I followed the flow. I followed you at university then, well, just the crowd down to London and now I have a job and I'm just kind of with Matt and he's kind of great and everything but I just want to be sure. I want to be sure that the life I'm choosing is the life I would like. So I wanted to see—"

"What the alternative might have been?"

"Does that sound daft?"

Chris shrugged. "No. You *look* daft. But it doesn't sound daft."

Posy glanced at her ruined shoes. "So. What is it like?"

"My life? Don't be stupid, Posy, I'm a bloke. I never think about it."

"Ha ha ha."

The sound of their voices against the cold air, no other sound but the sluicing of the waves on the rocky shore, made Posy want to whisper.

"Well. There's not a lot of women up here," he began.

"So you just had to settle—"

"Hey!"

Posy hung her head. "Sorry. That was rude."

"Yeah, and then some. She's just jealous, OK?"

Posy rolled her eyes. "Of an engaged woman. And there must be ten thousand other farmers for her to choose from."

Chris sniffed.

"Are you guys . . . are you going to get engaged?"

Chris shrugged. "Neh, I don't think she's fussed."

"Chris! She's treating me like a piece of dung discarded from the dung of a dung beetle! She. Is. Fussed."

Chris squinted. "Really? You think?"

Posy rolled her eyes again. They were halfway up the beach, and she could feel the chill seeping into her toes. "Duh! If she didn't care she wouldn't have done that evil eye thing with her fingers when I got up to clean the glass."

"You saw that, huh?"

"Yes, I did. If you've found your life here, maybe it's time to do the decent thing."

"Because getting engaged has obviously made you so settled and content."

Posy quickly changed the subject. "So. You'll show me a bit of Shetland life?"

"I certainly will," said Chris. Then all of a sudden, he grabbed her round the waist. "It's good to see you, Posy."

Posy cuddled him back. It would have felt weird not to. "It's good to see you too, Chris."

All of a sudden, she felt his mouth descending on hers.

"Chris! What the hell are you doing?"

Chris jumped back like he'd been stung. "What?!"

"Don't kiss me! Your girlfriend is in there. With a harpoon!

Probably. And I'm engaged. Did I imagine the conversation we just had?"

"Well, what am I supposed to think when you come all this way out of the blue and start talking about emotions and things?"

"You're supposed to think: here's a human being with their own thoughts and desires exploring their own destiny."

"And it's not like we've never done it before."

"You don't . . ." Posy was spluttering by now. "Just because you sleep with someone doesn't give you a free pass for the rest of your lives."

Chris pouted, completely unembarrassed. "I don't see why not. Once you've done it a few times, you should be able to come back whenever you feel like it, I reckon."

"Is Elspeth keeping you on a short leash or what?" asked Posy, walking smartly in what she thought was the direction of the boat.

"It upturns the chemical toilet. Plus she keeps talking about babies." He hurried to catch up with her.

"*Where* would you keep a baby?"

"I know. Swinging in a hammock from the roof probably. She's being very unreasonable."

"Hmm," said Posy. "Anyway, leave me alone."

"I feel sorry for this Matt," grumbled Chris.

"What, for the fact that I don't cop off with old boyfriends? I'm sure he'll get over that."

Chris looked at her. "Well, you really have changed, you know?"

Posy glanced at him. He hadn't. Not at all, in ten years.

"How did you ever even figure out how to get on to Facebook?" she said. "You're totally stuck in the dark ages." She gestured at the pitch black horizon. "Literally!"

"I know," said Chris. "I won't be doing it again."

"Good," said Posy. "Let's go back. Now, if I dared to link arms with you to avoid twisting both my ankles, will you promise not to pounce on me?"

"I still think that's a totally bourgeois and stupid rule about not being able to go back. What, you're going to be a reformed virgin on your wedding day?"

"Shut up!"

"OK," sighed Chris, offering her his arm.

"And you're going to show me the glories of Shetland tomorrow?"

"Uhm, yeah," said Chris. "Don't bother waking up too early. Although we've got a new Morrisons."

Chapter Nine

In the event, Posy was always going to wake too early. The clanking of the chemical toilet, the creaking of the boat, the creaking of Chris and Elspeth's bed next door—Chris was, Posy decided, simply *too large* to live on a boat.

So she had lain absolutely rigid, trying not to strain to hear the urgent whisperings coming from next door, mainly from Elspeth. She was pretty sure they were along the lines of, "When is this evil bitch bag from hell getting the fuck off our boat?"

Plus the little bunk was in a curved space so cramped and tiny it felt not unlike lying in a coffin. There was a shelf full of manuals just above her head so she couldn't sit up. The pitch dark made her feel queasy, as did the slight motion of the boat and the ominous noises it made. By five a.m. she would have given anything to be back home in her nice cozy Ikea bed. She missed Matt—she missed everything, out here bobbing on the harsh Northern seas. Feeling very sorry for herself, it took a long time for her to drop off, and she had a restless, uncomfortable few hours, with shallow dreams of drowning and death and Davy Jones's locker.

"Sleep well?" boomed Chris, as she finally made her way, sticky and unrested, into the main cabin, where she could hear tea—alas, no coffee, and double alas, no Starbucks—being boiled.

"Uhm," said Posy, conscious of her little stripy pajama bottoms and vest top. She was freezing. Elspeth was wearing a full fuzzy dressing gown loosely tied round the middle and great big fuzzy slippers. She looked like a cross between a bear and a bun.

Chris smiled. "You get used to it," he said.

Posy privately thought that having a bed you had to get used to rather went against every concept of comfort and relaxation that the principle of going to bed had ever stood for, but decided not to mention it. Today she was going to be positive, inquisitive, and not freak out Elspeth.

"Would you like tea? Or do you drink some strange southerners' drink in the morning made out of Japanese goat petals?" said Elspeth, stomping fuzzily over to the kettle.

Today was going to be harder than she'd thought.

"So I thought we'd go into Lerwick," said Chris. "It's the capital."

"It's got a Morrisons," said Elspeth, defensively.

"OK, smashing!" said Posy, hoping they weren't actually going to take her and show her the Morrisons.

Elspeth plunked a bowl of gray sludge in front of Posy, along with the tea. Posy eyed it carefully, knowing this was some kind of a test.

"Ooh, porridge," she said. "I love porridge." Posy had never had porridge in her life. Her mother was strictly muesli, for all three daily meals if necessary.

"Do you want sugar or salt with it?" asked Chris. Posy tried to work out how bland something had to be before you could do that to it, then wondered if it might taste like popcorn. That would be a good way to get it down. Pretend it was just soft popcorn.

"Salt, please," she said, tentatively.

Three spoonfuls in, Posy wondered if this wasn't perhaps some dastardly plot on Elspeth's behalf to send her to the bottom of the sea wearing concrete boots. People *ate* this stuff? It tasted like plaster. She glanced up, only to see Elspeth watching her maliciously. She pushed away her bowl.

"Thanks for that!" Posy announced cheerily. "It was *delicious*. Right, I'll go and get changed."

"But you've hardly eaten a bit of it."

"Oh yes, I'm on the . . . boat diet. You're only allowed three bites of everything. Works brilliantly for Jennifer Aniston, I've heard."

"You don't look much like Jennifer Aniston," observed Elspeth.

Well, you look like one of her minders, Posy wanted to say, but managed to restrain herself.

"No, Elspeth. No, I don't," she said instead, with a heavy sigh, then headed back into the coffin-room to get dressed.

"I am never ever ever ever ever coming to frigging Shetland *ever* again," she vowed to herself through gritted teeth.

"What was that?" said Chris, poking his head round the door.

"*Chris!* Get out, I'm getting dressed."

Chris rolled his eyes. "Posy! I have totally seen it, like a million times. And anyway, the door is so thin that if I wanted to I could probably see through it anyway. And you're dressed."

Posy heard a loud sniff from Elspeth, and felt guilty again.

"Get out! Get out! Get out!"

Ten minutes later she'd adorned herself in jeans and a huge fleece of Chris's she'd found hanging on a nail. It made her look shapeless and drab, but seemed to be the only thing sensible enough to keep out the wind. Elspeth noted that she was wearing it, she could tell. She didn't mean it to be a mark of ownership, she just didn't want to freeze to death, that's all. Elspeth was clomping around unhappily.

"So, uh, we'll be home later, yeah?" said Chris. Elspeth sniffed in response.

"Are you sure you can't come with us?" asked Posy.

"No. I have to do laundry."

"Do you have a washing machine?"

Elspeth laughed. "Yes, it's in the conservatory, next to the home cinema."

Posy pouted. "Well, at least you could get a service wash."

"No, we wash our own clothes here," said Elspeth.

"There isn't a single launderette on the whole of Shetland?" said Posy, cross.

"It's just nicer to do it in fresh water," said Elspeth. "More environmentally friendly."

"What do you do, hit stuff with stones?"

There was a silence, which Posy took to indicate that that's exactly what she did do. No wonder the whole boat smelled musty.

"OK, well have a fun day," said Posy.

They left in silence.

"You know," said Posy on the way to the car. "You'll think

I'm strange and mad, but I have the weirdest sensation that that girl may not like me very much."

"It is weird," said Chris, musingly. "Elspeth could have the pick of anyone, but she seems quite jealous about me."

"What do you mean, she could have the pick of anyone?" said Posy jealously. "*Really?*"

"Oh, any girl can have the pick of anyone," he said. "They're outnumbered here about six to one."

"Seriously?" said Posy. "I should send up Leah."

"Are you still seeing that crazy friend of yours? Wow, I remember her," said Chris, shaking his head. "Does she still dress like an explosion in a dustbin?"

"She's creative," sniffed Posy.

"She's a nutjob."

"And you know a lot about fashion."

Chris smiled.

"So where are we going?"

"We're here." Chris pulled up at what looked like a great mound of stones. "It's Scapa Flow."

"What's that when it's at home?"

"This is where the original settlers lived."

"On some stones?"

"Come on out and have a look round."

Chris parked up. The wind was blistering outside, and it was hardly light even now, at ten o'clock in the morning. Even though Posy could see the airport in the distance, there was no doubting that this was a wild, wild place. Flat, windy, and deserted, she absolutely felt perched on rock in the middle of the sea.

"Why did anyone settle here?" she breathed.

"Could you stop being insulting for two seconds?" said Chris. "This is my life you're talking about."

Scapa Flow turned out to be an incredibly well preserved settlement that dated back to the Bronze Age. Carefully constructed caves and holes revealed themselves, and a way of life quite, quite alien.

"So everyone just sat down a hole round the fire till spring?" said Posy.

"When they weren't being slayed by Vikings," agreed Chris, as they walked around.

"Amazing," said Posy. "And I think I have problems."

Chris raised his eyebrows.

"Don't do that! Stop it!"

"Well, come on, Posy," said Chris. "It's not a real problem, is it, you poncing about pretending to be looking at alternative lives. You've already made it quite clear you'd hate it here. So get over yourself and your spoiled little parallel universes. Of course if everything was as perfect with "Matt" as you say, you wouldn't even be here, but let's not talk about that, shall we? Let's just point and laugh at the funny island people."

They didn't talk so much after that. And watching Elspeth and Chris make lunch in the small enclosed space of the cabin, she noticed something. As Chris brought in turnips and carrots he'd grown himself on their allotment, and Elspeth started to chop, the two of them seemed to be taking part in an intricately choreographed dance that had been going on for years—Elspeth would put out her hand, Chris would fill it with the pepper grinder, or she would point and Chris would lift a huge tureen from a high shelf. There was an intuitive sense between them that she suddenly wondered if she and Matt had, given that neither of them could ever find the potato peeler, and Matt didn't really approve of carbs anyway. The way (as Elspeth rather over-patiently explained) that they ate in tune with the seasons, mostly what they grew, and how she made her own bread (Posy was eating it at the time and wasn't entirely sure whether she was eating the bread or the table mat) and caught their own fish from the sea was a full way of living.

"But you buy your pepper at Morrisons?" asked Posy.

"Oh, the new Morrisons is great," said Chris.

"Scapa Flow was interesting," said Posy, directing her comments at Elspeth.

"They say Shetlanders really discovered America," said Elspeth.

"Well, I'm not surprised they came back," said Posy. "This is great soup, Elspeth."

Elspeth looked taken aback by the unexpected compliment.

After lunch Chris jumped up, animosity apparently forgotten. "Come on then! You'll need some warm clothes."

Posy squinted. "Warmer than your duvet that I've been wearing all morning?"

"Oh yes," said Chris.

"OK, just bring me every single item of clothing you have. And all your towels. And any old newspapers."

The daylight had gone already when they all left the boat at three p.m. and started stomping up the road.

"Where are we going?" said Posy. She was wearing two woollen hats, some mismatched gloves, tights, jeans, two T-shirts, a jumper, and two coats. She felt like an upright pig. No wonder girls did so well up here. You could look like Elle Macpherson or Anne Widdecombe under all this and no one would ever know.

"Never you mind," said Chris, striding on ahead, illuminated by the rising moon. His great clumping boots, Posy noticed, were as ideally situated to this environment as they had been inappropriate hopping up and down library stairs in Leeds, or, she envisaged, stepping on commuters' toes getting on and off tube carriages in London. Once freed from the houseboat, his ludicrous size had room to stretch out; his legs could move and he could stand up straight.

Her phone finally picked up a signal, and it rang immediately. Matt.

"Hello?"

"Hey, hon, how's it going?"

Posy fit her phone between her two hats. "Not bad."

"You sound a bit muffled."

"I'm very far away."

"Yeah, that's not really how it works."

"Oh, yeah."

Posy looked around, heading up a deserted, stony cove in the middle of a dark afternoon. London could have vaporized and she would have been none the wiser.

"So, have you seen anywhere that might be good for a wedding?" asked Matt.

"Uhm, what? Uh, actually. No. Not really. I'm not sure if it's our wedding . . . uhm, temperature. It's actually pretty bleak up here."

"Well, obviously," said Matt patiently, as if explaining things to a child. "If it was really great and amazing, loads of people would live there."

"So how are you?" Posy could hear the chinking of glasses and laughter in the background. "Are you with Baz in the wine-bar? At lunchtime?"

"No, actually," said Matt. He sounded a little distracted. "One of my clients was having a party and I thought it would be good business for me to attend."

"What, so they can see a personal trainer get drunk in the middle of the day?"

"It's just a little reception," said Matt. "Nothing fancy."

"Same here," said Posy.

"Right," said Matt, and then there was a silence. Posy wondered if he was cozying up to his clients to see if they would back him. That wasn't really Matt's style, though, he was pretty straightforward. Sometimes *too* straightforward.

"OK then," said Posy. "I'll see you tomorrow night."

"OK, love," said Matt. And he hung up.

"Was that the great lover?" said Chris. "Telling you you were his one and only darling and not to run off and do anything silly in the braes?"

"Just checking in," mumbled Posy. Where was Matt? It wasn't like him to socialize at work.

"Well, that sounds lovely," said Chris.

"Shut up," said Posy. "Thanks for the lovely freezing walk in the dark. Can we go back now? Hey, Shetland doesn't have a cinema, does it? Because I am just in the mood for . . ."

But just as she said this, they crested the hill. Posy suddenly became aware of lots of noise she hadn't noticed before—drumming, and chanting. And as they walked over the grass-ridden dunes, she saw suddenly the peak of an almighty fire growing higher and higher in the air. Next to the fire was a beautiful carved longship, its dragon head prow held up straight and strong, and along its length, round shields painted red and green. Standing over it and hauling it on ropes were two lines of men, all bearded, dressed in furs and wearing horned helmets.

For a mad instant, Posy thought that she had fallen out of time; that she was witnessing the arrival of the Vikings, en route to America, or here to plunder what they could. Then she blinked rapidly and realized that it couldn't possibly be. She glanced round, to see Chris and Elspeth killing themselves laughing at her horrified reaction.

"Welcome," said Chris grandly, sweeping out his long arms, "to Up Helly Aa!"

Along the gray stone beach, with the clear, silver water reflecting the last traces of light in the sky, were hundreds of people, all rendered oddly genderless and shapeless by the heavy clothes they were wearing. Toddlers in Fair Isle jumpers and hats stumbled drunkenly up and down the stones, pointing at the fire with delight, as the Vikings pulled their furs closely around themselves and poured copious amounts of mead down their throats to keep warm.

Chris and Elspeth were immediately greeted by people they knew; they attempted to introduce Posy, but there were just too many of them, and Posy found their accents—Scottish mixed with Scandinavian, all cascading in a rapid singsong—beautiful to listen to but, often, difficult to make out.

Instead she sat back and enjoyed the scene, as more and more people came to watch the spectacle—an annual festival celebrating the Vikings, Chris had told her, rather redundantly. Chris had produced a bottle from his voluminous pockets and passed it to her. She was surprised to find it contained Bacardi and Coke, very much her favorite from uni when they were feeling flush. She hadn't drunk it in years and was very touched that he remembered.

"Thank you," she said, smiling, then drank deeply and almost immediately felt warmer.

"Go steady on that stuff," said Elspeth.

"Don't be daft! It's Up Helly Aa!" said Chris. "Everyone has to get stonking, otherwise you'll freeze to death. Just don't frighten the children."

Posy took another long swig from the bottle, then offered it to the group that had accumulated around them, who offered her theirs back. She moved as close as she could to the fire, feeling it warming her face and hands, although even the three pairs of socks didn't seem to be able to do much for her feet.

"*Welcome!*" roared a great Viking, obviously the chief. He had a beard that looked like it had been waiting all its life for this moment—full and bushy and red, with odd bits down the sides in plaits. "To Up Helly Aa! Where we remember and celebrate our great ancestors!"

"Are these the ancestors that came ashore and basically slaughtered everyone and did pillage and stuff?" said Posy, for whom the rum was beginning to take effect.

"*Ssh,*" said Chris. "Hey, listen, there's a reason the people here are taller than mainland Scots. All the Viking blood."

"OK," said Posy. But her attention was distracted as a large group of Vikings commenced hauling the wooden longship along its runners. Lying on top of the boat, dressed in full ceremonial Viking garb, his arms crossed on his chest, his shield on top of it, was a man. Posy's eyes went wide.

"That's not . . ."

"A real man. No. It's an effigy. They don't burn real men," said Chris.

"That *Wicker Man* film was not helpful," added Elspeth.

"Think of it as symbolic," said Chris. "It can be anyone you like. This year it's the EU Head of Fisheries Policy and Management."

Posy watched. Her eyes stinging a little from a lot of alcohol, smoke from the fire, and the howling wind, she looked at the figure on the boat and suddenly felt sadness and pity for it. Even though she knew it was ludicrous.

"Burning the image of a man," mused Chris, who had been liberally applying himself to the whisky bottle. "Have you ever done that, Posy?"

Posy looked at him. "No," she said.

"But that's what you're doing now, isn't it? Burning your past? Burning the memory of the other guys so you can marry this one?"

There wasn't a trace of bitterness in his voice, but even so, Posy realized he was right. As the chief Viking held up a flaming torch lit from the huge bonfire, and the other Vikings prepared to push the boat out to sea, she felt, suddenly, a strange lightness, as the boat erupted and the effigy itself took flame. The crowd cheered and the sight itself felt ancient and atavistic, as the men braved the freezing waves to let the boat catch the current and bear itself away.

"That's how I want to be buried," said Posy fervently.

"You're not allowed," said Chris. "I know, it's not fair."

"Well, promise you'll do it to me secretly in the middle of the night then."

Chris laughed. "OK. Yes. Me too. We'll have to secretly

build the longships in the dead of night. What about you, Elspeth?"

Elspeth looked at him, the firelight reflected in her eyes.
"I'll throw myself on yours, silly."

Chris kissed her, suddenly, just as the effigy flamed up
sharply as it caught light, and the boat sailed further and
further away, an outline of bright, flaring light against the all-
encompassing darkness.

Posy smiled to herself. Finally. This was what she was doing:
burning and celebrating the memories of other men who have
been, and leaving the life she was going to clean and new again.
She stood apart, as Chris and Elspeth embraced, no longer bick-
ering, but a solid, happy unit with its face pointed north.

Posy sneakily blew a kiss to the boat, now drifting toward
the northeast, as if finding its way back to its Scandinavian
home.

It was Chris, she knew, on that boat. And he, as she could
see, already was home. And it was time she went home too;
back to home, back to love. Matt.

"Are you ready," said Chris finally, turning to her, when the
boat was just a flicker of light on the distant horizon, "for a bit
of a hooley?"

Posy thought about it for five seconds. She was casting
off her old skin too; she'd said farewell to the old her, just as
Up Helly Aa celebrated the end of the old year. She should
celebrate.

"Yes, I am!"

The local pub was basically just a shed in the middle of
nowhere. But it had a fire blazing in the grate, local beer and
much whisky behind a makeshift bar, as well as a full army of

fiddle players and accordionists. It was also absolutely heaving, and so warm that everyone tore off their jackets and coats as quickly as they could.

"Do you all write your name in your things?" asked Posy, looking for a corner to dump her stuff, only to find it already completely overflowing with North Face jackets and oilskins.

"No," said Elspeth reprovingly. "We share." Then she took off the last of her jumpers to reveal, underneath, the most sensational red Viking dress—there was criss-cross embroidery all the way down the full bodice, before the velvet turned into a skirt. Let loose of her woollen tammy, her long, strawberry blonde hair cascaded in braids, and her makeup-free face, which Posy had registered as so pale and plain, suddenly formed the perfect accompaniment to her colorful hair and dress.

"Elspeth!" Posy exclaimed before she could help herself. "You look beautiful!"

For the first time, Elspeth smiled at her in a way that was neither nervous nor sarcastic. "Thank you," she said.

"I agree," said Chris, and whirled her off romantically, her braids whizzing, on to the makeshift dance floor. Posy fought her way to the bar and, after checking to see what everyone else was doing, put down a more or less random amount of money and picked up three whiskies.

When Chris and Elspeth failed to reappear, she decided on balance to drink them all, and before she knew it, she too was being twirled around the dance floor, by a very hairy and muscular Viking. She gave herself up to the incredibly loud sound of the fiddles and pipes, stamping and turning as close to everyone else as she could. The Viking knew what he was doing so she let herself follow him and, before she knew it, found herself red-faced and full of laughter.

"What's your name?" she gasped.

"Erik," he said, and she had no idea if this were true or simply his Viking name, but thought it was too funny to ask any more so kept on dancing nonetheless. The fiddles grew wilder and stranger—the music seemed no longer Scottish, but something older and more foreign, as if it came from the rocks themselves—and Posy found she needed to cool down.

Outside, the cold sobered her up immediately: it was heart-stopping. Erik the Viking immediately put his fur wrap around her.

"Thank you," she said.

"Not at all," he said, then, without warning, for the second time in two days, someone leaned in to kiss her. Maybe if you lived in a place where the weather was unpredictable, you learned to grab your chances while you could, wondered Posy, while she could still think. Or maybe it was just the Viking way. Yes, that was it—the Viking way.

"Hey!" she said, as his bearded head descended toward hers. She'd never fended off an attempted kiss from someone with a large beard before. Not to mention the horned helmet. "Hang on!"

"I can't hang on!" said the Viking unapologetically. "I'm a *Viking*!"

"Oh, I see your point," said Posy, frantically pushing him away. "But still. I'm not up for rape and pillage. I'm meant to be on a voyage of discovery."

"Well," said the Viking, "you might discover that you like kissing Vikings."

"I'm sure they're very nice," said Posy. "Thank you very much. But I think actually that I've had enough discovery for today and I should probably go home."

"*Nei!*" said the Viking. "*Nei! Ikke gå!*"

Posy sized up the situation quickly, and, as he bent in again, grabbed his horned hat and threw it as far away as she could.

"*Swina bqllr,*" said the Viking, and charged after it. Posy dashed back into the bar, put on five layers of completely random clothing—thus rendering her, as she had hoped, completely unrecognizable—and found Chris and Elspeth to take her home.

Posy is hungover.

Catching a flight the next morning felt both horrible, courtesy of a dramatic whisky headache—in the end, the three of them had sat up very late, she and Chris telling Elspeth hoary old university tales of derring-do—and an odd sensation Posy had of being trapped between two worlds, as if catching a flight shouldn't be possible in this tiny, old-fashioned corner of the country. Elspeth had softened up entirely, especially when she heard about the amorous Viking. It looked like the message had finally got through that she wasn't there to cart Elspeth's man back to London. That and all the whisky, of course.

"I can't believe I never got to see the Morrisons," she said to Chris, as he gave her one of his characteristic bear hugs at Departures.

"Next time," he promised. And as she grinned reluctantly, he said, "Or we'll see you at your wedding."

"Oh yes!" said Posy. "You know, we have something called Waitrose."

"Waitrose? Really? Will I like it?"

"I think so."

She hugged Elspeth. "Thanks for putting me up."

"That's all right," said Elspeth, graciously. "It's still funny to think of Chris going out with you for all that time."

"I know," said Posy. "But I think he was probably always just waiting for someone like you."

Elspeth smiled and looked embarrassed, and shuffled closer to Chris.

"OK, go, city girl," said Chris. "You can put your heels back on on the plane."

"I will do that," said Posy. Then she slept heartily all the long long long way down the British Isles.

Chapter Ten

"You have a rosy look to you," said Fleur, suspiciously.

They were sitting in Tiger Tiger, close to Posy's office. She couldn't believe how busy and crammed London was, even though she'd only been away for the weekend.

"You do," said Leah, who was wearing a tunic that made her look really pregnant, even though she was incredibly slim. Posy reckoned it would be a good thing if it meant no men bothered to approach them, in case they were talking about breast pumps or something. She needed some girl talk.

"No, I don't," said Posy. "No one tried to, like, snog me or anything. Honestly."

Leah and Fleur swapped looks.

"I mean, it was just a bit of fresh air . . . in the open air . . . countryside et cetera."

"Can we buy Posy some more wine?" asked Fleur hopefully.

"I don't want any more wine. I drank too much wine. And whisky. Mostly whisky."

"And?" said Leah.

"And nothing. It was nice actually."

"Nice?"

"Nice. For a small rock in the middle of the ocean."

"And what about El Stinko?"

"Stop calling him El Stinko, Fleur! It's not funny and is actually quite offensive."

"It's not," said Fleur. "It's useful and descriptive. And it means when you're in a room with him you don't need to check to see if it's him because you'll already know it's El Stinko. So it's more of a timesaver than anything else."

Posy took another small sip. She was still suffering, two days on, from her whisky hangover. Matt had been out working when she'd returned the day before, and she'd hardly seen him. She was glad. She didn't like the idea of lying to him, plus she wanted time for the red bristle marks to fade from her cheeks.

"So?" prompted Leah. "Was he living ferally and desperate for a glimpse of civilization?"

"Did he need you to save him from his freezing, bear-like existence?"

"Chris is *fine*," said Posy. "He lives on a boat."

Leah squinted. "You mean, he has a boat to live on?"

"Yes."

"But he doesn't live in, e.g., the Caribbean or the Mediterranean or western Australia . . ."

"No."

"Or the Bahamas or Hawaii or . . ."

"OK, you've made your point. The boat was quite cozy, actually."

"Once you got used to the—"

"FLEUR! Shut up now!"

Fleur pouted. "I was only saying." She gave a big sigh. "Why

107

am I sitting here with you two killjoys when I could be getting in touch with my inner guardian angel?"

"That's a good question," said Posy. "Why aren't you?"

Fleur pouted.

"And he's got a nice girl in the Shetlands," Posy went on.

"Aha!" said Leah. "What's she like? Does she look like you?"

"Or does she not look like you but he's made her have lots of plastic surgery to look like you?" said Fleur.

Leah and Posy stared at Fleur until, finally, she got up and left, muttering something about a party they weren't invited to.

"What has got *into* her?" said Posy. "She's being unconscionable. Just so rude all the time!"

Leah shrugged. "I know, it's strange. She's taken this idea of you talking to your exes really weirdly."

"Well, it wasn't her place to decide if she liked them or not."

"I know. Maybe she's jealous."

"Of me? Fleur is *never* jealous of me. In fact, she never misses an opportunity to rub in exactly how much better than me she is in every single way."

"Well, she wouldn't bother doing that if she wasn't jealous, would she?"

Posy thought about it. "Hmm. Maybe not. But she's always been the pretty, popular one."

"Yes, and look. There you are, taking a measured, mature look at the main relationships in your life, prior to settling down with a lovely man."

Posy briefly thought about her wild Viking hooley and blushed somewhat.

"Whereas she's still ditzing about here and there, dating boys who pretend to be in bands, hanging out in Camden, for goodness' sake—she's not a teenager anymore, but she could earn more from a paper round."

"Hmm," said Posy again. "I suppose that's one way of looking at it."

"Plus, she enjoys being really really really annoying."

"And that's the other."

"So was it worthwhile?" asked Leah. "Did you discover what you were looking for?"

"You know," said Posy, "I really didn't think I would. At first I thought it was just gruesome and horrible and that Chris needed rescuing and it was all awful."

"Yes, all that horrible countryside and wildlife and fresh air . . . how could that possibly compare with the overpriced craziness of SW1?" said Leah.

"But then, I kind of figured out . . . well, it suited him. His girlfriend is, like, *really bossy*, but he likes that. And he tinkers a bit here and there and has an oil stove and lots of time to read books, and it was a really nice kind of life."

"Just not the one for you."

"No. But, yes, I do feel better. No hard feelings, no regrets . . . it was a long time ago."

"Good," said Leah. "I'm glad it went so well."

"He hasn't changed a bit, not really," said Posy.

"Did he think you had?"

"Yes," said Posy.

"For the better?"

"Hmm."

"Hmm," echoed Leah. "Did you fancy him?"

"No," said Posy. "Well, about as much as I did when we broke up. We were like siblings by then."

"OK, good," said Leah. "Well, I'm glad it all worked out."
She paused. "Are you going to tell me who gave you that stubble
rash on your chin then?"

"No!" said Posy firmly. The Viking had slightly left his
mark when he'd swept in. "Let's talk about our engagement
party."

Margie looked sniffy when she got into the office the following
morning. She never, Posy reflected, skipped an opportunity to
get at her. Today she was wearing a tightly fitted short jacket
over unflattering trousers, with a large cat brooch with spooky
amethyst eyes winking at everyone.

"Enjoy your holidays, did you?"

"I took two days off," said Posy. "I cleared it with Gavin."

"Yes, well, I set up holiday rotas every year in January, and
it's not appropriate for people to take leave at such short notice.
It's very unfair to the rest of the staff and . . ."

Posy tuned Margie out while endeavoring to still look attentive. Sometimes it was the only way. She liked the office, even
more since Gavin had started working there, but Margie had
never ever forgiven her for *him*, even though it was years ago
now. She thought about Chris, being his own boss and working
his own hours, answerable to nobody. Her job had a lot going
for it, but yes, sometimes that would be nice. Of course, that
was a lot easier to do if you could grow your own turnips in the
back garden and didn't mind living off them for most of the
winter, but still it seemed, when Margie started having a go, an
enviable existence.

Gavin bounced in. "How goes it then, Posette?" he
breezed. "Tell me your mystery mission put you off the whole

ridiculous idea for life. Well worth two days out of anyone's schedule."

Margie retreated, looking wounded.

"It was nice, actually," said Posy. "Useful to see that domestic harmony can be achieved under almost any circumstances."

"Yeah, right," said Gavin. "You know what the witch has done now? She changed the password on all my bank accounts and bills. So now I can't get anything done."

"Ooh, that *is* harsh," said Posy, taken aback.

"I know. I've already lost the internet service and the satellite telly. Probably be the water next."

"Mightn't she just have changed the password to something? Something you can guess?"

Gavin frowned. "What, like "Gavin is an arsehole"?"

Posy shrugged. "It's possible."

""I hate Gavin"?" mused Gavin.

"Could be."

"And that, Posette," said Gavin, pointing at her in front of the whole office, "is why we hired you. Smart thinking like that. I'll be in my office."

"I thought you'd come round to the idea of this party," said Matt that evening. "Something *in London*. Nice. For us and our friends and families."

Posy snuggled up to him, enjoying being home and cozy and familiar, as outside, against the seventh-floor window, rain hurled itself incessantly. "I'm glad we're not on a boat," she murmured, half asleep.

"Uh, me too," said Matt. "Although rowing is a great cardiovascular . . ."

"Ssh, Ssh," said Posy. "Stop it. Shall we book a room above a pub?"

"And tell the world."

"And tell the world."

And she turned her face to his on the sofa, and, feeling calm, kissed him full on the mouth.

Chapter Eleven

Posy hopes everyone is coming to the party!
Comment: 17 people like.
Comment, Annie: See you there!
Comment, Pete B: Wouldn't miss it.
Comment, Margie: I wasn't informed of any party, but
obviously wish you well.

"What are you wearing?" Posy entered the tiny bedroom, putting on her fail-safe purple party frock that made Leah sigh with resignation every time she saw it, but made Posy feel confident and small(ish) of waist.

Matt looked up from where he was practicing a new stretch. "What do you mean?"

"For the party that you wanted. What are you wearing? Maybe you should get a purple tie and we could be like Posh and Becks."

Matt looked at her. "Is that what you would like?"

"*No!* Apart from the expensive watches and stuff."

"I hadn't really thought about it. My dress trainers maybe? Something boxfresh?"

"Matt. You're thirty-four. Soon to have a wife. Boxfresh is no longer an adjective you need."

"OK, smarty pants. Tell me how it is in London again. Us Blackpool idiots know nothing. Do I need a top hat? I don't even know where to buy a monocle."

"What about a shirt?"

Matt shrugged his shoulders. "My mates will tease me."

"What are you all, *nine*?"

Matt's friends from the gym were quite tribal: they liked football, body building magazines, and trying to pull the more attractive of the gym bunnies under the nose of Mr. Headingly, their boss. Posy found them a bit intimidating in a group—all her friends went on about how fit they were all the time.

"Well, who's coming then? The Lord Mayor to do an inspection?"

Posy shrugged. "The usual, really. The uni lot, the girls from the office."

Matt looked perturbed. "Are they all going to get pissed up again and launch themselves at the guys? It's a bit embarrassing."

"Why?"

Matt shrugged. "'Cause some of your friends are . . . you know."

Posy did and she hated him saying it. "You mean they're not twenty-five years old with the BMI of a hamster? And the brain of a hamster?"

"Well, they spend all night saying they reckon my friends are thick, then they get totally pished up, show off their gigantic knockers and launch themselves at them."

"That doesn't sound so bad."

"OK. I suppose as long as they're warned. Who else is coming? Your mum?"

Posy nodded. "Probably. With her lemon face on."

"Aren't parties good for the psyche?"

"Not when you're propelling your eldest daughter into a life of slavery and misery."

"Oh, yes. Will you make me a cup of tea?"

"No."

"OK. What about your dad?"

Posy shrugged, applying her makeup in the mirror over the chest of drawers. "I asked Mum to tell him about it."

It was all right for Matt, he had two nice parents who loved him dearly. Wasn't the same thing at all.

"So don't you care if he comes or not? He is your dad, Posy. You are a bit—"

"He won't." Posy shut her eye shadow with a snap. Matt would never understand. His dad had never walked out on his wife and family. He'd never had to watch his own mother crumple and fall apart.

They'd met, in fact; she and Matt had run into them on Oxford Street one day. Her dad's second wife Marian was there, with their overgrown son Jason, and they were walking into Garfunkel's. Posy and Matt were on their way to Niketown.

"Oh Christ! It's my dad!" Posy had said, to Matt's surprise, trying to push them into the store.

"*Posy!*" Marian had always tried to be warm toward both of the girls, which, as a heavily dyed, large-bosomed blonde who'd stolen their dad, they treated as ridiculous. "How lovely to see you here!"

"We live in London," said Posy. "Hi . . ." She didn't really like to say Dad. "Hi, Jason."

Jason grunted. "I want chips. Real chips."

"I'm sure they'll have real chips," said Marian, stroking the back of Jason's beefy shoulders. Jason was twenty then. She turned to Posy, looking worried. "Do you think Garfunkel's does real chips?"

"I've no idea," said Posy stiffly. She knew she was being rude, but she found it hard when her whole body went rigid inside. What he had done to them and her mother.

"Hello," said Matt, stepping forward with his hand outstretched. "I'm Matt."

Posy's dad, Ray, had shaken it. "Hello," he'd said with a smile. "Are you . . . ?"

"I'm Posy's boyfriend."

Later, Posy was so proud of Matt for the calm way he'd dealt with the situation. At the time, however, she was mortified. Her father was just so obviously pleased.

"Oh, hello! How nice to meet you! We never get to meet any of Posy's young men, uh, not that . . . anyway. We're in town to take Jason to the football."

"Oh yes? Arsenal?"

"Of course!"

"I like Gallas," said Jason, launching into an incomprehensible (to Posy) discussion of tactics. Her father and Matt joined in, all gesticulating excitedly.

"What are they like, those men of ours?" said Marian, affectionately. "It's good for Jason to get out and about. He's so sensitive, you know."

Posy thought Jason was possibly the least sensitive example of humanity outside of Simon Cowell, but didn't mention it.

"Hmm," she said.

"He's lovely looking, your bloke," said Marian. "Seems nice too." She studied him a bit longer. "You know, it's funny," she said. "He reminds me a bit of your dad when he was younger."

"You are joking," said Posy.

"Oh no. He had hair once, you know."

"Yes, I remember," said Posy sourly.

"We'd . . . we'd love you both to come out to Essex sometime," said Marian. "Anytime. You don't have to ask, just pop in."

Posy's dad overheard. "Yes, we would. Plus I have to explain a few simple rules of football to this young man here."

"Ah, no, I don't think so," said Matt, smiling. "Your father, Posy, appears to be laboring under several terrible miscomprehensions."

Jason snorted. Ray smiled.

"Listen," Matt added, "don't suppose you'd like to join us for lunch?"

Marian nodded excitedly.

"We have to get on," Posy had said.

Matt looked disappointed. "Really?"

"Yes. We have to get those trainers."

"I have forty-five pairs of trainers. It's not that urgent, surely?"

But Posy had been adamant. Matt hadn't understood at all when she wouldn't speak to him all the way home.

"What's up?" he said. "He seems nice. They all did."

"Well, he isn't," Posy had said. "He left me when I was

eight years old. And Fleur was four. For her. So no. He's not that nice."

And after that, the conversation was closed.

So Matt knew when to leave it alone. He'd tried to prod her about her father before, and got absolutely nowhere. He bent to his trainers, the Converse that Posy liked because they reminded her of her favorite Doctor Who.

"You're not really sure about this party, are you?" asked Matt.

"Yes, I am, I'm fine!" said Posy.

"What's up? Don't your mates approve of me?" He pulled her to him.

"They think you're far too good for me . . . I'm joking."

"You look nice."

"Thank you." Posy stroked his handsome face. There was nothing to worry about. Nothing. He wasn't like her dad. Nothing like him.

"How bad can it be?" said Matt.

The party, given that she wasn't exactly looking forward to it, turned out busier than Posy had expected. Well, obviously there were a clutch of gym bunnies from Matt's work, whom Posy had always made a point of avoiding. They were standing around the bar dressed in Adidas—Posy often wondered what the point was of all that incredibly painful working out and starving yourself if you were going to cover yourself up with trackie bottoms like Kerry Katona on a bender. If she was a hard-bodied size six she would wear Herve Leger and a ballgown to pop down to the shops. They stood together drinking smoothies and looking faintly contemptuous, eyeing up the bodies of the other girls.

Well, excuse *me* for people trying to have fun at a party, thought Posy crossly.

Although was that Joyce from her office getting the punch funneled down her neck? Good! It was only seven-thirty. Posy put on her best smile and decided to be nice to everyone, as she was princess of this party. And to think she hadn't even been sure about Matt, or getting engaged . . .

"Hello, Kaylee, Staycee, Haylee, and Cayree," she said, smiling. How did they even get their ponytails to swing in unison like that? Had they had a meeting? "Thanks for coming!"

"Congratulations," said one of them—it could have been Kaylee, Staycee, Haylee, or Cayree—without really allowing a smile to crack across her orange face.

"So you got Matt," said another. "Well, he's always been popular."

Posy wondered what that was supposed to mean.

"Yes, what was your secret?" said another, in a slightly snarky tone. As always when she went near a gym, Posy was instantly aware of every tiny piece of cellulite on her body. She realized her ambitions to be a delightful princess to everyone all night were perhaps a tad unrealistic, and it wasn't even eight o'clock yet. Focus. What Posy really wanted to say was *Oh, didn't he tell you? He hates that over-worked-out look. Thinks it's a bit desperate. Likes something a bit more self-confident and feminine.* After all, they were asking such rude questions. Instead, she smiled politely and muttered, "Oh, it's a really filthy trick I picked up in Bangkok," and started to back away, scouting for the tray of mini-sausages. They were watching her strangely regardless. Well, it didn't matter now, did it? Matt was hers, hahahaha, and she didn't have to have those snot-faces looking down their noses at her. So there.

She headed back into the main body of the room, feeling wicked and excited. Matt was across the other side, talking to someone else in a tracksuit. She sighed. Maybe she could ban tracksuits from their marriage. Perhaps unlikely with a personal trainer . . . She went over to him and gently pinched his bum.

"Ow!" yelled Matt.

"Hey, it's my bum now," said Posy. Matt looked a trifle embarrassed, but put his arm round her. "Uhm, sweetheart, this is the boss of my gym, Mr. Headingly."

Mr. Headingly was so well-preserved he looked absolutely dreadful. Between the carefully dyed hair, the eye lift, the ingrained tan, the too-white teeth, the honed figure and the manicure, he could have been any age from forty to a hundred and five.

"Nice to meet you," said Posy. "Do you run that whole gym?"

Mr. Headingly let out a loud laugh, showing off his stupidly white teeth. "Do I run that whole gym?"

Matt laughed too. Posy shot him a look to ask him what the hell he was laughing at, but he couldn't return her gaze.

"So, is that a no?" she ventured.

"Lady . . ." He seemed quite overcome with fake mirth. Posy wanted to glance at her watch. "You tell her, Matt," he managed eventually.

"Uhm, Mr. Headingly has five gyms," said Matt. Posy couldn't quite see why that was so funny. If he'd said, "Mr. Headingly owns every gym from here to Sydney, Australia, and also the Olympics," well, that might have been something strange, but . . .

"Wow," said Posy. "Five gyms. That's amazing."

"So, what do you do to manage to tempt my top personal trainer here?"

Matt looked at her, grinning. Posy felt a little flicker run across her.

"You know, I wish everyone would stop asking me that! I don't have any special tricks. Except for, you know, all the filthy ones."

Mr. Headingly laughed again. "Oh yes, you chunky girls are always right goers."

Posy froze. Matt did too, right between his boss and his new fiancée. Thankfully Leah came bouncing up, wearing a top that appeared to be made out of Licorice Allsorts. She had the kind of body mass index Mr. Headingly would approve of (it was the law for working in fashion), which meant two glasses of the fake champagne in her empty stomach and she was on the point of falling over.

"Matt! *Matt!*" she yelled, slurring slightly. She caught sight of Mr. Headingly and tried fitfully to focus. "How *old* are you?" she blurted, before Posy grabbed her arm.

"Now, that's a good question," said Mr. Headingly, puffing out his chest, clearly waxed, through the hippy Indian cotton shirt he was wearing. "What would you reckon?"

"Sixty-one," said Leah.

Mr. Headingly took a step back. All the jocularity had gone out of him and he looked winded. "Uh, yes. Sixty-one," he muttered. "Exactly. Uhm. Well done."

But Leah had already turned away. "*Matt.*" She launched herself at him.

Posy closed her eyes in embarrassment. She suddenly remembered why she hadn't really wanted a party at all. Too sensitive, the two worlds coming together. Too much opportunity for people to point fingers and ask questions.

"I just want to say," said Leah, clutching his shoulder very tightly. I just want to say it's not even a quarter to eight and all my friends are steaming, thought Posy. Her mother wasn't even *here* yet.

"We can't . . . we never thought Posy would *ever* get married. We thought she'd be, like, alone forever after all the disasters she had."

Oh great. Fucking great, thought Posy. This was exactly what she needed right now. "*Do* shut up, Leah. And you and whose committee thought this anyway?"

Matt was looking increasingly worried.

"Oh, *everyone* who knows you. We thought you just weren't the marrying kind, *you* know. You've said it yourself."

"So I was, what, the grow old alone and bitter and eat myself to death kind?"

"No . . . yeah . . . anyway, doesn't matter now, does it?"

Another friend of Matt's wandered by, in black sports shorts so tight he'd actually caused a ripple effect as he moved through the crowd. Leah immediately put her hand over Posy's eyes.

"You're not allowed to look at those anymore! No strange winkies now you're getting married!"

Posy batted her hand away. "*Best friend!* Could you please *stop this*!"

The man slouched up to Matt.

"Hey, heard you were getting married, man. Couldn't believe it. Are you mad?"

"Clearly," said Posy.

"God, all those women who request you specifically."

Matt started to go pink round the ears.

"All that exercise," he went on, "know what I mean?"

Posy glanced at Mr. Headingly. "You know, first three times I got married . . ." he was saying.

Posy wandered off. What *had* they put in the punch? Over by the snack table, her boss Gavin, the huge buff Aussie who never took any shit off anyone, was . . . was he *crying*?

"What's up?" said Posy kindly. She felt like crying herself. Where were all the congratulations and presents?

"Oh, nothing," said Gavin. "Just seeing you all so fresh and hopeful . . . but only I know that it all turns to shit in the end. All of it."

Posy had known Gavin was going through a divorce, but she hadn't realized it was this painful. She'd thought he was coping with it in the same bluff way he coped with everything. Now, watching the tears leaking down his sozzled, red face, she could see perhaps this wasn't so.

"She burned our wedding album," he said. "So I'll never see what our wedding day was like ever again. Which is a good thing, obviously."

"She was clearly a crazy person," said Posy, trying to be reassuring while also trying to remember whether parties weren't meant to be, like, fun.

"Divorce turns everyone into a crazy person," said Gavin. Suddenly, he grabbed at her hands.

"Promise me," he said, urgently. "Promise me you'll never put yourself in that position. Promise me you could never be somewhere you could hurt someone that badly, or let them hurt you."

"Uh, OK," said Posy.

Gavin squeezed her hands tighter. "Don't get married! I beg you! Please! Promise me!"

Posy was rarely overjoyed to see her mother stalk into a room looking snooty. But tonight she was.

"Gavin, I have to go and see my mother."

"Is she married?"

"Divorced."

"*See?! See?!*"

This was getting worse and worse. With the ghost of Marriage Future echoing in her ears, Posy shook out her hands and gave a big sigh. Gavin had lumbered off in Matt's general direction. Oh Christ. This was turning into a disaster. Her university friends were, as predicted, lining the walls, trying to simultaneously look down on, and pull, Matt's fit gym friends. It didn't look very nice, especially as the female gym bunnies were still hanging out and laughing.

"Posy!" came her mother's voice imperiously from the other end of the room. Many of Matt's friends turned round to see who was shouting, then looked back at each other, sniggering. All right, Posy wanted to say, so my mother has a carrying voice—get over it, tracksuit boys. Instead she hurried up the hall.

"Mum."

Jonquil gave her a light kiss. "I don't see any chains."

"No."

"Or shackles. Have people been giving you cleaning products for gifts? And did I tell you—do *not* close your own bank account."

"Mu–um. Be nice. For five seconds. *Do* you want to come and say hi to Matt?"

Matt's parents couldn't make it down from Blackpool in

the end, though they would come for the day itself of course. They were very old and rather sweet and the two times Posy had been up to see them she couldn't believe how calm their house was—filled with pictures of their small cocker spaniel, about whom they talked more than their only son. Nobody ever picked a fight about Iraq, or the rights of women in Yemen, or brought up female circumcision at the dinner table. Mrs. Farmer even cooked proper dinners, things like shepherd's pie and lasagne, proper full meals that had started life looking like one thing and ended up as something else. And she didn't seem to feel it was launching herself into a life of slavery to do it. When Posy had mentioned that she had been the family cook, Mrs. Farmer had looked extremely shocked, as if this were quite cruel. Her mother, on the other hand, had been terrified that Matt would want his dinner cooked by her, a fate almost as horrifying as being called Mum.

"He's not going to call you Mum."

"I don't even like *you* calling me Mum."

"I know that, Mum."

However, at least she'd turned up, as had Fleur, with, Posy noticed with a sinking heart, a whole posse of her hippie girlfriends, who were all in their twenties, droopily dressed and beautiful as rosebuds. She saw the gym boys immediately drop their desultory chat with her thirty-something friends, stand up a bit straighter and look a bit more interested. Oh God. That meant all her single friends would now get absolutely sloppy drunk and start fights with the blokes who were no longer chatting them up. Great great great.

"Yes, I will come and see Matt," said her mother. Posy thought back to the last time they'd met, after she'd told her mother about the engagement. Matt had actively sulked. It was only Sunday lunch.

"You know, it's a bit early to start being really happy not to have to see your mother-in-law," Posy had said before they arrived.

"She doesn't like cooking for me," said Matt.

"She doesn't like cooking for anyone!"

Matt looked uncomfortable. "OK. Well then, I don't really like the way she asked me if getting into sport was a way of not being in touch with my true feelings, and distracting myself from everyday life."

"Oh that," said Posy carelessly.

"The first time she met me."

"It's kind of her job," said Posy, feeling awkward. It was OK for her and Fleur to complain about their mum, but she didn't really like anyone else doing it.

"Yes, well, I don't ask her to hit the floor and give me twenty every time I see her, do I?"

"You *should* do that," said Posy. "That might be good."

Matt had pulled on his rugby shirt and looked up at her. Posy reflected once again how handsome and muscular he looked. He really was a catch.

"She doesn't think I'm good enough for you."

Posy sighed. They were going to be late if they were going to fall out about it.

"That's not true," she explained patiently. "She doesn't think *marriage* is good enough for me."

"And how is that different?"

"Can we not argue about my crazy mother?"

Matt kissed her. "OK, calm down. I didn't say your mother was crazy, that was you."

"No, but you didn't correct me either, just now, when I said it."

Matt held his hands up in defeat. "OK, OK, I give in."

Sure enough, it had gone about as well as she'd expected. Her mother had even asked him if he'd read Freud, for goodness' sake. That was just being vindictive.

Matt came over to her beckoning hand.

"Hello, Mum," he said now. Posy closed her eyes.

"Jonquil will be fine," said Jonquil. "Or Doctor Fairweather, if you must."

Matt glanced at Posy.

"I believe I must," he said. Posy gritted her teeth and took a slug of her punch. This was turning into an extremely long evening.

She glanced round. She'd asked her mum to ask her dad but it didn't look like he was going to show. Which was fine, of course it was. After all, he'd missed just about everything else, and if he turned up now, Jonquil would probably start chucking stuff at him anyway. Far better not to have to bother about that at least. Marian had sent a card, but she'd barely glanced at it.

"I see *he* isn't here," said Jonquil, annoyingly chiming with Posy's thoughts. Even though they'd been divorced for over twenty years, he was still *he*. Jonquil lowered her voice to what she thought was a whisper, although, it being Jonquil, it was still about one hundred decibels.

"Shows what *he* thinks of marriage, darling."

"Fleur!" shouted Posy. "Can you get Mum a drink, please?"

As Fleur languidly disengaged herself from a crowd of admirers (being watched beadily by Posy's older friends, lining the bar and drinking absurdly huge glasses of wine) and sashayed over, Posy decided that a huge glass of wine was exactly what she needed. She joined her friends with relief, who escorted her over to the low cozy banquettes at the back.

"How did you manage it, Posy?" asked Shell, her old flat-mate. "You were always such a mess with blokes."

"I wasn't!" said Posy.

"You were! Remember Adam?"

"Forget about Adam."

"And what about that other bloke?" said Joyce from the office. "Who you were so nuts on nobody saw you for a year and a half."

Posy stiffened and took a long draught from her wineglass.

Leah came careering over, obviously completely pissed.

"Did she tell you what she's doing?"

"No!" said the girls. "What?"

"Nothing," said Posy. "I'm getting married."

"She's looking up her ex-boyfriends!" gabbed Leah. "She's tracking them down through Facebook! To say goodbye before she gives it all up."

"No way!" said Joyce, looking respectful. "Wow. Giving them a second chance?"

"It's not like that," said Posy.

"It is too," said Leah. "She even went up to see one in Scotland. Well, come on, Posy, it's not like everyone doesn't know you're settling for Matt—he teaches gym, for Christ's sake."

Posy glanced around. Her mother was by the bar talking

to Fleur and looking annoyed. Gavin was sitting on his own in the corner, tears pouring down his face. One of the girls from the office had forced herself on one of Matt's friends, and they were snogging by the door. The noise levels had reached insane levels. Everyone else was yapping obliviously. Couldn't they see this was awful, a total disaster? What were they all talking about anyway? The two of them and how badly matched they were? Could this get worse?

"SPEECH!" shouted Leah.

"No way," said Posy.

"No, I mean, I'm going to make a speech."

"How much wine have you had?"

"SOME!"

"Please, please don't."

But it was too late. Leah had already stood up on a chair and was wobbling about a bit. She clapped her hands. The room went silent. Posy felt her heart in her mouth.

Leah looked around the room. "Welcome, everyone," she said loudly, "to Posy and Matt's party!"

Posy felt very exposed, like she should be standing next to Matt and they should have their arms around each other, but he was miles away, trapped behind Mr. Headingly on the far wall. She grimaced at him.

"Now those of us who know Posy thought she would *never* get married."

Posy could hear her mother tutting and dropped her head in her hands.

"After those losers, some better-looking than others." Leah paused for laughter. There was none. "So thank *fuck* she's met someone who'll put up with her!"

129

There was scattered applause at this. Posy could see the gym girls sneering. Oh God.

"OK, so her mum is very snotty about a P.E. teacher, but I think she's *wrong* about that."

Posy could feel her mum stiffen across the room.

"Matt is a totally fantastic bloke, Posy doesn't know how lucky she is. Why she's haring off all round the country looking up her ex-boyfriends is a *complete* mystery to me."

Posy's heart stopped in her chest. Matt was staring at her from the other side of the room, and she at him, but she couldn't make a sound come out of her mouth. Neither could he. The whole party was silent, just staring at them now. Leah fell off the chair and Fleur darted forward to pick her up.

Quietly and steadily, light on his trainered feet, Matt backed away. As he left the room, Posy unfroze and dived after him out into the February night. It was freezing. Every shop window was festooned with red hearts advertising Valentine's Day. The street outside the bar was quiet and empty, just the two of them, although Posy could already hear their friends clattering down the stairs.

"MATT!" she screamed.

He turned toward her. In the streetlights, she thought she could see a tear sparkling off his face. It couldn't be, surely.

"What?" he said.

"Don't . . . that was just Leah spouting shit. It was total rubbish. Total crap."

"I know what your friends and family think of me," said Matt.

"But *I* don't think that," said Posy. "Isn't that the important thing?"

"I don't know," said Matt. "Did you go to Scotland and see your ex-boyfriend?"

Posy paused. "It wasn't like that."

"You told me you were looking for a venue for our wedding and you went to see an ex-boyfriend?"

"Yes, but . . . not that one."

He let out a guffaw. "Oh, well, that's all right then. As long as it wasn't *that* one—the one you *really* like."

"No! Matt, no, it's not—"

He held up his hand. "I think that's all I need to know, don't you?"

Chapter Twelve

Posy is totally over so-called friends.
Comment: Like.
Leah Kone: I'm SO sorry. PLEASE pick up.

Leah had been beside herself, she really had. What was meant to be a lighthearted speech about Posy and Matt getting together had gone horribly, horribly wrong. She'd called a million times until finally Posy had turned her phone off.

Posy had caught another cab back but when she went in Matt was curled up in bed, either truly asleep or pretending. She'd stared at the laptop, but managed to resist it. Surely, surely, surely they could sort this out in the morning. She'd undressed and clambered into bed, aware of the warm, solid feel of him there. It felt good. She stretched out her arms and he squeezed away from her, as far in the bed as he could get. It would be better in the morning; it must. She'd get up early—very unlike her. Get breakfast. Suggest they do something energetic, like a jog or a brisk country walk. He'd like that, wouldn't he? Wouldn't he? Every time she thought about the previous evening, her head wanted to burst with embarrassment. All of those people thinking those things . . . But she wasn't. Was she? Was she? What was *wrong* with her?

In the morning she trailed out to the coffee shop, feeling as if a huge cloud of gloom was sitting on her shoulders. Her phone rang again.

"Hello?"

"Posy? Posy, I am *so, so sorry.*"

Posy paused, filling her coffee with sugar. "Did you write that speech?" she said carefully. "Did you plan to say all that?"

"No! I just . . . I was pissed and I thought it would be funny."

"Hilarious. But then, I suppose it's only what you've been saying to me all along."

"I feel awful," said Leah. "Awful. Please tell me you've made up and it's all fine."

"Well, he's not talking to me yet," said Posy. "But I am getting him breakfast. And . . . and of course I did lie to him about Scotland."

"I was just jealous," said Leah bitterly. "I just . . . I just can't understand why you'd jeopardize what you have."

"Well, I suppose you're right," said Posy. "I know it's an odd thing to have done. I just hope he understands."

"Me too. He will, Posy. It'll be fine. He'll understand."

"I hope so."

"Course he will, he loves you to bits."

"Yes," said Posy, feeling slightly more optimistic. "Yes, yes, he does, doesn't he?" She rotated her engagement ring thoughtfully.

"Come see me later, please, I'll take you out."

"I hope not," said Posy. "With any luck Matt and I will be staying in bed all day."

"I have Starbucks," she announced loudly, entering the flat and realizing how husky and hungover her voice sounded. It wasn't good. But Matt still wasn't moving out of the bed.

"What?" she said, feeling a clutch of fear at her chest. "Matt, please. Can you wake up and talk to me? I know you're not asleep."

Matt sighed.

"Look, can you just turn round?" said Posy. She rubbed the corrugated cardboard of the cup between her fingers. Suddenly she didn't want coffee at all, even though her mouth was suddenly, desperately dry.

Matt did. Posy's hopes had been raised after chatting with Leah—he'd realize it was just silly drunk talk—but he did look terribly miserable.

"Leah just called. She's really really sorry for talking all that rubbish, and—"

Matt looked like he was about to sigh again, then stopped himself. "Posy. Posy, look."

Posy sat down. "What?"

Matt shook his head. "I had no idea you felt this way. That you were so . . . what the *fuck* were you doing going to see your ex?"

Posy bit her lip. "Because . . . well, it seemed like a good idea. To close a door on the past. And I just wanted to be sure. To make absolutely sure that I've moved on and I'm ready, I promise."

"So was it—"

"No. It wasn't him. It was Chris."

"The big chap you dated at university?"

"About a hundred years ago, yes. It was nothing, nothing at all. I just wanted to be sure of you."

"But why . . . why couldn't you just talk to me about it?"

Posy hung her head. She didn't know the answer.

"Did you sleep with him?"

"*Fuck* no."

"Well, don't act as if it's an unreasonable question."

Posy stared at the floor.

Matt spoke slowly, as if trying to compose himself. "You know, I didn't want to be in your life to be the one who is just normal. Or 'good enough.' Or no trouble, or there to take care of you because you're tired of messing up, which was all news to me, by the way, but all your girlfriends did manage to get the point across throughout the evening, thanks for that."

Posy stayed quiet.

Matt looked up. "When we were up that mountain . . . I mean, it took quite a lot, you know. I didn't just do it on a whim, or because I thought you could fix me or anything like that. I did it because I loved you heart and soul and was willing to dedicate my entire life to you."

This was a long speech for Matt, and Posy didn't know how to react. Except to remember herself, bouncing around the party like some queen of the world who'd managed to haul some daft sap into marrying her, with a terrible sense of embarrassment and shame.

"I was . . ." she said tentatively. "You know Leah was just talking bollocks?"

Matt shrugged. "*In vino veritas* and all that," he said.

"That's nonsense," said Posy. "I speak constant bollocks all the time when I'm pissed. What about that time I tried to convince you that butterflies were girls and moths were boys?"

Matt's mouth twitched, but he stifled it. Then there was a long silence. Matt heaved himself out of bed and moved toward the chest of drawers. Then he turned to face her.

"Posy," he said, resolutely. "I'm not breaking up with you."

Posy's eyes widened and her mouth dropped open. She felt her heart fall down a lift shaft.

"Shit! You're breaking up with me!"

"I'm not breaking up with you. What did I just say?"

"You said, 'I'm not breaking up with you' in a way that made it totally obvious that you are in fact breaking up with me!"

Posy felt the first hot tears rising to the surface. She glanced down at her hand.

"Hang on!" said Matt. "Don't throw that Starbucks at me! Hear me out!"

"If I do throw the coffee, will you be nice to me again?" said Posy. She felt like her chest was opening up, exposing a huge raw chasm, a great pain, to the whole world. Sniveling hard, she ran up to him. "Matt?!"

"Listen. *Listen*. I was thinking. I'm just . . . I mean, it wasn't just what you said last night."

Posy didn't believe him. She'd ruined it, her and her big gob, just like her mother always thought she would. Oh God, her mother. How was she going to tell her mother? Oh God, her mother was going to be *pleased*. She choked out a painful sob.

"Matt," she said.

"I mean, it was everything else—your family, and, well, just people seemed so amazed at us getting married that I thought, Maybe this isn't the right thing for us right now . . . ?"

"What do you mean, "right now"? We haven't set a date or anything."

"I mean . . . maybe just take a little time out to see if we think this is what we want?"

"But . . . but you said—"

"I know what I said," said Matt. "And I meant it. But then I heard what *you* said. And I'm just . . . I mean, my mum and dad have been married for thirty-five years, but I don't think they've found it easy, you know? I think they've had to work at it a lot."

"And mine just couldn't be bothered?" said Posy, bitterly.

"Come on, Posy, I don't mean that. But they do say kids of divorced parents find it harder to stay married and, you know, I just don't want us to make a terrible mistake. I really, really don't want that to happen."

"So you're leaving me."

"I'm not leaving you. Actually I was hoping I wouldn't have to leave you . . . I don't really have anywhere else to go."

"So, what?"

"I was just thinking we should take a break for a little. I have a lot of work on and won't be about; we can take any wedding stress off ourselves, and you can think about what it is you really want—me, or some normal, upright guy that could be anyone you've pulled off the streets to mend your broken heart."

Posy winced, realizing just how much she'd really hurt him.

"Matt," she said, "Matt, I'm so so sorry. If I could take back what I said, what I did, how I've been, I would. In an instant. I love you. I love you *so* much."

"Thanks," said Matt. "That's nice of you to say and every-thing. And I would hope it would be enough. But right now, Posy, I'm not sure that it is."

Posy felt a huge lump swell in her throat. "No!" she said. "It can't be! It was just me, being an idiot!"

"Well, an idiot is good enough for me," mumbled Matt.

Posy couldn't believe he was serious. "Come on," she said in a panic. "Let's just go back to bed."

Surely this would work. OK, she could probably do with a shower, and he certainly could, but the prospect of a bit of hangover-lifting nookie—that would make everything all right, wouldn't it? Wouldn't it?

Matt looked at her sorrowfully.

"No. No, thanks, Posy."

"So what did you do?!"

Leah was so horrified and upset she'd forgotten to drink her happy hour cocktail. The umbrella in her drink was exactly the same color as the slightly unfortunate Ra Ra skirt she'd chosen to wear. The effect was very Club Tropicana.

Posy turned back to the cocktail. Getting cocktails with Leah had seemed like the right response at the time. Matt had gone out for a run, and she couldn't face sitting in the flat—*their* flat—by herself. Not when Matt was moving to the sofa. It was unbearable. But now, coming out somewhere filled with laugh-ing people without a care in the world, felt like the saddest thing on Planet Earth.

"I did what anyone would do," she mumbled.

"What, took off all your clothes and tried to drag him into bed anyway?"

Posy nodded.

"Then beg around the room, completely naked?"

"Obviously."

"Did you bark like a dog?"

"In fact, I didn't bark like a dog."

"Oh," said Leah. "Well, could have been worse."

"Oh God," said Posy. "What am I going to do?"

Leah shook her head. "I just can't . . . I mean, I can't get my head around it. Can't you sue him for breach of promise?"

"I suggested that," said Posy. "He said that threatening him with legal action probably wasn't the best way to get him to change his mind about things, on the whole."

"But where's he going to go? Is he leaving you to tell everyone?"

Posy winced. "Well. I thought I might just not tell anyone. Weddings take ages to arrange anyway, don't they? I'll just tell them I've had a bit of a hold-up with the napkin rings or something."

Leah nodded. "But you've told me now, though. I mean, you know I'd do my best and everything . . ."

"But you wouldn't be able to help spilling?"

"I'd do it in a very sympathetic way and everything."

"Hmm. But you'd feel really sorry for me and stuff."

"I would." Leah smiled. "Don't be daft. I won't tell a soul."

"Doesn't matter, my mother will sniff it out a mile off. Plus, I ran out of my own engagement party." Posy mused for a second.

"I think this is truly her fault," she said. "She's always saying it's the parents' fault anyway—everything."

"Yeah," said Leah. "So is he going back to Blackpool or not?"

"Well," said Posy, "he has his job here and stuff."

"Yes?"

"So, well, and you know, we're not *really* breaking up."

"Uh oh," said Leah.

"So I said . . . well, he can sleep on the sofa. Just, you know, till we've figured things out."

"You didn't even get to throw all his multi-colored tracksuits out of the window then cover them in petrol and set fire to them?"

"It's you that wanted to do that though," protested Posy.

"From the second I set eyes on them," agreed Leah.

"I think it's good," said Posy. "Nothing too much will change, then he'll forget what happened."

"Which wasn't that bad," said Leah.

"Which wasn't *that* bad," agreed Posy, feeling slightly more positive. "Then he'll fall back into bed with me one night, hurrah, and remember that he totally loves me and everything. And it will be fine. Yes." She took a large sip of her cocktail, feeling slightly more positive.

"Yes," said Leah. "That's what'll happen." She glanced at Posy's hand. "Where's your ring?"

"Uhm, he asked for it back," said Posy, deflating again.

"Oh fuck," said Leah. "He really has broken up with you, hasn't he?"

She got another round in.

*

"Oh, Posy," Matt was saying, in the kind voice she knew so well. "I know you're upset and everything, but I have a five a.m."

"Well, I'm sorry to disturb you," said Posy, through her tears. "It's just, like, my fiancé has broken up with me? The man I was going to spend my whole life with and marry and everything? And it's—I know you'll find this strange—it's made me quite sad?"

Matt sat down on the bed, gingerly, in case she tried to haul him in again.

"Do you think I'm not sad?" he said.

"*You* have a five a.m.," said Posy.

"Posy, I'm heartbroken. I've told you already. I thought I was everything to you—sun, moon, stars. But I'm not. I'm some normal bloke you've managed to snare into your crazy world. How do you think that feels?"

"Ultimately get-overable?" sniffed Posy.

"I don't know," said Matt, gently patting her on the shoulder.

"Don't touch me," said Posy. "You're not allowed."

"OK," said Matt, getting up.

"Maybe you should move out if that's what you think," said Posy, throwing her worst fear at him.

"Posy. Sweetie. It's our place. I can't go home, I can't commute from Blackpool. We'd have to sell up, go our separate ways. Are you sure you want that right now?"

"So you want to break up with me *and* send me home to my mums?"

"No," said Matt. "I think until we've sorted everything out there's no reason you can't stay here. We're civilized adults, aren't we?"

Posy looked at him. "Are you saying there's hope?"

Matt shrugged. "Not if you get pissed every night till two a.m., probably not."

"Well, if I'm going to be staying here, I have to be allowed to cry."

Matt looked at her for a long moment.

"We're all allowed to cry, Posy."

Chapter Thirteen

Posy is resolute and totally fine and nothing is
    happening in her life.
Posy Fairweather relationship status: In a relationship.
Matt Farmer relationship status: It's complicated.

It was a cold, sunny February Monday morning. Despite the
hangover when Posy woke, Matt gone from his side of the bed,
she felt a little better, somehow. She checked the trainer count.
All there. He hadn't gone yet. And while he was still here, there
was still hope.

She finished yesterday's muffin, left untouched, and dressed.
OK. Something bad had happened with Matt. But he was still
here. And in a sense the fact that it had come up—that she
wanted to go and see her exes—was a good thing. She had kept
something from him, but now he knew all about it. And the sky
had not fallen in. He would come to understand, wouldn't he?
Why she wanted to see Chris? And why, deep down, on some
level, she felt she still had to see . . . him.

Well that, for now, could wait. Along with wedding magazines, and frocks, and arguing with her mother—all of that, just for now, could take a rest. And she could fix this. She could. It was fixable. The trainers were still under the bed. She did love him. It would come good. Surely.

"Heard I missed a great party," said Margie as she walked into work the next day.

"Good morning, Margie. Yes, it was great, thank you," Posy said, staving off the others' concern by explaining it as a passing tiff, easily remedied. That was the best way. Smooth it over, forget all about it. Nobody would mention it.

There it was, sitting in her inbox—the summons.

As usual, in her mother's deliberately formal emailing style, as if out to prove something about her unflinching superiority toward the technical form:

```
Dear Posy and Fleur,
I would be delighted if my two daughters could
join me for supper at home on Tuesday evening.
RSVP.
Jonquil.
```

Immediately, the phone rang.

"What have you done now?" demanded Fleur. "I thought you said it was just a tiff."

"Nothing!" protested Posy. "I don't know!"

"Supper at home!"

"I know."

Jonquil could not, as she often informed them, run a top-class therapy practice and cook too, and, in fact, it was sexist to expect the woman to do the cooking just because she was in the house all day. What had led Posy to cook had led Fleur to alternate between infuriating raw food fixations and periods where she seemed to exist entirely on fruit shoots, wonton, and *pain au chocolat* without gaining an ounce.

"I mean . . . what about that time she served us onions with water?"

"That was soup."

"She *said* it was soup. But actually it was some onions in hot water."

"I know," said Posy, "I could cook. Or maybe we could bring a take-away?"

"Then you suggest it and she'll get all cross, like, "Don't you think I can make dinner for my daughters?" and we say, 'No,' and then she puts that face on and says, "How long have you been feeling this hostility?"' said Fleur, grumpily. "And then the take-away is always horrible and Mum thinks it's for prisoners and down and outs and makes snobby remarks and no one is happy."

"That's true."

"It's not right. I'm not coming."

"Well, thanks, then I'll get it all."

"Well, don't you go either."

"And then next time it will be worse."

Fleur sighed. "Well, there's one good thing." She thought of it suddenly, perking up.

"What's that?"

"It'll definitely be you she's having a go at."

"Why?"

"Obvious, isn't it? You piss off to Scotland, then have a big fight with your fiancé and we get summoned. I shall sit back, look wise, and make psychological observations."

"Will you?"

"Oh yeah, I will. I'll break down your defenses till you're begging to help."

Posy is dining en famille.

Posy and Fleur met at the tube station.

"Can we just go and have a quick treble gin and tonic before we go in?" said Fleur, who was equipped with a Tupperware box full of her own supper.

"No. What's in the box?"

"Raw squash and sprouting bean salad."

Posy sighed. "Fuck, I'd rather eat Mum's stuff."

"Come on, if you get a bit drunk you won't even taste it."

Posy considered it. The idea was tempting. Unfortunately, the last two times she'd got drunk the effects had been somewhat unpredictable, so she decided against it.

"Nope. Faster we're in, faster we're out. And I've brought a bottle of wine."

"One bottle."

"Yes."

"That is *not enough*."

The lights were on in the sitting room window and, in a childish reaction, Posy remembered how pleased she would be to see those coming home from school—it meant her mother was in the house, and not upstairs seeing clients in her office with the brass plate on the wall where they were never ever allowed to go. The sitting room lights weren't on very often, but tonight, against the encompassing cold, it still felt like coming home.

From the outside, the place retained some of its grand air—wide stone steps led up to the entrance of the tall Hampstead redbrick, and the neighboring houses had all been expensively developed, with topiary trees lining the passageway and large front doors painted in heritage colors, with shiny brass knobs.

Their house, on closer inspection, looked like it might be derelict. Piles of newspaper for recycling blocked the top step, along with discarded mail, odd boots, and the occasional stick belonging to a neighborhood dog.

The doorbell had had an OUT OF ORDER PLEASE KNOCK LOUDLY sign on it since Posy was at secondary school. How hard was it to repair a doorbell? she wondered, not for the first time. Was it really so unbelievably tricky and time-consuming that it was better to make people rap on the door for twenty minutes every time they came round instead?

"Helloooo!" the girls hollered. Nothing stirred in the house.

"Maybe she's gone out," said Posy.

"Yes, well, it's funny, I thought she'd be waiting on the doorstep in a flowery pinny holding out a tray of freshly baked scones," said Fleur.

Soon, however, there was a familiar high-heeled tread on their familiar creaking stairs with the peeling-away carpet—a death trap—and Jonquil was flinging the door wide.

As usual the contrast between the dusty house and Jonquil looking glamorous was a big one to take in. She really was lovely, reflected Posy, far prettier than she herself was, having inherited her father's heavier jaw and smaller eyes. Fleur was much more like her—high cheekbones, a perfectly straight nose, and a wide mouth. The effect couldn't fail to be pleasing, even if she was fixing them with a gimlet eye.

"Ah, there you are," said Jonquil. "I thought you were going to be late."

"Well, we're exactly on time," said Posy, kissing her. "Like always. So you didn't have to worry."

"Fine, fine."

There was no smell of cooking in the narrow entry hall, which was piled up thickly with mail, brochures, invitations to gallery openings, and leftover Christmas cards. Pictures—all originals, many valuable small oils by artists Jonquil had picked out early in their careers—were hung willy-nilly on every spare inch of wall space, their frames thick with dust. Posy breathed in the homely messiness of it. Whatever her reservations, this was still home.

She thought about her and Matt's plans to move—he was taking on more clients all the time, he was extremely popular, and Mr. Headingly had tipped him for big things, apparently. They had thought maybe they would move out of town a bit, get themselves a nice little house somewhere. Well, they *had* thought that. Before ... before this *temporary unpleasantness*, Posy told herself firmly. They kept their apartment very tidy, though. Posy liked everything to be just so, and Matt was organized. See, she thought, we *do* have *lots* in common. Like folding things.

She sighed. He'd gone out without saying where. It was probably work. Probably. God, she missed his body at night.

"What's for supper?" she asked.

"Stir-fry," said their mother. Fleur and Posy exchanged glances. That didn't sound promising.

"I've brought my own," said Fleur gaily.

"Oh, very good," said Jonquil, distractedly leading them into the kitchen. At least they couldn't insult her about her cooking, she cared so little about it. And, as she was always pointing out, she was still the same size she'd always been and could have got into her wedding dress, had she not had it ritually burned.

The kitchen dining room was a huge space at the back of the house, with windows looking over the immaculate garden. Jonquil loved gardening and took it very seriously. The garden was an exquisite haven from the tumble of the indoors, delicate and beautiful, with wildflowers and a herb rockery. It was as elegant and regular as the interior was messy and disorganized. Posy was sure there was some deep-seated reason for this, but wasn't too sure she wanted to get to the bottom of it.

"Roll on spring," their mother said. "I do hate all this mulching. Fleur, what are you wearing?"

Fleur was wearing a micro mini with a huge oversized jumper over the top. She looked sixteen, not twenty-eight.

"Some couture, blah blah blah," said Fleur to curry favor. "Did you see it in *Vogue*?"

"Oh!" said their mother, pleased. "Very good."

"Who does the jumper belong to?" whispered Posy.

"I didn't catch his name," said Fleur. "But I did catch his sweater!"

"And his pubic lice?"

"Shut up."

Posy opened the bottle of wine and poured them all a large glass. "Thanks for having us to dinner, Mum."

"Ah, yes, supper," said their mother, looking around distractedly. "Are you *really* hungry?"

The girls looked at each other.

"We could call for a take-away," said Posy. Their mother looked horrified. As far as she was concerned, take-away was simply Not Done. Posy often thought that if her mother could take all her meals in pill form, she would.

"Well, quite, Posy," said their mother. "Then we can all put up our hoods and go out and do some cheerful-slapping."

Fleur and Posy rolled their eyes.

"I'll start chopping," said Posy, pulling open a kitchen cabinet. Out fell a huge sheaf of unfiled bank statements. "Mum, do you think it's right to keep bank statements in your kitchen cupboards?" she complained.

"Aha," said their mum. "Well, do *you* think it's right to go haring off out on your fiancé and going to look up your ex-boyfriends on the World Web World? Haven't you ever heard of letting sleeping dogs lie? After that speech Fleur told me all about it."

Posy straightened up. "Subtle, Mum. Very subtle. Nice timing, nice gentle introduction."

Fleur was crouched on the ground trying to look innocent and coax a mouse out of its hole by offering it some squash.

"Fleur, for God's sake. What's the first rule of Sisters' Club?"

"Never talk about Sisters' Club?" Fleur mumbled into her sleeve.

"YES."

"That's very passive-aggressive behavior, you know," said Jonquil.

"So?"

Fleur poked up her head. "Actually she was asking loads of nosy questions about me, and it was a good diversion to talk about you instead."

"*That* is why you dobbed me in it? Cowardice?"

"Hey, I'm not the one stalking my exes online."

"That's because your hard drive isn't big enough for all six million names."

"Girls, girls." Her mother handed them each a wineglass. "Let's sit down."

"In front of our delicious supper," said Posy. Jonquil ignored her and walked over to the dinner table, which was piled high with files.

"After what Fleur told me—" she said.

"You mean Judas," said Posy.

"I know I've told you this before, but . . . you don't have to get married if you don't want to."

Posy sat down with a sigh. "Mum. Listen. I do want to get married, OK?"

"Just not right now?"

"Yes, actually, now."

"But not to him."

"Mum, *stop it*, OK? It's not really your business."

"No, I'm only your mother who watched you two run out of your own engagement party."

"It was nothing. Just a storm in a teacup. Honestly, what's the big deal? I mean, I think I'm trying to take a rational balanced look at my life right now and everyone else keeps treating me as if I'm a dangerous loon."

"What does that tell you?" said Fleur from the floor.

"Are you talking to me or your best friend the mouse?" said Posy crossly.

"Did you really go all the way to the Hebrides to see Chris?" asked her mother.

"No."

"Oh, thank God."

"It was the Shetlands."

Jonquil rose. "I think I'll just make a sandwich. Would anyone like a sandwich?"

"I'm fine, thanks," said Fleur, smugly opening her lunch box. Posy decided to give in gracefully, stay seated, and keep quiet. The silence in the kitchen, as Jonquil pulled out white bread, tomatoes, cheese, and mayonnaise—her default attempts at motherly feeding—seemed endless. And she wanted to kick Fleur under the table.

"I just want to say," said Jonquil, "that if you're worried about married life beforehand, it . . . it definitely doesn't get any better afterward. That's all. I see it day after day. Marriage is just too difficult for long-living contemporary society, it just is." She looked down at her knife, suddenly mumbling in a way that was most unlike her. "I just don't want you to get hurt again, Posy. Not like that. I am still your mother."

Outside, imperceptibly, the freezing cold had done the trick and, gently in the lamplight, snow had begun to fall, landing on the birdfeeder and gradually obscuring the path.

Posy found herself thinking about her dad.

She often wished she'd paid more attention to him when he

was at home. Run to greet him at the door, rather than continu-
ing to watch *Press Gang*. Clung onto him on the rare occasions
they'd gone on family outings and walks. Sat on his lap, even
when she was too big for it.

But he was just her dad. A familiar-smelling presence that
left at eight and came home at six and had a glass of wine and
wasn't, as far as she knew, the least bit different from all the
other dads at school and perhaps in the whole world.

She supposed in retrospect that he and her mother didn't
speak very much, but she hadn't thought much of it at the time.
All her mother seemed to do, she reckoned, was get at her, so
she wasn't surprised her dad wanted to stay out of her way too.
And Jonquil's presence was so very *there*, with her "How did that
teacher make you feel?" and "But you have to understand that
Clemency may have been *saying* that she didn't want to be your
friend any more while hitting you over the head with her milk
bottle, but she didn't necessarily *mean* it." It seemed entirely
balanced for her dad to be more of a background figure, who
only liked to give her the occasional tickle and say, "Everything
OK down there, Posy girl?"

He'd grown up in a family of three boys and been sent
to boarding school very young, she knew, and her mother
complained endlessly in later years of his emotional unreach-
ability and closed-off nature, but Posy wondered sometimes
if that wasn't something they had in common after all; they
weren't entirely easy people to get to the bottom of. Fleur and
Jonquil bore their hearts on their sleeves—if they had a disaster, the world got to share it; if they were happy, then ditto.

Happiness was more complicated to Posy, she thought. She
seemed to have an in-built, questioning self-consciousness that

stopped her ability to just "be" in the moment. Here she was, with a nice boyfriend—fiancé—ex-fiancé. Oh god!—lovely boss, everything in life lining up, and she was running off on wild-goose chases around the country.

The morning her dad had gone she hadn't even noticed. He'd left the house as normal at eight a.m. Jonquil had evidently had clients all morning and, in the clutter, hadn't even discovered the note until after the girls had come back from school. Posy could still see herself, as she sat there remembering: her mouth full of Jammie Dodgers, trying to watch *Danger Mouse* on a tiny telly (Jonquil thought the concept of telly was common), as her mother gripped at the kitchen table and gasped. It was the first time Posy realized that a pain inside could hurt just as badly as one on the outside. Her mother had crumpled as if she'd been punched in the stomach. Fleur had been doing an interpretive dance and hadn't noticed. Posy had leaped up, alarmed.

"What is it, Mummy?"

"Call me Jonquil," her mother had gasped. Her father had never gone along with the name thing. Posy still had to double-take when she thought of his real name. Raymond.

"What is it, Jonquil?" Posy had obediently repeated, feeling as if she didn't want to know.

Her mother had straightened up painfully slowly, like their grandma getting out of her bath chair in the home for retired genteel ladies they religiously visited once a month to allow themselves to be pinched and preened for inspection.

"It's . . . it's nothing, darling." Jonquil sat down, clutching the letter in her hand.

"Is that from school?" said Posy, who suffered from a

persistent belief that her year's form teacher, Mrs. Fitzgerald, didn't like her.

"No . . . no," said Jonquil. "No, it's not the school."

In fact, the letter—although Posy had never seen it, due to her mother suddenly taking up smoking again and burning it compulsively in her ashtray—said simply that Ray couldn't take it anymore; that he couldn't bear to live his life ignored, and that he was going to take a bit of time to himself to work out what he wanted to do.

What, it turned out, he wanted to do was start dating a rather brassy woman about ten years younger than their mother, after what even Posy realized at her age was a completely inappropriate period of time. Marian may have been nice and she may have been horrible, but it would never matter to the girls, who immediately decided to stick together like glue and hate her en masse, forever, which was a terrible shame, because when Marian and Ray got married, just a year later, and moved to Essex and had a baby boy called Jason, Posy and Fleur never really got the chance to know their new baby brother, and Posy, at least, would have liked to very much.

Access visits had started off as awkward affairs—Posy often read, ruefully, in adult life, agony columns in which separating couples were advised to go speak nicely about each other in front of the children so as to minimize confusion and bitterness. In their home, all-out war was declared. Jonquil would sit through dinner and point out, using a variety of psychoanalytic methods, every small point of failure in Ray as a husband, father, and, indeed, lover.

"You need to know the truth about the world," she would

say, waving a cigarette wildly over their Dairylea sandwiches. "And about men."

"But Fleur is six," Posy would add, quietly.

"I am not really six," Fleur would add. "It is only my disguise for being a pirate queen, for now, until I am ready to take on my true bydentity."

"Identity," Jonquil would add blankly. "And that's another thing. The man had no sense of identity."

There hadn't been a formal decision to break off contact. And Posy knew, and was grateful, that Ray had continued funding her education until she'd left college. She just wished that he'd fought a tiny bit harder for his daughters, that was all.

Yes, they'd taken him for granted, but weren't you supposed to take your parents for granted? Assume everything would always be OK and that they would never let you down? And the older she got, the less she understood. Jason was twenty-two now, still living at home in Welwyn Garden City, playing a lot of Playstation and showing an incipient weight problem. He was nice enough, looked a lot like Marian. They didn't see much of him, or Ray, but whenever they did have stilted, awkward get-togethers—normally about twice a year, when Ray would have a "family barbecue" and Jonquil would sniff about how *déclassé* it was and refuse to ask them any details about it when they got back, even though Posy could tell she desperately wanted to know everything and, depending on how her and her mother were getting on that month, would tell her or not—Ray wouldn't cuddle her, exactly, more like give her an apologetic squeeze. She and Marian would politely ignore each other. And they would never, ever talk, not properly, and sometimes it was agony.

"I won't get hurt," said Posy now, decisively. "Look, it's snowing!"

"So, why the wild-goose chases up and down the country?" Jonquil asked.

"I just wanted to see how Chris was doing, that's all."

"Weighing up your options," said Fleur. This time Posy did kick her.

"I always liked him," mused Jonquil.

"You did not! You called him a woodworking bear!"

"Did I? Affectionately, of course."

"Well, it wasn't a goose chase, just a . . . I was just interested, that's all."

"If you were really into this whole wedding thing, you wouldn't be interested," said Fleur sagely. "You'd be too busy doing flower arrangements and blah blah blah things, and ooh I must have lavender serviettes and ooh all my bridesmaids must be the same height:weight ratio."

"I would not be like that!" exclaimed Posy.

"You would, everybody is. If you loved him, that is."

"Can't you go outside and make a snow angel or something?" said Posy crossly.

"Anyone would think you didn't want me here helping and giving advice."

"Fleur, I don't want you here, "helping" and giving advice."

Fleur pouted. "Well, just as long as you don't go and get mixed up with Adam all over again, that's all."

"You're not going to see Adam," said Jonquil. Posy reflected that Leah's parents hadn't asked about her boyfriend status for three years. This made Leah worry that they thought she was a lesbian. "He's a bounder."

Posy rolled her eyes, but didn't deny it.

"He was, Pose," said Fleur. "A real nob-end. You totally wasted your time there."

"That's rich," said Posy. "What about you and that Cossack?"

"Dmitri was from a wild gypsy race," said Fleur. "He couldn't be tamed."

"He couldn't be taught to pee in the toilet," said Posy.

"Anyway, this isn't about me and Dmitri, who had a wild inner passion you could never understand."

"For British visas," said Posy.

She hadn't really been planning to see Adam—well, he'd crossed her mind, but she had enough problems here as it was—but the onslaught was making her petulant and contrary. She was hardly going to cozy up to *Adam*.

"Really, darling," said Jonquil. "Adam is the most dreadful wide-boy. It's a ridiculous idea. Don't put yourself through this. If Matt isn't making you as happy as he ought to, focus on that, not looking around to see what else is out there."

Posy bit her lip. Being ganged up on was only going to make her more stubborn.

"I know," she said eventually. "I know that staying in love with someone for a lifetime is really difficult. I'm interested in how people manage it, and how it would have been. I don't think it's weird to have a look at different lifestyles, before I embrace my own."

Jonquil and Fleur exchanged glances.

"Well, dear, you're the psychotherapist . . . Oh no, that's me," said Jonquil.

*

"Can we go and get some dinner somewhere?" complained Fleur as they trudged back to the tube in the snow. "That Ethiopian place will still be open."

To her surprise, Posy was furious. "I can't believe you've been talking about me to Mum," she said, trying to control her fury. "I can't believe you two sat in there and ganged up on me about my perfectly reasonable personal business."

Fleur tutted. "You know why."

"And so what if I *did* see Adam. He was hardly serious, if I *was* to go and see him." Posy had been planning on giving up the whole thing, actually. But her mother and sister's intransigence was driving her crazy.

"But it's *not* Adam, is it? It's—"

"*Don't* bother."

"You still can't hear his name, can you?"

"Shut up."

"You're going to see Lord Voldemort."

"Well, I can't and I won't."

Fleur blinked. "Oh my God, he's not on Facebook, is he? You can't find him! Trust him to live off the grid. I suppose he did always follow his own rules . . ."

"Don't *you* get nostalgic about him."

Fleur sighed. "He was quite something."

"Shut up."

"I never understood why he went for—"

"*Shut up*, Fleur."

Posy was trembling. Her sister had just gone too far. Again. It was unlike Posy to get so enraged and Fleur took heed for once. They walked on in silence.

"So, uhm, you're not going to take me out to dinner then," said Fleur eventually.

"No," said Posy.

Fine, thought Fleur. So I won't tell you.

And she promptly forgot all about it.

Posy is thinking that some people should mind their
   own beeswax.

Comment: Like.

Comment, Fleur: Fleur is thinking that some people
   ought to be sectioned.

"Hey," said Matt, not unkindly, when she got home. "How's your mum?"

Posy grunted.

"That bad, huh? Don't tell me, she told you she'd always truly wanted one of her children to be gay, so it has to be you?"

"No."

"She wants to use you as a test case in a book?"

Posy shook her head.

"OK. How was it? Did you tell her about us?"

"What's to tell, Matt?"

Matt shrugged and looked awkward. "I don't know, Posy. I really don't. I think I need some time."

"How about fifty years?" said Posy. "Please. Come on. Let's just work it out together. After we're married. It'll be fun. Come on!"

She could hear the desperation in her voice. Matt backed away.

"I'm not . . . I'm not ready yet, Posy."

"Oh, *crap* in a bucket," said Posy, as Matt started folding open the sofa bed. It took up the entire sitting room. She picked up her laptop and hared off to the bedroom, slamming the door behind her.

She logged on. Checked who was online. And there he was. Adam Linden, with a little green dot next to his name. Shooting the door a cross look, she typed.

Hi there!

Immediately it pinged back

    - Hi, babe! Long time!
    - Yeah! Fancy a drink sometime?
    - Sure! Shoreditch House?

It couldn't be that easy. Bloody hell. And nobody else called her babe. Nobody called anybody babe, these days, did they?

Posy blinked. She couldn't help it, she glanced behind her, feeling guilty. No sign of Matt. It must just be a hangover from the old days, that she was feeling her pulse race a little faster, felt a little wobbly. She was reliving being twenty-three, that was all.

And why shouldn't she go? Her family had already given up on her as a bad job, it was only a drink, and Matt was paying her no attention at all. She bloody just might. It was perfectly innocent, and she could hardly make things worse by seeing him.

Right, she would give Matt one last chance. Just as she thought that, she heard an anguished groan come from the bathroom.

She got up. The bathroom door was, unusually, closed.

"What's up?" she called.

Matt didn't answer, so she pushed it open, feeling strange. A week ago, she wouldn't even have asked.

Matt was lying in the bath, looking oddly strangulated. The breath coming out of his mouth was visible. As she looked closer she could see that the bath had lumps in it.

"What are you doing? You look like the end of *Titanic*," Posy observed.

"Go away, please."

"What *are* you doing?"

"I'm taking an ice bath, if you must know. Good for the muscles, aids mental focus and concentration."

"Is the mental focus and concentration on saying, *Fuck, this is cold*?"

"No."

"How blue do you have to be before you can come out? Turquoise or more of a "night sky"?"

Matt grimaced at her.

"I'm leaving! I'm getting out."

"Maybe," he grunted, "this not-moving-out thing isn't actually working all that well."

Posy slammed the door on him. "Fine!" she yelled. "Move out whenever you like. To an *igloo*!"

Great, babe! See you there!

Chapter Fourteen

Posy is going shopping.
Comment: Like.
Leah likes this.

"What do I wear to Shoreditch House?"

Posy had decided to meet Leah for an emergency lunch stop cum shopping expedition.

"I need to, you know, totally blow Adam's socks off and look completely cool without looking like I'm trying too hard or that I'm trying to get off with him or that I'd just go and get off with anyone, or—"

Leah rolled her eyes, but there was no doubt about it—she felt slightly responsible for this.

"OK, OK, calm down," said Leah. Posy felt mollified at this until Leah added, "Have you thought about leopard skin? It's back again, but this time with a twist."

Posy blinked at her. "Leah. Nothing 'with a twist,' OK? This is me you're talking to, not the editor of Italian *Vogue*."

Leah was wearing black leggings that appeared to be made out of rubber, and a tulle top in pale green.

"How did you get into those leggings, by the way?"

"I get up early and refuse fluids," said Leah. "OK, try this." She pulled what looked like a rather pretty fresh sailor-collared top from the rail, until Posy noticed it was actually a woollen playsuit.

"What?" Leah clocked Posy's horrified expression.

"What?! I'd look like Andy Pandy: the Prostitute Years."

"It's sassy!"

"It's an arrestable offense. Are you going to concentrate, or am I going to Gap on my own?"

Leah shivered at the mere mention of Gap.

"No, no, OK. But this is Shoreditch House, all right? Not grab a granny night at Tiger Tiger."

Posy rolled her eyes. "It was a mistake, remember? In fact, wasn't it *you* who pulled—"

"OK, OK, let's keep moving. How's it going with Matt, incidentally?"

"I'm picking out an outfit to meet my ex-boyfriend in. How do you think it's going?"

"Is this just to spite him?"

Posy considered it. "No! Honestly, I still . . . I mean, I do . . . OK, Adam and I shared some pretty shallow times together, but I still want to *know*. What it might have been like, what I was like—this is all I ever wanted till it got blown out of proportion."

"Mmhmm."

"And Matt is still being a completely reasonable . . . argh. He's being tough."

"For a good reason."

"Yes, I *know* that."

Leah looked bashful. "I'm sorry. It's my fault."

"No, I think maybe some time on our own might be useful to get this out of my system, you know?" Posy glanced at her hand and Leah gasped.

"He really took your ring off you?"

"Yeah. I thought doing it might make him feel so bad he'd dash over and put it on again and we could forget all this. But he hasn't. So. Let's go."

"Oh, Posy, that is so sad."

"*Don't* make me cry. Make me look gorgeous."

In tribute to spring—OK, it still felt like the depths of winter, but it must surely be round the corner at some point—they compromised on a fresh, shorter-than-Posy-would-normally-choose little dress with a floral pattern.

"Wear it with fishnets and big clumpy boots," said Leah. "And tear some holes in the fishnets."

"Won't I look like Blossom?" said Posy.

"Nobody that goes to Shoreditch House is old enough to remember *Blossom*," said Leah.

"Well, that *does* make me feel better," muttered Posy, but she did like the dress when she put it on. It made her look young and, well, ready to party.

Leah regarded her in the big mirror. "Ready for Adam then?"

"Stop sounding disapproving," said Posy. "I'm not going to pull him or anything."

"Mmmhmm," said Leah.

"I'm not."

Leah put down the pile of skirts she'd pulled out just in

case she could persuade Posy to go for something a little more adventurous.

"Well," she said, "apart from you two going out and getting bladdered and having nookie, what did you ever really have in common? Really?"

Posy remembered. It must have been, what, six or seven weeks into her time in London. She'd found a room in a shared house with some girls from university she didn't know very well, and a job basically running out for coffee at a low-level direct mailing company. At the time, though, that had felt like a huge success. She was earning, and living independently. She missed having a boyfriend but the newness of everything—finding her way around London; figuring out the best place to stand so she'd get on the right tube carriage; getting jostled around the West End on weekend evenings and eating cheap Chinese food in China Town—meant she didn't miss him quite as much as she'd expected.

And although the girls hadn't turned out to be quite the *Sex and the City* sophisticates she was hoping for—why, she wondered, move to London if your sole aim in life was to never miss an episode of *EastEnders*? Maybe to feel closer to the cast?—she'd already been out for a few drinks with people from work, had got back in closer touch with her sister, who was doing some ridiculous homeopathy course in Chelsea and had lots of cool friends who somehow looked on Posy as being madly staid for actually having to get up five days a week (Posy managed to conveniently forget that she had only recently held the same opinion herself about anyone with a real job), and, in general, was loving life in the capital.

One night in the flat, Brinny, a rather stolid quantity surveyor, had come in saying, "Oh, yawn. There's a huge uni get-together next weekend in Fulham. That sounds absolutely gruesome. I can't imagine who would want to go to that."

Posy's ears pricked up. In fact, ever since the night of the university ball—when she felt she was getting a glimpse of everything she'd missed for the three years she'd stayed in with Chris—she had been quite keen to meet up with some of the people she'd never really got to know. Carla, for instance. She bit her lip. She wouldn't, of course, admit to herself that she was quite interested in, well, she had occasionally wondered what was up with that arrogant posh boy . . . not that she cared or wanted to see him, of course, it would just be nice to widen her contacts in town.

"Oh, I might drop in, spot a few familiar faces," she said casually.

Which was how she found herself, a week later, in an unfamiliar part of town—west London, which was much more salubrious than the slighty dodgy suburb she was flatting in—dressed up nervously and sitting on her own. Brinny hadn't fancied it, and Posy had hung back as late as she'd dared, only to find in the pub she was still miles too early and had to nurse an incredibly expensive glass of wine as all around hordes of screaming—and wildly attractive—young Londoners about town greeted each other confidently. She conjured with the idea of trying to keep seats for people—but then, what people? What if it was all people she no longer recognized? After all, she hadn't even been directly invited. It was technically a free-for-all, but what if it wasn't? What if Brinny had got the wrong end of the stick and it was someone's totally private birthday party or something like that and everyone would turn up wearing matching party hats, and—

Posy had just about convinced herself to leave, when she heard her name being called over the roar of the pink-cheeked crowd.

"Pose!! POSE!!"

It was Carla, looking the same as ever—enthusiastic and slightly mad. Posy doubted she'd ever been so pleased to see anyone in her life, and leaped up. Unfortunately she spilled her wine over herself in the process.

"Uh, hi, Carla!"

"Posy! I didn't know you'd be here!"

"Uhm, no, me neither . . ." said Posy, her voice trailing off. Her heart suddenly caught and jumped a beat, as she spotted who was following Carla, carrying a bottle of champagne and two glasses—wildly flash in itself. It was him.

As Adam saw her, his mouth unfurled into a huge wolfish grin. Posy felt ridiculous, like a schoolgirl at a disco. He must have known all along, however much she tried to be standoffish.

"Well, look at you," said Adam. "Perhaps we'd better get you out of those wet clothes."

Posy grinned nervously. And after that, Carla was forgotten—and engulfed, into a large group of people Posy barely recognized but who turned out to have been there the whole time, all of them bragging excitedly about their new lives and careers in the smoke.

Adam, however, didn't do any of that. He grabbed his champagne bottle and the two glasses and somehow procured a little corner booth which cut down on the peripheral noise of twenty-somethings living it up. After a while it was so stagey and funny and new to Posy she couldn't help giggling.

"What's so funny?" demanded Adam. "You must tell me."

Posy couldn't. And she couldn't help it: it was sexy, and charming. He had such an absolute assumption that he was going to sit her in this corner, get her tipsy then pull her. And, weirdly, it made him incredibly attractive, this focus. She looked at him. He wore his very dark hair long so that he could push it back raffishly with his hand, a smart, navy-blue suit with a blue tie, loosened, and a white shirt, the clean cuffs of which showed beneath the buttons at his wrist, along with an old, expensive-looking gold watch. The black hairs on his arms crept over the band of the watch in a way that fascinated Posy for reasons she didn't understand. He was so different from big soft sandy Chris. He was lean, and venal, and almost certainly not as nice. She liked him.

"Nothing is funny," she said, suddenly chastened. He looked at her intensely.

"Nothing? What about my hilarious work anecdotes and charming manner?"

She smiled. "Oh, sorry, was that you trying to be charming?"

He rolled his eyes. "I think I'd better get you another drink."

Posy watched him move through the bar, confidently, smoothly, waving hello to a few aquaintances but not stopping, taking his good leather wallet out of his back pocket. He was, she decided, by some margin, the best-looking boy there. It wasn't a question of whether she was going to sleep with him. It was only a question of when—and what he was going to teach her when she did.

"So," he said as he returned, bearing two ludicrous-looking cocktails. "Tell me about you. Where did you grow up?"

Posy squirmed. She didn't really like talking about it. People either got highly interested in her mother's job, or had had the same thing happen to them and wanted to tell her about their dads. Either way, she didn't like it very much.

"I was raised in the mountains by wolves," she said.

"Wolves, huh?" said Adam, raising a heavy eyebrow.

"Yeah, they were great. Though it's hard to find the milk now. I miss it."

Adam grinned. "Do you have particularly sharp teeth, or . . ."

Posy smiled. "Oh, yes. And a vestigial tail."

"*A-dam*!" It was Carla, looking peeved. "We're all going to eat, want to come? They can probably fit seventeen of us in at Napule."

Posy glanced at her watch. Who were these confident people who didn't have to keep track of the last train home? Who had enough money to eat out at the last minute? Who were perfectly sure that a restaurant would be happy to seat seventeen people at ten-thirty at night? What had she missed out on while she and Chris were busy stirring lentil stew in their little terraced house?

"Are you going to come with us?"

The invitation was quite clearly not aimed at both of them. Adam shot a quick look at Posy, who kept her face studiedly neutral. It was a long way back to Clapton.

"Neh," he said, stretching lazily. Posy felt her heart leap, and told herself off for appearing too keen—heck, for *being* too keen. But, on the other hand, what if he vanished now and she never heard from him again? "I think I'll just eat olives tonight."

170

Carla looked from one to the other, her face an unhidden mass of disappointment. In a strange way, this galvanized Posy. If this gorgeous, popular girl wanted Adam, then obviously she was OK to want him too. She wasn't accidentally getting off with a weirdo she didn't know very well; he was indeed what he appeared. A sexy, confident man whom suddenly she wanted to kiss very much.

"Fine," said Carla rudely. "See you around." And she turned on her high heels and left.

"I have no idea who that just was," said Adam, and even though Posy thought that was a little cruel, she found herself laughing anyway.

They drank more, laughed more, and it felt like seconds before the bar was closing and they found themselves turned out into the dark night.

"Which way are you headed?" asked Adam, his eyes glinting in the streetlights.

"East," said Posy, which was easier to explain than the distant suburb she lived in, which nobody had ever heard of—at least nobody in Fulham, she was sure.

"Ah, shame," said Adam, and Posy felt her heart plummet. "I'm not far from here . . . but the other way."

"Oh," said Posy. They stood there. Earlier rainfall had left the road glistening and wet, and quiet, as the tubes stopped running and even the bright young things went home on a school night.

"Of course?"

He didn't have to say any more. He just put out his hand. In a skipping heartbeat, Posy put out hers and took it.

His flat was surprisingly nice—Posy had never met anyone

her own age who employed a cleaner before. It was set in the upstairs of a large house, and he shared with a chap called Charlie, who worked in international finance and was never in the same country two days running. Mountain bikes were hanging on the wall, and ski equipment was propped up in the cupboard of his large room, with an enormous bed.

"Coffee or wine?" he called from the smart, modern kitchen.

"Uh, wine?" she said, her voice quavering slightly as she looked around. All the walls were filled with collage pictures of him and all his millions of friends: skiing, getting drunk, messing about on boats and obviously having loads and loads of fantastic experiences she'd never managed to have. There were lots of sexy girls in the pics too, holding up glasses of champagne while wearing bikinis, or looking pretty at weddings. And there was Adam, looking incredibly tanned and lithe, diving off a rock, or performing a huge ski jump. How on earth was she going to compete?

Adam brought through two glasses of what was clearly very nice expensive wine, even though Posy knew nothing about wine.

"Oh, don't look at those," he grimaced. "Are you thinking all my friends are idiots?"

"Well, you put them on the wall," she countered.

"So I did."

"Is it like a competition to prove you have friends? Should I count them?"

"In case you think I'm a lonely saddo?"

"Yes."

"Well, actually, I cut them all out of magazines, and replaced some of them with my head."

"I was thinking that." She took a sip of her wine, as Adam went to the expensively wall-mounted CD player.

"What kind of music do you like? I don't have any Spice Girls."

"Only the Spice Girls, I'm afraid," said Posy. "I actually have them tattooed on my back."

"Can I see?"

He put on some Van Morrison, which made Posy smile even more—could this be any more of a cliché? Then she wondered briefly how many girls Adam had brought back with the jazz and the wine and the charm, and wavered again.

"What?" said Adam.

"Nothing," said Posy, looking round. "It's just this is such a bachelor pad. I was wondering how many girls get to listen to your Van Morrison collection."

Adam's face was a comical mixture of faux-innocence and genuine confusion.

"Oh, Posy," he said. Then he came toward her and put down her glass. "Why do you think I've been following that dreadful Carla around? Because I thought I might get the chance to see you again."

Posy blinked. "Really?"

"Of course! She's horrendous. I couldn't believe my luck when I finally saw you in the bar tonight. I nearly peed my pants."

Posy smiled. "*Really?*"

Adam shrugged. "See? Would a practiced seducer confess to you about nearly peeing their pants?"

Posy smiled. Adam put out his big, masculine hand, with the dark hair curling round the watch strap, and caressed her chin.

"You are . . . you are too cute, do you know that?"

"Cute?" said Posy. "Like a Disney creature, or what?"

"OK, stop talking now," he ordered. And he moved in closer, until their lips met.

This is what Posy had managed to successfully explain to the girls. Not that, in fact, the Van Morrison album was indeed a tried and tested routine—as, she suspected, was his line about peeing his pants. Not that his friends in the pictures turned out to be as attractive and snotty as they looked. But that, for the first time, she truly, really felt her body come alive; felt what it was capable of with a confident, sexy man, who could make her feel confident and sexy too. Who could, in fact, make her feel things she hadn't even believed were possible, after years of comfy, comforting Chris. This was something else altogether. This was slipping off to the toilet in nightclubs. This was turning up at his office in a basque. The heady, overwhelming excitement of the first incredibly good sex of Posy's life came off her like a flame. She lost weight; her skin gleamed. She was sure she walked differently, and that it would be immediately evident to anyone she passed that they were at it almost continuously.

So he was often late—he worked hard—and rarely, again, as attentive, as funny and interesting as he had been that first night. Posy wondered sometimes whether she shouldn't have made it a little harder for him, let him chase her a bit further. He was a wolf, after all: sexy, handsome, charming, and an alpha male. Posy felt practically addicted to him—to the wild, heavy-boozing nights; to the feel of his long muscular body against hers. He never came to her place; in the hours in between their meetings she haunted the narrow streets of Earl's Court.

He didn't call her terribly regularly; they were hardly, she supposed, even official boyfriend and girlfriend. But when his number showed up on Posy's very first, expensively acquired, and much treasured mobile phone, with its antennae on the end, then she felt alive. She would drop her friends at short notice, travel miles across town at any time of night, endure any number of tedious sports-based evenings and nights out with his female friends, who clearly saw her as a transient dalliance and treated her with according disdain. Just for the feel of his rough cheeks, his fine features; the expensive aftershave mingling with the taste of alcohol, the sharpness of his shoulder blades. Even the way he hung his suits up carefully in his cupboard sent a shiver of desire down her spine.

In sober moments (of which there were not many that giddy summer), Posy knew things weren't perfect. She'd never met his parents, for example, even though they lived in London, and he had shown no inclination to meet her mother (which was probably wise, she conceded). He never took her anywhere on her own after that first night; it was always him and a huge gang of friends, and she was permitted to tag along, be ignored, then go home with him at the end of the night and have sex with him. It was as opposite to the cozy, settled, taking-turns-at-the-dishes conventionality of her life with Chris as she could possibly imagine. There were never any dishes with Adam; they ate out every time they met up, and the cleaner picked up the coffee cups in the morning.

But he was so funny, so exciting. She discovered parts of London she would never have seen otherwise; went to some wild parties and mostly enjoyed herself. But something gave her an inkling, some feeling that this wasn't quite . . .

"He used to call you up like pizza," Leah was saying.

"What?" said Posy, returning to earth in front of the mirror.

"Look at you! You're miles away. It's just the same as it always was with Adam. He calls up for you like pizza and you go running to get there in thirty minutes or less."

Even though it was years ago, Posy still felt her ears go hot.

"I do . . . I did not. That's not true. Adam and I had great fun together."

"And I have enjoyed many pizzas."

Posy squinted. "Is that what you thought at the time? I always reckoned you were quite envious of us."

Leah raised her eyebrows. "You think that."

"But he was a good-looking bloke . . ."

"Posy, he totally loved himself so much you were never going to get a look-in."

"Well, yes, there was that—"

"Do you really think he's changed?"

"Well, won't it be fun to see?"

"I hope so. What about Voldemort? He must be next on your list, surely?"

Posy retrieved her credit card from the assistant and slipped it neatly back into her wallet. "Oh, well, I don't know. I don't even know where he is."

"You mean there's someone in the world who's *not* on Facebook? I thought they'd introduced it instead of identity cards. I can't believe he's escaped the net."

"It's not funny. He just chooses to keep himself off the grid. I think it's rather noble actually."

Leah rolled her eyes. "I'm sure you'll track him down."

Posy bit her lip and fingered where her ring used to be. "Hmm."

Posy hid herself away from Margie in the office that afternoon. However sympathetic Gavin might be, she didn't think she was going to be getting much work done. Even though she felt things had gone, in the end, quite well with Chris, she didn't feel at all as confident about Adam. He was so swift, so sure of himself that it was often hard to predict what he was thinking. After Chris, who always made sure you knew exactly where you stood, his mercurial personality had been both compelling and a worry. He wasn't the marrying type; she'd always known that. But would he tell her what he'd really thought of their time together? And whether his life was so much better without her? Was everyone's?

She was glad the flat was empty when she got home. Even though she had nothing, she told herself fiercely, to be guilty about with Chris—except not telling Matt about it before rather than afterward, and really that was semantics, wasn't it? *Wasn't it?*—she had *nothing* to feel guilty about with Adam. So why did she feel so guilty? Horribly, horribly guilty. But the desire to see Adam outweighed the guilt, after all.

Still, she would put on blusher and eye makeup to go out with anyone, even Fleur. Probably not this much, but she was going to a smart place and she needed to make a bit of an effort.

She glanced at Matt's gym kit, slung over the back of a chair, and frowned. He was usually so meticulous, it wasn't like him. Must have been in a rush somewhere. She put on the pretty dress and looked at herself in the mirror. Not bad. Not twenty-three again, but not bad.

Chapter Fifteen

There was no doubt about it, Shoreditch House was intimidatingly smart, and full of incredibly young, trendy, famous-looking people who had obviously never heard of the words "credit crunch" in their lives. There was even a swimming pool on the roof, surrounded by cool people smoking. There was nobody in it. Posy wondered how body-confident you would have to be to change into your swimming togs and go splashing about in front of everyone. Presumably people just fell in whenever they got drunk.

She wouldn't have been surprised to find Adam with his usual entourage; she had hardly ever seen him not surrounded by thousands of friends. On his own he could withdraw, become less of himself, abandon the extrovert, cheeky, voluble character. But surrounded by his crowd, his gang, he could finally be himself. As if he felt his personality always needed backup before it could truly let rip. The few dinners out they'd had just the two of them had felt awkward, stilted. They usually had to get drunk instead, and just turn them into elaborate rituals of foreplay—having dinner as a couple was a joke, of course, and couldn't possibly mean anything at all.

Otherwise it all took place in a gang; a gang to which she didn't really belong, of shared (rubbish) jokes, shared outings, meals, experiences. Posy, brought up to believe that following the herd was essentially weak and an admission of failure, found it all inexplicable, but she couldn't ignore the nagging voice that told her that Adam was happier in company because he didn't want to be with just her. Ever. That, in fact, she was tolerated, certainly not cherished, and, even more certainly, not loved. And that was six months of her life, she reflected sadly, as the attractive waiter checked the name on the reservations sheet. A long time to hang around, not really being loved or really loving in return. The passion, the excitement, she had adored that. But the man, she supposed, she had barely known. No wonder Leah and Fleur didn't want her to see him. She thought again about Fleur's anxious face. It wasn't like her to show so much concern for her big sis.

To her surprise, there was only one person on the shiny banquette inside, sipping a cocktail carefully. He hadn't changed that much in nine years—the dark hair was shorter and flecked with gray, he had gained weight and his face looked a little weary, though that might just be the extremely low lighting. She was glad, as she caught sight of the intensely glamorous denizens of the club flit about the room, that she had bought the new dress. The floral pattern was definitely flattering, and the evening, while not warm, was mild.

"Adam?"

He leaped up nervously, as if he hadn't been expecting her.

"Posy!" He shook his head. "You haven't changed a bit."

"Neither have you," said Posy, lying slightly. Closer up, he did look more ravaged, a little craggy round the edges. Dark shadows under his eyes looked like late nights, long working hours, too much coffee. His teeth were a little yellow too.

"Hey," she said, as he leaned in and they gave each other an awkward social kiss on each cheek.

"It's been too long," said Adam. "Really we should have met up before."

Posy wanted to say, "Yes, but you dumped me, remember?" but didn't want to spoil the mood before they'd even started, so just smiled instead.

"What are you drinking?"

Adam looked at it. "Not sure. Some house specialty cocktail."

Typical Adam, to order without even glancing at the menu. Posy was glad he was less attractive. Very useful. He didn't measure up to Matt, who always seemed to be bursting with health, even if it seemed occasionally entirely *too* much health.

"OK. Can I have one?"

Adam nodded. "Definitely." And, as if by magic, a waiter appeared. They sat down.

"So what have you been up to?" asked Adam, as Posy played nervously with the strap of her handbag. She wasn't sure how to launch in; how to start. Maybe if she drank her cocktail quite swiftly, that would give her inspiration.

"Oh, you know," she said. "Working, blah blah blah."

Her drink came. It was delicious. She downed most of it quickly and decided to plow straight on in.

"And I'm getting married."

Adam smiled. "So I hear. And see."

Posy held up the ring. She'd snuck it out of the cupboard and put it back on. She couldn't help it; she loved it so much. It was so beautiful. And tonight it would be her magic amulet; her protection.

"Yes, it's a bit naff, but I like it."

"It's not naff," said Adam, looking slightly affronted on behalf of the male gender. "It's an engagement ring."

"Yes, I know, but the whole concept is a bit naff, don't you think? Like some people get engaged to be engaged."

"I think if you meet someone you feel strongly enough to dedicate your whole life to, you should celebrate it," said Adam, ordering them more drinks. "Truly."

"And I don't want you back if that's what you were thinking," she added hastily.

Adam looked totally surprised. "Uh, sorry?"

"I don't want you back."

"OK."

"OK."

"We were never married."

"No, I know that."

"So . . . ?"

"Never mind. Forget I said it."

Posy felt embarrassed for shooting her bolt so quickly. Still, it seemed necessary—Chris hadn't got the point for ages.

"I thought we were just catching up," said Adam, taking a deep draught.

"We are! We are!"

181

"That's what Facebook is for, isn't it? Round up the old muckers and all that?" He stretched out his legs and smiled at her.

"Definitely! Yes. YES."

"Good."

He lifted his new glass and they clinked cheers to one another. Actually, thought Posy, watching him run his hands through his thick hair, he hadn't really changed at all.

"Where's your entourage?" asked Posy, desperate to change the subject.

"What do you mean?"

"You know! Everyone you hang around with all the time."

Adam still looked totally stymied. "I don't know what you're talking about."

"Dyl. Chas. Lugs. Maxine."

"You mean my *friends*?"

Posy began to feel this wasn't a particularly fruitful line to be taking. But funnily enough, sitting down and staring him straight in the face, it was just like the stories she had read as a child. When you confronted your fears head on, they weren't as frightening as you'd thought. It was, after all, only Adam—charming, handsome, feckless Adam. So she had got dumped. It wasn't the worst thing in the world, was it? As she looked into her cocktail, all that silly part of her life—which had felt so important at the time—suddenly seemed so distant. She felt slightly heightened from the alcohol, and untouchable, safe from the Adams of this world.

There had hardly really been an end to the relationship in any case—he had just got, steadily, further and further away. He would occasionally allow her, gratefully, to sleep with him after big nights out, but it was indifferent at best. She, in her turn, dressed up more, desperately trying to engage herself with his hobbies (horse racing and skiing, both borderline impossible to merely fake an interest in, but she did her best). She offered to cook for him, or look after him when he was sick—things which had always made Chris very acquiescent and grateful. He wasn't interested in either. When he went away for a weekend with all his friends, telling her there wasn't room, Leah and Fleur begged—begged—her just to end it, but she felt like she didn't know how. There was no exciting alternate world she had to go off and explore. Adam's London was all she knew. To be without someone, however distant, felt too terrifying to contemplate. Amazingly, she felt if she were alone at twenty-three she might be alone forever. Chris had loved her—hadn't he? Or was she simply a handy warm bed to him as well? She drove herself crazy trying to figure it out. Was she too fat? Too ugly? Boring? Too short/not short enough? Too London? Whatever these things, she simply battened down the hatches and waited for the inevitable.

She never got the chance to ask. After the final weekend away, after which Adam had waxed lyrical about girls who played tennis called things like Minge and Pony, he gave up calling or speaking to her at all. And when he did, finally—when she had gone round to his flat to see him—he looked at her with those sharp, amused, shallow eyes and said, simply, "Oh, Pose, it was fun, wasn't it?"

"No!" she desperately wanted to say. "No, it wasn't fun at all! You're being a total arse!"

But she didn't, of course. She just shrugged and said yes, as if she wasn't that bothered either. He'd looked relieved that she wasn't putting up much of a fuss. Not sad, or disappointed, or wistful—pleased.

"You should have thrown a glass in his face," said Fleur afterward.

"I know. But they were at the Conran Shop," Posy had said. "Argh, he was *such* an arse. He shouldn't have looked so pleased. I know he pulled those women too."

And she had slunk out, showing a brave face as if that would help somehow, for when he called her in a couple of weeks or so, realizing his terrible mistake and anxious to give them another go. It never happened. All, it turned out, she had to do in the end was avoid loud overpriced bars in west London over-populated by screaming yahoos and drunken rugby-loving idiots and she would never, ever have to see him again.

"So," said Adam, pulling her back to earth. Eight years ago she would have been desperate for this chance, this moment, to tell him a few things, or whack him about the head. But today, not so much. "What's this about then?"

He ordered another couple of drinks. Posy realized this meant they were going to be getting drunk. And fast. All her good intentions would be in jeopardy. Oh well, why should they break their usual habits?

"I don't know. But I never felt we had a proper ending," said Posy, trying to say what she'd meant to.

"Well, we broke up, didn't we? Didn't we?"

"Yeah, but you just said, 'See you later,' and then I never saw you again."

Adam stared into his drink. "Oh, I thought it was quite an easy end to a casual kind of thing . . ."

"Hmm," said Posy.

"Would you have rather I said, "See you later, I want to nob lots of other people and not feel guilty"?"

Posy thought about it. "Well, at least it would have been a good reason, rather than leaving me to think I was the ugliest, stupidest, shortest girl on the face of the planet."

His face looked stricken. "Is that what you thought?"

Posy shrugged. "I didn't know what to think, did I?"

"Damn you, Facebook," said Adam, then smiled ruefully. "It is nice to catch up, though. OK, I'm sorry. Can I be sorry? Will that be enough? I mean, I really am actually sorry. You were—are—great and everything, I just wanted to explore, you know, that's all it was. Come on, I'm much nicer now, I promise."

"Did you?"

"Did I what? Screw around? And how." He shook his head gleefully at the memories. "It was ace. Did you?"

"No!" She slapped him hard on the knee. "I sat indoors for a year watching *Ally McBeal*."

"You did not! You idiot."

Posy reflected on it. "I was an idiot, wasn't I?"

"And how! You're a great girl, you should have been out there, flashing it about a bit."

"Curses," said Posy.

"Then you probably wouldn't been mooning it up the place now."

"I suppose."

Posy shook her head. She felt the cocktails begin to take effect too. Had she just been overthinking this the entire time? And if she'd been overthinking this then surely she'd been overthinking . . . *him*, as well. This was fine, this was easy, no

185

problem. He was just a man, not the right man for her, but nothing to worry about. And if this was the case with Adam, shouldn't she also slay the dragon that was . . . Well. Anyway, she was definitely feeling more relaxed.

"So, what else have you been up to?" she asked, eating a nut from the dish in front of her, then stopping when she realized nobody else in the entire room was touching the snacks.

Adam shrugged. "Well, after I got divorced, I—"

"Whoa!" said Posy, spilling the bowl of nuts all over the table. "Back up! Back up! What do you mean, you got divorced?"

"Well, it's when two people—"

"No, I mean, what . . . I didn't even know you'd got married."

"Didn't you?" He looked confused.

"No, because you broke up with me, remember? So . . ."

"OK, we've been through that bit," said Adam. "Oh yes, I did get married. In fact, you knew her but she didn't want to have you there."

Posy looked at him. It couldn't be. "It wasn't . . ."

"Carla, do you remember?"

Posy shook her head in disbelief. "You married *Carla*? That girl that followed you around like a limpet?"

"Carla? Did she? I never noticed."

Posy rolled her eyes. "She followed you around like a crocodile stalking its prey . . . is that what crocodiles do? Wow, I can't believe it. Wow. And I thought you liked me playing it cool!" she said, slightly knocked by the news. All this time she thought Adam was too selfish and thoughtless to settle down with anyone. But no, it turned out he just didn't want to settle with her.

Adam still looked utterly bamboozled. "I had no idea she liked me so much."

"Because you're an idiot!"

"Then why did she treat me so badly when she got me?" he wondered.

"How did she treat you badly?"

Adam squinted. "Well, maybe I started it . . ."

"Did you forsake all others, wanting only her?" asked Posy mischievously.

"Well, before we got married, she just treated everything like such a laugh," said Adam. "Honestly, I never thought she'd mind all that much."

"Did she mind?!" asked Posy. "Carla *never* had a laugh! You unbelievable tart! Don't tell me, was she boring too?"

"Does it help if I tell you she took my house?" grumbled Adam.

"Yes. A bit."

"It's not funny."

"It's not." Posy frowned. "You'd think she would have known what you were like."

"I know!"

Posy shook her head. "Adam Linden. I would never have thought you'd get down the aisle."

Adam held up his arms, helplessly. Posy felt sad suddenly. Other people seemed to find it all so simple.

"So what," said Posy, leaning forward, "what made you propose? What made you do it?" She thought about Carla— friendly, pretty, enthusiastic Carla. Well, it made sense, she supposed. With her fashionable clothes and tidy ways and, well, Carla was obviously just better wife material. She thought of Carla with her manicure and her fashionable clothes. And those girls at the gym, of course . . . all taut and buffed to a high-tan sheen. She wasn't like that, would never be like that. She wouldn't have made a good corporate wife for Adam. OK, so she wouldn't humph around in a sack like Elspeth, but still, she wouldn't fit in. She looked around her, at all the slender glamorous types. She didn't fit in with him.

Matt, though. He was surrounded by these kinds of people all the time and yet he liked her. Just her. Hmm.

Adam rolled his eyes. "Oh, she told me she was pregnant."

Posy was so surprised she felt her mouth fall open. "She did *what*?"

"Yeah. And did a lot of crying and stuff. Then I said, 'Well, I suppose we could get married,' and she burst into tears again and rang everyone and before I knew it I had a morning suit on." He shook his head at the memory. "It *was* fast."

"So, hang on," said Posy. "Do you have a child?"

"No," said Adam, setting down his drink. "She lost the baby at six weeks."

"Oh, that's very sad," said Posy. "I'm sorry."

"Yeah," said Adam, "it was really sad. Carla said the best way to get over it was to throw herself into planning the wedding."

"Oh, that's awful," said Posy, still sympathetic.

"Yeah, I know, we had color swatches and everything."

"I mean . . ." Posy abandoned the train of thought. "Was it a big affair?"

"Totally massive. Disgusting, in fact. Doves and almonds and all sorts."

"Red Arrows fly past . . ."

"Yup, all of that."

"Why *is* it that the more extravagant the wedding, the shorter it lasts?" wondered Posy aloud. She realized she was doing exactly what she had promised herself she wouldn't: getting drunk with Adam in the room.

"Because big weddings are really really boring for absolutely everyone except the bride and the bride's bloody mother and they cost a bloody fortune," said Adam bitterly.

"You're not over it," said Posy.

"*It* I am over," said Adam. "Paying the damn thing off and losing my house I would say I am not. Teach me to try and do the decent thing."

Posy raised her eyebrows. "The man beneath the cad."

"I would . . . I would have liked to have met the baby," said Adam, quietly.

They sat there in silence, and Posy reached out and patted his hand gently.

Adam looked at her out of the corner of his eye. "Actually I'm on a mission to rediscover my inner cad. Fancy joining in?"

Posy couldn't help but laugh. "Come on, Adam, I am ancient now and you've had me already. You can let it rest."

In answer, Adam picked up their drinks and insisted they move over to where, Posy hadn't even noticed, a DJ had started playing.

"Well, in any case, you must dance with me. I've poured out my whole terribly sad story, I deserve a little mercy."

Posy realized she hadn't really danced for . . . well, how long? Her and Matt had kind of stopped dancing. It just didn't seem like the kind of thing that couples who'd been together a long time did anymore, which felt daft when you thought about it, like giving it up along with sex. She wondered, if you drew a graph, whether or not you would see a direct trajectory. Before she could follow the train of thought too far, Adam had grabbed her arm and was spinning her around.

"Hey, baby," he joked. Something incredibly naff was playing—Robbie Williams—and Posy felt the cocktails course through her veins. Around her, gorgeous young starlets were dancing self-consciously, in an incredibly sexy way. Posy decided that under the circumstances, the best thing to do was let herself go with the flow, and with a shimmy she brought her arms up above her head.

Adam grinned at her. Vulnerabilities abandoned, he was back in full wolfish mode. Posy realized she'd forgotten what it was like—it just seemed so very long ago. But he was a great dancer, of course, sexy without being show-offy, un-self-conscious without being horribly uninhibited. As she twirled in and out of his arms, stopping to occasionally sip her drink, she realized that for the first time in weeks, she could put the soul-searching from her mind. For once, she wasn't having a really terrible time. She could live in the moment; enjoy herself. As the music got louder and the room got sweatier, she found herself moving nearer to Adam, and when he moved closer and closer amidst all the young people and the smell of aftershave and alcohol, Posy gave herself up to the headiness of it all; losing herself in being twenty-three again, without a care or a thought in the world, without a mortgage, a broken engagement or fear of an uncertain future, without a little crease in the middle of her forehead. Her short skirt billowed as she leaned into him eagerly. There was a pause in the music.

Harshly, sharply, her phone rang.

"No phones on in here," said Adam, breaking off with her

briefly. Indeed, she could see disapproving looks all around the dance floor.

A cool breeze off the roof blew into her face as she escaped the dark room. She swayed gently against the external fire escape.

"This is your come-home alarm call," said Leah's familiar voice.

"What?"

"Come home! You've been out with Adam for too long! He'll put you under his spell!"

"No, no, it's fine," said Posy, realizing she was slurring her words. "I have to turn my phone off."

"Oh God, it's worse than I thought," said Leah. "*Come home.*"

"No, it's fine."

"Are you getting off with him?"

Posy didn't want to listen to Leah right then. She wasn't getting off with him anyway.

"You're thinking about getting off with him, aren't you? *Come home* or I'm coming to get you."

"I'm fine," said Posy. "He's been through a very painful divorce."

"I'll put you through a very painful headlock if you *dare* go home with—"

Posy felt the breath on her back, and a familiar strong arm come round her waist to caress her and, with one swift move, take her phone and switch it off.

"Hey!" she protested.

"What did I tell you? No phones in here," said Adam. The view over London from the fire escape was breathtaking. The towers of the City loomed up over the illuminated glow of

St. Paul's and the dark streak of the river. Adam kissed the back of her neck.

"You do like looking at views," he muttered, and she was taken back to the very first night they had met.

"Stop it!" she said. "Stop it at once."

Chapter Sixteen

"Oh *God*!" Posy pounded her screaming head against the pillowcase. It didn't help. "*How*?!" she moaned out loud. "How could I have been such an idiot?"

She marched to the window. Adam was living sixteen stories up in what was obviously meant to be a cool penthouse block near the river, but actually felt more like a big glass box. That divorce really had hit him badly. Her phone rang. She considered throwing it out of the window, but settled on ignoring it.

At least it wasn't Matt. That would have been the worst thing. She sighed, running her hands through her tangled hair. Matt, who would have had all his worst fears confirmed that she was indisputably *not* the marrying kind.

London didn't look sparkly and exciting from a great height anymore. It looked gray and miserable and horrid, full of identically dressed people marching glumly off to work.

Oh God, what a horrible horrible disaster. She looked down. At least her clothes were still on. Of Adam there was no sign.

Oh God. Oh my God, she'd really done it now. Chokingly she started to cry.

"What's up with you, sexy pants?"

She turned round slowly. "I can't believe . . . I can't believe I came back with you."

"What are you talking about? Four of those cocktails and you weren't capable of going anywhere on your own."

"What was *in* those things?" said Posy, grasping her head.

"It's a secret recipe," said Adam.

"That's because it's illegal," said Posy. "Oh. Oh God."

"It's not that bad."

"Adam, I'm *engaged*! And I woke up in your bed."

"Yes, and I woke up on the sofa, you idiot. I know you think I get about a bit, but I can assure you I find near-unconsciousness very unattractive."

Posy's hand shot to her mouth. "You mean, we didn't . . ."

Adam rolled his eyes. "No, but thank you for your six-hour lecture on how much you love Matt, and I liked the way that every time you got to the end of telling me about it you'd go back and start again. That made it even better."

"Oh Christ," said Posy. "I am sorry."

"Not at all," said Adam. "Actually, I found the first couple of hours quite fun."

Posy looked down. "No more mystery cocktails."

"I think that sounds like a good idea."

Her phone rang again.

"You're there, aren't you?"

"Hello, Leah," said Posy, with a resigned sigh.

Leah sighed as well and made a disappointed sound.

"It's not what you think," said Posy.

"Oh no?"

"You're a gorgeous hunk of woman!" shouted Adam from the kitchen doorway.

"Shut up!" hissed Posy furiously.

"Last night was incredible!" continued Adam relentlessly.

"Posy, look, you can get through this." Leah's voice sounded anxious on the phone. "You're not a bad person."

"She's a very naughty girl," said Adam.

After she'd explained everything to Leah (who didn't necessarily think getting pissed with your ex-boyfriend was a great idea either, something with which Posy was in full agreement), Adam had very sweetly offered her a bath—which she'd accepted—and one last opportunity to get off with him, which she'd declined. He even suggested breakfast—it was Saturday so he was working anyway but having taken off the top layer of hangover grime, Posy wanted out as quickly as possible.

"Well," Adam had said politely, dropping her off at the tube station. "It was nice to catch up. Anytime!"

Posy saw, once again, her dreams of coming across as an adult, sensible woman with her own life and confidence, breathtakingly admirable and incredibly sorted, leaving Adam winded with admiration and respect for her life choices and wishing he hadn't been so hasty all those years ago . . . oh, for *fuck's* sake.

"What are you shaking your head for?" said Adam.

"Oh, nothing," said Posy, "nothing at all. Good luck, Adam."

"Oh yeah, sure," he said, and kissed her jauntily on the mouth. "You too, eh? Keep in touch!"

*

Back at the flat, Matt's clothes were carefully and neatly hung up on the washing line. Adidas jogging pants; hi-tech running clothes with little pockets for water and watches and timers and iPods and netting and all sorts of things. No note for her, no query about where she'd been or why she hadn't called. Nothing at all. Nothing. Tired, hungover, ashamed of herself, she sunk into the second bath of the day and cried big salty tears.

Matt only stopped by briefly, around lunchtime, to change. He eyed her up, but pointedly didn't ask where she'd been.

The evidence, thought Posy, was probably written in the tear stains in her eyes. Or didn't he care?

"Where are you going?" she asked timidly.

"I'm having a coffee with a client," he said, looking awkward.

"Oh," she said.

"Oh," he said. "Yeah." Then he looked at her, suspicion in his eyes. "Good time last night?"

Posy swallowed hard. "Oh, it was nothing, just had a few drinks, stayed with a friend."

"You don't need to tell me, Posy," said Matt. "It's your business."

"But I want to . . ." said Posy.

"I have a client," said Matt sadly, walking on out. Posy wondered if he'd seen her rumpled dress—her outfit of shame from last night. Had he taken something from that?

"Matt!" she called desperately. "Are we going to talk or what?"

Matt looked at her, shaking his head. "You're never here."

"I'm here now."

"And it's two p.m. on a Saturday. I have a client. Sorry."

Posy is having a lie-down.

"Well, you've really fucked it now," said Fleur, sitting on the end of her bed.

"Ssh," said Leah. "That's not helpful."

"What? She was engaged for five minutes and she spent a holiday with an ex and then the night with another ex. You're not cut out for marriage."

"That's too harsh, Fleur," said Leah. "It just means she's not cut out for *this* marriage."

"Could you stop talking about me like I'm not here?" said Posy. "It's not helping."

"Well, you are playing the invalid," pointed out Fleur.

"I can't get up."

"Shagged out?"

"Shut it."

"Where's Matt?" asked Leah.

"Don't know," said Posy. "He just says "out" these days and vanishes."

"He must be up to someone," said Fleur.

"Matt? I don't think so," said Leah.

"Oh, come on—"I have to think it over" means "I have to go out and see if there's anyone better out there." Just what you're doing, in fact."

"I," said Posy grandly, "was just being a complete fucking

idiot. That's not the same thing at all. Do you really think he might be cheating on me?"

"You have to be going out with someone to cheat on them," said Leah.

Posy let her head bang back down on her pillow. "Things are just getting *more and more complicated*."

"Do you think Matt will want to buy you out of the apartment?" asked Leah.

Posy put the pillow on her head. "Oh *God*, I don't know."

"Can you buy him out?"

"No. I owe tons of money on my Visa. This was a stretch anyway. And he's raking it in with his private clients."

"Oh," said Leah.

"Especially after I bought those flights to Scotland."

"Oh."

"All I can see," said Fleur, "is that you just have to cut your losses and run. You must see that. It's all over."

"Well, yes, but I've never felt the urge, like you, to get by in a touring caravan."

"That's because you don't have a free soul."

Leah looked worried. "Fleur might be right, you know. Maybe the marriage was just too much after everything—"

"What?! You bought me the bridal mags! You've been collecting "special buttons" for my dress!"

"I like special buttons," said Leah.

Posy stared out of the window. "Maybe. Or maybe if I just saw this through . . . finished it up."

Fleur and Leah glanced at each other.

"Well, the last two times you've done this it's gone *brilliantly*," said Leah. "So do go ahead."

"I am completely wasted as your sister," said Fleur, getting up. "I wish I had someone who appreciates me and my *good advice*."

"Although," said Leah, stopping and turning in the doorway. "Maybe if just once, just *once* you said his name, that might be a start. Help you move on somehow. Somewhere."

"Yes," said Posy. Because it was time, she thought. It was past time.

Chapter Seventeen

It had been Victoria Station again. Where she met everyone. Where everyone passed through sooner or later.

'This time, however, had been different. Well, seeing Margie was no surprise—that was a perfectly normal morning. She was usually earlier than Posy, but once a fortnight or so Posy would bump into her, stomping across the concourse like someone had just peed on her shoes, heading directly for the muffin stand. But that morning, she wasn't alone! Not only that, but she had a man with her . . . and not just any man. Not at all.

It was four years after Adam. Since then there had been men, nice and otherwise, in and out, but nobody she'd really felt for. A lot of them were like Adam, in fact—fashionable, fun, flashy, but she wasn't thinking about letting them get close. She didn't want that again. And she hadn't really met anyone . . . no one that made her heart really bounce, no one that made her bubble with excitement inside. As her friends started to pair off, Posy was starting to wonder if perhaps it was going to be like this for her, after all—maybe she just wasn't destined to fall in love like the rock songs, or the poets. Maybe love like that was for nineteen-year-olds, and here she was, washed up at twenty-seven and just never going to be the type, never destined for a "great love." It made her feel sad, sometimes.

She'd moved on in flats and was sharing with Leah, which was fun, even if she had to occasionally make sure she didn't use a very avant-garde hat as a teacup. She felt much more comfortable with her friends, her life; she liked her new job at the insurance company. Everything was mostly fine. If she had someone to love, she thought right then that morning in Victoria Station, she *did* have someone to love, he would look *exactly* like him.

The man walking with Margie was tall and rangy, slim without being puny, with huge chocolate-brown eyes and slightly unruly curly hair that straggled over his head and needed a cut, but actually looked just perfect as it was. His eyebrows arched up on his wide forehead and his stripy Breton T-shirt was spattered with paint. It wasn't very often Posy fell for someone at first sight. Never, in fact. But her very first sentiments on looking at this man were very simple: *if Margie is dating this man, I will want to die.*

Normally Margie and Posy merely nodded at one another at the station. Being a few years older than her, and single too, Margie had decided when Posy joined the office that she needed to instruct her on the ways of the wiser woman, and was constantly trying to get her to buy a cat so they could do "cat chat" and gossip about the younger women in the office. Posy very much wanted to be one of the "younger women in the office" and usually tried to have none of it. This morning, however, after checking her lipstick, Posy went up to her, beaming. She couldn't help it, she told herself. This man . . .

Even if he was someone else's, she needed to have a closer look.

"Hi, Margie!"

Margie, not to be outdone, smiled regally. "Hello, Posy. I was just coming in to work."

"Mhm," said Posy, but she wasn't really listening. Up close, he was even better. He had a couple of lines round his eyes that suggested amusement, and full lips that looked like they smiled easily. Margie, however, wasn't going to be bullied into introductions. But her face. Was she . . . was she *simpering*? This was very unlike her. Snapping she did a lot, Margie, and complaining sourly. But simpering? There was no other word for it. It wasn't a good look on her.

"Well, bye then, Almaric," she breathed.

Almaric? thought Posy. Yeah, right. I wonder what his real name is. Steve, probably. You could melt in those eyes though.

"Steve' gave a shy, incredibly sweet smile.

"Sorry," he said, addressing Posy directly. "I didn't realize Margie was in such a hurry."

Posy started, shocked at being addressed out of her reverie.

"She likes to be on time for work," said Posy helpfully, then cursed herself for not thinking of a witty rejoinder. *She likes to be on time for work*. Great job, Posy. Really sparkling out there.

"I could have guessed that," said "Steve."

"*I* just think it's appropriate behavior in the workplace," said Margie grumpily. "Unlike some."

"Steve' and Posy raised their eyebrows at one another.

"Hi," he said, putting out a long hand, with delicate-looking fingers. "I'm Almaric."

He glanced at her face. "I know, I know. Please, it's all right, you don't have to mention it. No, my parents weren't hippies; no, I'm not making it up; no, it's not some kind of sealant. It's a family name. You can call me Steve or something if you like."

Posy grinned at how accurately he'd read her.

"In fact, I do like it," she said.

"Steve."

"Yes."

"Or there is also Alfalfa, Alabama, Pain-in-the-Neck, Al—"

"Was school fun for you?"

"Yuh."

"BYE," said Margie loudly. "See you next week. Come on, Posy, we don't want to be late."

Posy raised her eyebrows again. She couldn't help it, she didn't want to go anywhere out of the orbit of this fascinating man.

"I'm Margie's pottery teacher," offered Almaric.

"We're just friends," said Margie, as if Posy had been insinuating something. Posy nodded, but inside her tummy suddenly started dancing a little happy dance. Was Almaric holding her eye for a little longer than was entirely necessary?

"You're a potter?"

"You need a class?"

This was getting more overt by the second. After the grimness of the London dating scene, Posy was amazed to find herself enjoying a proper flirt.

"That's amazing! That's *exactly* what was on my agenda for today. That and nothing else. I *have* to find a pottery class!"

Almaric grinned. "Well, Margie has my number."

"Actually, you wouldn't give me your number," said Margie, looking crosser by the second and glancing at her watch. "You said you never gave it out to clients."

Almaric's lip twitched. "I don't?" he said. "Oh yeah, I forgot. That's right. Sorry."

There was a pause.

"I'll just have to hope to run into another pottery teacher in a station with someone I work with," said Posy seriously.

"I hope you do," said Almaric. He glanced at Margie and Posy could have sworn he was wishing she wasn't there so they could swap numbers. They lingered a second more.

"Well, fingers crossed," said Posy.

Almaric smiled at her as she and Margie crossed the station concourse. Posy couldn't resist the urge to glance back, just once, but he'd gone. But inside, it was the oddest thing. She knew she would see him again. She wasn't even sad when she didn't get his number.

"He's very in demand," said Margie, fluffing up her bosom. "You wouldn't manage to get a pottery class with him anyway."

"I don't really give a stuff about pottery," said Posy.

Margie looked at her. "Why, fancy him or something?"

"No," said Posy.

"No, he's probably not right for you," said Margie. "Has loads of girls after him all the time anyway. Us older ladies need to hang back!"

"Do *you* fancy him?" asked Posy, stung.

Margie sighed and stopped walking for a second. "Yes. I fancy him a lot. Really a lot. Can we stop and get some muffins?"

Posy was intrigued.

"And I think he likes me too, definitely, it's just that he has, you know, so many students it's hard for him. That's why he doesn't have a phone or anything."

"Like the Queen," said Posy helpfully, choosing blueberry.

"Yes," said Margie. "I'll have two double choc-chip please. So I've arranged to have extra classes early in the morning, you know, so we can really get familiar with each other."

"That's a good idea."

Posy felt mean, pumping Margie for information on the chap she was after herself. But somehow, she just couldn't help herself.

"Is he a good teacher?"

"He's amazing," said Margie, glowing. "He's really patient, and he does all these amazing sculptures and things."

"Of pots."

"Well, OK, yes. They're pots. But they're really nice ones."

"Is he a bit like Patrick Swayze in *Ghost*?"

Margie bit her lip and stifled a giggle. "Ooh." She looked up. "Well, maybe just a *bit*."

"So he sits behind you and—"

"Sometimes."

"Maybe I *should* get myself to this pottery class," said Posy. Margie glared at her. "I saw him first!"

Posy would have felt guiltier about muscling in on Margie's teacher if Margie hadn't then marked her up on the office calendar for being late, even though they were both, clearly, late, claiming that she'd just wanted to keep everything nice and efficient. Posy had finished her muffin too, while Margie had both of hers left.

This wasn't the best justification in the world for Posy

trying to pinch Margie's favorite pottery teacher. But a week of slightly pathetic lingering around the exact same spot in the station at exactly the same time was getting her nowhere (except having to walk to the office every day with Margie), so after a quick perusal of *Floodlight*, the evening-class guide—there weren't too many Almarics listed—she decided, given her alternative Thursday-night plans (watching Leah trying on hats at late-night shopping, followed by a long post-mortem over half-price cocktails about whether or not wearing a hat was offputting to men), to take herself off down to the Adult Institute. OK, this seemed a bit desperate but it had been so long—possibly forever—since she'd felt this strongly about someone. She couldn't help it.

She wasn't enrolled, so decided to come by at the end and take a peek in. This was very unlike her, but for some stupid reason . . . Well, OK, she couldn't help it. He was the hottest man she'd seen in possibly *ever*. And now she was going to feel like a stalky idiot.

Wearing jeans and Converse, as if dressing down would make her look less psychotic, she headed through the dusty gray corridors of the old school. Classes of various people were reading out loud, or listening to teachers, or crocheting things. It was all incredibly interesting-looking and made Posy feel she should probably take a class in something, rather than focusing all her attentions on following *EastEnders*, looking for a boyfriend, and getting drunk with Leah.

Finally, on the third floor, she found him. He was sitting at the front of an Art class, using a wheel. His face was entirely concentrating on the long vase he was pulling out of the clay, his fingers long and beautiful. Posy was transfixed. As were, she could see, the faces of the eight female classmates, including Margie, who were sitting in front of their own wheels, but watching him intently. One, Posy thought, actually had her tongue hanging out. He was wearing an old checked shirt over a white T-shirt smeared with clay, and he had small pieces of it on his high forehead, which didn't seem to bother him at all. Finally, he completed the piece—a perfect oval, a smooth shape reaching up out of the raw matter—and took his feet off the wheel. The class actually applauded.

"Now you try," Posy could see him mouth, and as the women set their feet to work, splashing merrily with water and clay, he moved around them all, touching and shaping their endeavors so they could start to grow out of the gray sludge. She couldn't take her eyes off him. He walked between them so carefully and elegantly, laughing, using his fingers to reshape and improve the work, handling the material with a casual mastery and complete focus that made her bite her lip. She couldn't remember finding anyone so attractive.

As he rounded the back of the class, he caught sight of Posy staring through the window, and his eyebrows shot up. Posy immediately realized she should have come up with a better excuse for why she was there. But the fact was, she didn't have one. Since she'd met him, even though it was only for a moment, she'd wanted to see him more than anything. That was it, that was her excuse. She couldn't do any better.

Almaric excused himself to the class and came to the door. Margie shot her head round and although Posy tried to duck out of sight, she didn't quite manage it.

Almaric closed the door behind them.

"Hey," he said.

"Hey," said Posy. She felt her face flaming red all of a sudden. But he didn't seem cross or annoyed to see her there; genuinely puzzled if anything.

"Did you come about the class?"

"Uh, yes."

"It's kind of full."

"Uh, that's OK. I don't really want to take a class."

"I don't really want to teach one," said Almaric.

At that moment, out of nothing, something passed between them—a glimpse, an understanding. It was so instant, and felt so absolutely right, that Posy almost couldn't believe she'd seen it. But a part of her knew exactly what he meant, and her heart leaped with joy in her chest.

"Can I . . ." she started. "I mean . . ."

His gaze was intent. He had soft brown eyes, downturned slightly at the corners. He had none of Adam's confident shrewdness, nor Chris's intelligent distraction. He was just beautiful, plain and simple.

"Yes, please," said Almaric. He glanced at his watch. "I finish in twenty minutes."

"I'll wait."

"I'm not sure I can."

Both of them were blinking quite quickly. Posy felt her heart rate scurry.

"There's a pub round the corner—"

"I know it," jumped in Posy.

"No, not that one, that's where everyone goes." It was as if they hardly needed to talk; they could understand one another with barely any words.

"A little further on. The Yorkshire Gray."

*

When he arrived, looking dishevelled, twenty-five minutes later, Posy was shaking. This seemed such a mad, ridiculous thing to do. She didn't know this man, not at all. What on earth was she doing? What must he think of her just turning up like that, all weird and . . . it was just wrong. She should just go home. Definitely. But somehow . . . she just wanted to see him. She couldn't help it, she needed to find out.

"Hey." He looked awkward too. Incredibly so, in fact.

"Sorry," said Posy. "This is a bit mad. I shouldn't have—"

"No, no, you should," he said. "Would you like a drink?"

"Yes, please," said Posy. "Wine."

"What color?"

For a second, she just looked at him. She had no idea how to answer the question. She'd been focusing on the line of his eyebrows, and how on anyone else his forehead might look too high, but on him it just looked . . .

"Oh," she said. "I have no idea."

He grinned, helplessly. "OK. Why don't I get the middle one?"

"OK."

It was a warm evening and they sat on the terrace of the pub with a bottle of chilled rosé between them. And talked. And talked. It couldn't spill out fast enough, somehow; as if they were both in a race to share as much of themselves as possible. She learned all about his four older sisters, his mother's arthritis, and his father's pride when he became a potter ("Shortly followed by disappointment when I had to keep borrowing money to pay rent"). And oddly, she told him everything: about her mother's practice, and the dad she just didn't know, her half-brother, her crazy sister. And he laughed and they both laughed and they found things in common that they couldn't have imagined, from their teenage taste in music (both rubbish imitation goths) to shared Westlife-phobia to a joint adoration for Harry Hill.

The whole time Posy felt the oddest sensation, like she was hurtling at full speed toward the most extraordinary fairground ride of her life: a delicious freefall. When he got up to go to the loo, she stared after him, in a state of disbelief, completely and utterly shocked that this thunderbolt had walked into her life.

A fear grabbed at her chest: he couldn't be single. He couldn't be. Women were always single; men never were. There was absolutely no way some woman—not Margie, though not for lack of trying—hadn't leaped on him like a hungry cougar the second he'd waved goodbye to his last super-model at the airport. I mean, thought Posy, *look* at him. The way his bum curved into his jeans, his ludicrously long fingers and the way they pushed his hair off his forehead, his eyes a wide dreamy brown. Posy shook her head. He couldn't—there was absolutely no way on earth he was single. None. That was the rule in London. And it was going to kill her. The luckiest bloody witch—or chap—in the world who had him, and she or he had better know how lucky they were. As soon as he came back from the loo, she was going to ask. She had to.

"Would another bottle of wine render us completely incapable?" Almaric was saying, with a regrettable look on his face.

"Incapable of what?" said Posy. "Are you scheduled to drive an HGV later?"

Almaric grinned, showing his lovely teeth, and headed back

to the bar. He put a shirt around her in case she was cold and, when she complained, insisted that it was his friend Smithy's, and she must have it, even if he caught hypothermia. Him or Smithy. Oh no, this wouldn't do. This couldn't. Because if she didn't find out right now, Posy was going to want to kiss him. In fact, she wasn't sure how she could *avoid* kissing him. And that could end very messily indeed.

"Almaric?" She stood up.

He turned back. Posy spoke very quickly so the words all ran together.

"Are-you-gay-or-married-or-have-a-girlfriend-or-just-broken-up-with-someone?"

She realized her face must look like a picture of hope and vulnerability. But she couldn't help it. When it came to this man, this man whom she didn't know at all, she was an open book. She felt that she couldn't hide anything.

Standing at the bar, Almaric twisted almost comically back to her, staring her full in the face. For a second she was sure he was going to ask her to repeat herself, and she wasn't sure she had the nerve. Maybe she should just pretend she'd said something else, and slink out . . .

But his face smiled again, then he bit his lip. As if making up his mind about something, he strode toward her.

"E," he said.

"What do you mean?"

He was very close to her now, they were chest to chest, or rather, she was chest to stomach; he was that much taller than her.

"E?" he said again, a shadow passing across his brow as if he was worried that his joke had backfired. "None of the above?"

They stared at each other, heartbeats apart, for a long moment.

"Are we rushing?" said Almaric. "Am I rushing? Is this too much?"

Posy couldn't do anything except shake her head in disbelief.

"I think," she found herself saying, completely against her will, "I think I've been waiting all my life for you."

Immediately, everything in her life that wasn't Almaric, or talking about Almaric, took on secondary importance. They hadn't slept together then—not that night, not that first night. It was as if they'd both known on some level that there was no rush; that the whole world was there for the taking. So they'd kissed on the terrace, tasting the dusty London summer sun on their lips, and the sweet pink wine; kissed and chatted and laughed and kissed until the pub closed and turfed them out and they found themselves, hand in hand on quiet city streets, giggly and a little drunk. Posy looked at him, wide-eyed.

"I have to go," she said. "I have work tomorrow and normal life, and all those things."

Almaric nodded.

"We could set your office on fire."

"We *must*," said Posy. "I can't think of anything else better to do."

Almaric smiled.

Even now, years later, Posy could remember dimples in his smooth cheeks like it were yesterday; the way he looked at her then, as if she was the most amazing, the most wonderful, precious jewel in all the world. It was one of the sweetest nights of her life.

Chapter Eighteen

"You're off on one again, aren't you?" said Leah.

It was two days later. They were having lunch and Leah had asked once more if she was going to find him. "I don't think you ever stop thinking about him. You never have."

Posy shrugged. "Yes, thanks, I have your take on the whole affair. It was the first time I fell in love, OK? The first time I fell in love properly. And it was like lightning; it was exactly like everybody always says. It was like being hit by lightning. It's the only time that's ever happened to me. So I think I'm allowed to, you know . . ."

"Obsess about it and jeopardize all your future relationships?"

"Reminisce a bit."

"I'm just saying that until you get Lord Voldemort out of your head, then I'm not sure you and Matt have a chance. Which means . . ."

Posy stayed quiet.

"Hmm," Leah sighed. "OK. All right. I admit it."

"What?"

"That maybe you should go and see him."

Posy looked at her. "Oh my God, someone agrees with me."

"Well, maybe life is like a blister. Sometimes you just have to prick it with a pin and let the goo come out."

"Maybe it is. Some people like doing that, you know."

"It's true, I like doing that. Because it hurts, but then you feel better afterward."

"I hope you're right," said Posy.

"But there's one thing you have to do."

"Tell Matt?"

"Are you two speaking?"

"No," said Posy miserably, nudging at her cappuccino. "Funny, I thought we'd be picking out china patterns by now."

"You need to talk to him."

"I know."

"And there is another thing."

"What?"

"Say his name."

"He used to say, 'Call me Steve.' Can't I call him that?"

"No."

"It was a stupid bloody name anyway."

"Say his name." She drained her cappuccino.

"Almaric," she said. "His name is Almaric."

"And he wasn't all that," said Leah, but too quietly for Posy to hear.

Chapter Nineteen

Dear Aunt Cathy,
Although I am in a good relationship, I have been
checking up on my exes on Facebook. I can't seem to
stop myself. One in particular I am desperate to see
again. Do you think this would be a good idea, just to
close the door on the unfinished business in my life?
P, London.

Dear P,
Oh dear. What a terrible muddle you are in. Facebook,
MySpace, and Friends Reunited have all become so
popular, and it is human nature to wish to find out
what happened in the lives of people you have known;
particularly those you have been close to.

It is, however, a temptation entirely worth resisting
if you can. The temptation to give in to grass-is-
always-greener syndrome can be terribly strong,
especially if you compare past relationships, without
worry or responsibilites; when you were younger and

215

more innocent, to the day-to-day realities of being part of a couple. But that is what maturity is. Rest assured, the golden haze you attach to the past would soon become commonplace if you were picking up his socks every day!

If you genuinely feel you cannot work on the relationship you have, then perhaps you need to look inside yourself and ask what, exactly, is missing, and why you can't be happy with what you have.

Dear Deirdre
Although I am in a good relationship, I have been checking up on my exes on Facebook. I can't seem to stop myself. One in particular I am desperate to see again. Do you think this would be a good idea, just to close the door on the unfinished business in my life? P, London.

Dear P,
Perhaps the first thing to do is to spice things up in the bedroom arena with what you have at home. Try a naughty secretary outfit—being taken on the computer will be much more fun than spending all your time in it!!

Posy is BLAH BLAH BLAH BLAH. >:(

*

But he wasn't there. That was the problem. He wasn't on Twitter. Facebook. MySpace. Bebo. You couldn't even Google him, apart from a passing mention in the evening-class brochure from years ago; he wasn't teaching there now. Nothing. He was completely off the grid. Who didn't turn up on Google, at least, here or there?

Everyone in the world was connected. Everyone was about. Except for him. He had vanished off the face of the earth.

Posy hated the very idea of it, but she knew it had to be done. She was going to have to endure the sneers and happy superiority. The "I told you so's. And she may not even get what she wanted in the end. But she was going to have to talk to Margie.

At work, she steeled herself and bought two chocolate muffins. Then she thought again and bought three. There was no nice way around it or of thinking it. When Almaric captured her heart, and she his, she broke Margie's. It didn't matter that Margie wasn't Almaric's type, that he hadn't looked at her, however many private classes she took, that Almaric was Margie's crush. It only mattered that Margie had seen him first, had practically warned Posy off, and Posy had sluttishly rushed in and snaffled him anyway. Posy understood that this was how Margie saw it, and indeed endured without complaint the many, many work demerits that were to follow in the years to come, from the first time—Posy couldn't even think of it without wanting to wince—when Almaric had turned up to surprise her at the office, with a huge bouquet of delphiniums, and she had rushed out of the building and thrown herself into his arms, unable to bear even the eight-hour separation of the working day. And yes, Margie had seen it, and Posy had been so wrapped up and senseless in love she hadn't even cared—in fact, worse; she felt that Margie should be as happy for them as she was, that everyone should be incredibly fascinated by every tiny detail of Almaric: his favorite muppet, what an amazing cook he was, the location of the most perfect freckle he had low down, just below his right ear . . .

She had been hideously selfish, overflowing.

"You must shut up now," Leah would say. "And I *like* you."

Posy hadn't listened, of course, her every spare second was for Almaric, and his for her. She had never been so happy, never. And now, it had come down to this.

She absent-mindedly ate two of the muffins before she'd even got in the lift, then when she saw Gav, offered him the remaining one immediately.

"How are you?" she asked, but she didn't really need to. His year-round Australian tan, topped up when he went home at Christmas (skin cancer, he'd informed her, was something only weaklings got) had faded, leaving him gray and weary, his thinning hair whitening at the temples. He looked beaten up, kicked in.

"That witch," he said. "Do you know what she's done now?"

Posy shook her head.

"Well, we have to share custody of Sprinkles, right?"

"Sprinkles?"

"Our Maltese Terrier. She's the most beautiful little dog, right . . ."

Posy was slightly worried he was about to start crying right there in the lift.

"Anyway, *she* says, right, *she* says that she'll keep the dog, but when she . . . she . . . dies . . ."

"Your wife?"

"Sprinkles."

"She . . . my *wife* will have her cryogenically frozen. Then when technology develops, they can bring her back to life and then it's my turn to have her. And I can pay for the freezing."

"Oh," said Posy. "Oh dear, that sounds terrible."

"Don't . . . *don't* get married," said Gavin, taking her arm in a serious gesture. "Not unless you want to pay to freeze a dead dog."

He left her behind outside the elevator, brushing chocolate muffin crumbs off herself. Posy walked into the office.

"Margie?"

Margie looked up, her eyes blinking behind her spectacles. Immediately she glanced at her watch.

"I'm not late," said Posy defensively.

"So what do you need?"

Margie was wearing a tight skirt suit, with a large cat-shaped brooch on the lapel.

"I like your cat," said Posy.

"Yes," said Margie. "My cats keep me company now I've lost my true love and everything."

"Actually," said Posy, biting her lip, "as you *probably* remember from the way I lost a stone and walked about with a black beret pulled down over my face, it was three years ago. Why don't you go out with him now?"

"He wouldn't go out with anyone else from this office," said Margie immediately. "It wouldn't be right."

"Is that what he told you?"

"No, but it's totally obvious."

"Uh huh," said Posy. "Actually, Margie, I wanted to ask you . . . have you heard from him?"

Margie's eyebrows shot up. "Almaric?"

"No, the Prince of Wales. Yes, Almaric."

"He won't take you back, you know."

The fact that Margie knew absolutely nothing about the circumstances of their break-up, and therefore had not the faintest idea as to whether Almaric would have taken her back or not was wildly irritating, but Posy tried to swallow it. All through their break-up she'd managed to avoid Margie—who had made it clear she had many important thoughts on the topic, if Posy would only listen—and gradually it had faded into the background. Except here she was, scraping up all the old wounds again.

"I don't want him to take me back," said Posy. "I just have to speak to him."

"He's probably married to some really beautiful woman now . . . and they'll have really beautiful children," said Margie. "Although Almaric could always see beyond physical appearances. It didn't matter to him."

"Yes, apart from him being an artist and thus totally concerned with physical appearances," said Posy. "Do you know where he is? I've looked online, but I can't find him."

"No, you wouldn't be able to," said Margie, irritably.

"So you know?" said Posy. "You know where he is?"

"Why do you want to see him?"

Suddenly Posy wished she was a tough-talking action figure from an American television series. What she'd really like to do was square Margie up against a wall and threaten her with deadly torture until she gave her the information she required.

"It's a long story," she said, smiling sweetly. "I'd send him your good wishes."

"I did a lovely sculpture of one of my cats," said Margie. "Maybe he'd like to see it."

"I bet he would," said Posy, wondering whether Margie even knew.

"But he's not very good at answering letters," said Margie.

"You write him proper letters?" asked Posy. "You've been doing it all this time?"

"Only Christmas cards and things," said Margie. "And pictures of the cats."

Posy sat down. She'd had no idea.

"You write to him all the time?"

Margie shrugged.

"Oh, Margie," said Posy. "I'm so sorry. I didn't realize you loved him so much."

Margie dropped her gaze. "Well, you had him."

"If it helps, it wasn't just to spite you. I loved him too," said Posy. "Very much. Really."

"Was it worth it?" said Margie. "Honestly?"

Posy smiled. "Oh yes. Yes, I think on balance, all the getting my heart trampled into the mud, the never quite getting over him, the messing up my future relationships and any chance at happiness . . . Yes, I think, he probably *was* worth it."

"Yes, he would be," said Margie decisively. "How could you have let him go? If it had been me I'd have locked him up in a wardrobe and never let him leave the house ever again till we both died."

"I should have thought of that," said Posy. "Maybe I'll take some handcuffs with me."

"It's quite far," said Margie. "And you don't have any holiday leave left."

"I know," said Posy, looking down. "I was hoping you might . . ."

Margie blew out air so her fringe flew up.

"You'd *better* not make him sad."

"I'll try my absolute best," said Posy.

"Will you take my sculpture?"

"Of course."

Margie nodded, then went to her desk. She took out a key ring with Garfield on it, and carefully and secretly opened a locked drawer, then a locked cash box inside the drawer. She withdrew a piece of paper.

"Here," she said simply, passing it over.

All this time, thought Posy. All this time she thought Almaric was locked up in her heart; the name she couldn't even say. And all that time he was right here, locked in a box. She wondered how many other women in the world were walking around with Almarics in their heads. Two per office . . . at *least*. That seemed an awful lot.

"Thank you," she said, softly. "Thank you. I won't forget this. I bought you a muffin, actually. But I accidentally ate it."

"So you had something for me but you took it?" said Margie. "Don't worry, I'm used to it." She went back to her desk. "It's a long weekend. That's all, OK?"

Posy nodded and Margie marked it carefully on her wall planner.

Chapter Twenty

She wasn't going to get caught out again by the weather, like she had been in Scotland. Posy packed a bag with the warmest, most comfortable clothes she could find. Even if it was March in—what was this place called? She couldn't pronounce it, that was for sure. What on earth was it about her that made men want to seek out wild lonely places afterward? Betws-y-coed. North Wales. Posy had never been to Wales. She had no idea what she was going to find when she arrived. Worst of all, there was no simple way to get there.

A small voice in her wondered if she shouldn't give up. But she wasn't going to. She'd come so far now. She was going to meet her final man. Matt was never there these days anyway, always working or out or avoiding her, she reckoned. Every day that passed, their relationship seemed to vanish further and further into the distance—it was finishing. Not with a bang, but with a whimper. Her heart was slowly crumbling. And if the reason, if what had spoiled everything for her, was her lasting feelings for Almaric then she had to confront them once and for all. She had to clear it up. And she needed to get there to do it.

Well, she might as well ask.

"Matt?"

"Hmm?"

He was in the kitchen on the computer. Whenever he was in one room, she made sure she was in another. It was like living in two bedsits. Both of them had to always pretend to be thoroughly engrossed in whatever they were doing and not watching the other at all. Due to the layout of the flat, with its open plan kitchen/sitting room and door onto the bedroom, there were very few angles where you were out of view. It was intensely difficult to look that engrossed in Facebook for that long, and both of them had taken to retreating to the bathroom whenever possible. It hadn't got to the stage of leaving one another notes on the fridge door quite yet, but Posy was slightly concerned that it might. In her most nonchalant tone of voice possible, she said,

"Uh, I need to . . . Can I borrow your car?"

There was no way around it. Leah used her little Mini every day to ferry about prom dresses and feather boas to fashion shoots. Fleur couldn't drive. Her mother's old Vauxhall was a death trap and as she never used it she could never remember where it was parked and always forgot to renew her parking permit, so it spent most of its time at the Islington car pound.

Matt, on the other hand, did jog to most of his appointments, and they were all in central London; he could take the tube if he needed to. And he wouldn't mind, would he?

Matt looked up, a slightly pained expression on his face.

"Pepe?"

Posy rolled her eyes. "Matt, if I wouldn't call your car by its name when we were together, I'm hardly going to start now, am I?"

Matt bit his lip. "Uh huh."

Even though, strictly speaking, he could have got by without his car, Posy did know how much he loved it. It was a beautiful old red Alfa Romeo with pure Italian style in every inch of it. Matt must have spent more than the cost of the thing just to keep it on the road all these years, but it was a perfectly tuned, nippy little growling monster of a thing, and his pride and joy. Posy remembered how hurt he'd been when she'd accused him of having a poser's car when they first got together. She'd instantly retracted it. This car was his little work of art; he always kept it under a tarpaulin, and was happy to spend Sundays polishing it up. Posy had always found something incredibly retro and touching in this when he went out to tinker, or talked longingly one day of having a garage. It just made him seem so much of a man, a dad; so grounded. So she patted the car occasionally too, and complimented it all the time. In return Matt would occasionally—and grudgingly—let her take it to Ikea or the supermarket, fretting nervously at the windows all the time.

"I need to . . . there's something I have to do," said Posy. She looked at him straight in the eye. "It's to do with us."

"What do you mean?"

"There's some things I need to clear up . . . from my past."

"Like going to see some ex-boyfriend nob-end?"

"Well, a bit like that."

It was odd, Posy thought, that she had been prepared—willing—to share her entire life with this man, but she hadn't shared, in fact, some of the most important things. Like, for example, the first time and how it felt, that time she fell in love and how, when it broke up, she thought she was going to die.

She flashed on it suddenly. The first tiny crack: Almaric, coming into the pub, looking awkward. After she smothered him in kisses she'd asked him what was the matter.

"I don't have any money."

"None?"

"None." He sniffed. "Shall we go for a walk?"

"I wanted to go to the cinema."

"Oh," he said. "Shall I wait outside? You can tie me up if you like. Just leave me a small bowl of water."

"No, of course not. Let me pay for you to go to the cinema."

"No, thanks. I'll get a reputation."

They'd stood, looking at each other.

"Well, can I buy you a drink?"

"Half a cider? Or a lemonade?"

Posy had laughed. "You are hopeless. Can't you become a famous potter?"

Almaric had shrugged. "Name me one."

"That one that dresses up like a woman."

"Oh yeah. I can't afford the outfits. Anyway, who cares?"

"Not me!" Posy had said gaily, going to the bar, stopping on the way to kiss him full on the mouth. He hadn't reciprocated.

Had she, though? Was that the first time she'd spotted a chink? Noticed a difference between them? And if she had the time again, would she take him up on that walk? Or walk away?

Matt rubbed the back of his neck.

"Do you think this is helping, Posy?"

Posy came up to him.

"Matt," she said, looking straight into his face. "I am trying everything. I am doing the best I can to save us. I am trying to find stuff out about me, stuff that happened in the past . . . see if I can become the kind of woman you deserve."

Matt blinked.

"So I should lend you Pepe? To go look up your exes?"

"It's up to you," said Posy, turning away. What more could she do? She was trying, but it looked like Matt just wanted to stay here, forever testing out new ways to do knee curls—biding his time, almost, until she gave up, until she left.

"But do you know what's not helping?" she asked, turning back. "Coming home every day to nothing. To you not wanting to talk, not wanting to make it better. Just ignoring it. Not loving me, not forcing me out; so what *do* you want? Huh? Do you want me to leave for good?"

"Well, every time I think we should talk, you disappear and I find out you've been with another man."

"Well, isn't that a coincidence."

Matt looked down.

"Do you want me to leave?" she asked. "Are you just trying to think of yourself as a nice guy and waiting for me to move myself out?"

"What, because I'm not taking myself off on "voyages of discovery" with old girlfriends and other people's cars?"

Posy was stung. "I just want to know how you feel."

"Posy, is it really me who needs to change?"

His face looked so wounded, she wanted to stroke it. Or smack it, she wasn't entirely sure.

"No," she said. "You are perfect, your car is perfect, everything is perfect. Obviously I'm best off out of your way."

She marched over to the bedroom and grabbed her coat and her bag. She'd figure it out.

Just as she reached the door, Matt said her name, softly.

"What?" she said, turning round, miserable.

Matt threw her the car keys with some force, and, for once, she caught them. His phone rang. She stayed, watching him. A client. Of course it was. His voice grew soothing and kind. The difference in tone cut Posy to the quick. He used to speak like that to her—joking and teasing her, sweet and funny and organized. She did miss it. She missed it, him, so much. But as she looked at him, her gaze filled with yearning, he turned away and continued his call in the other room. Staying for one second longer, her hand almost outstretched toward him, Posy finally turned on her heel and left the flat behind.

There was something healing for the soul, Posy thought, swishing down B roads past green fields and forests in a beautiful red car. At first paralyzingly nervous, the thought had come to her: could Matt really hate her more than he did already if she banged up his car? Once she'd moved out of the maelstrom of London traffic and onto the motorway, attracting several admiring glances on the way—for the car—she'd concluded he probably couldn't.

Now she felt like she was flying down the winding country roads. Always a city mouse, she'd never really given credence to the idea that driving was anything other than a road-clogging, unenvironmental, unnecessary extravagance. Out here, with barely another car on the road, only the rumble of the engine and the soft swish of the trees outside, she could see the appeal all of a sudden. The radio veered in and out of any recognizable channel, occasionally playing long melodious strings of Welsh. Suddenly, Posy felt freer and happier than she had in weeks.

She remembered the day she and Almaric had taken off to the seaside, running through the freezing cold water, screaming their heads off and laughing till she thought she would be sick. She remembered the day Matt had taken her potholing. It had been absolutely cold and miserable. She sighed.

Almaric. He was, he had been, the man for her. She had never been so sure of anything in her life.

The first time they'd lain in bed together, they'd just gazed at each other, unable to believe in the reality of the other. She'd traced his face with her fingers, then held his—his exquisite, long fingers—while he'd done the same to her, feeling almost awestruck and worshipful. His slender body, with its pale skin and dark hair, his huge eyes, his wide mouth. He was undoubtedly the most beautiful man Posy had ever slept with. She didn't ever quite believe it. Perhaps that had been the problem. It was like sleeping with a movie star or a pop star—too good to be true.

"I'm very lucky," Posy had said one night.

It was just one normal night, or as normal as life could be in the whirling heaven that was Posy's life. They'd been out at a concert, snogging all evening, right up the front just by the stage. The bass player had even given them the thumbs-up. The noise and the crowd had been incredible. She had never wanted it to end. They were at her flat—his was effectively a hovel. Even though there were about nine girls in Posy's flat, competitively not eating cheese, it was still better than Almaric's bunk bed.

"You are," said Almaric, snuggling into the duvet.

"I know."

"I know that."

Posy sat up on her elbow. "What do you mean?"

"What do you mean, 'What do you mean?'" Then he said pointedly, "I am very tired," and tried to grab back the duvet.

"Do you think I'm lucky?"

"What? You said it."

"Don't you think you're lucky?"

"Well, yes, obviously."

"But . . ."

"But what?"

"But you think I'm luckier?"

"Can't we have Stupid Conversation Hour another time? Like, never?"

"No!" said Posy crossly. "I want to know what you meant."

"Argh! Women!" said Almaric, and made pretend snoring noises.

"You think you could have any woman you wanted and I'm lucky to get you."

Almaric continued snoring loudly but there was a smile playing around his lips.

"Actually I could have any man I wanted," said Posy. Well, obviously, not *any* man. But she resented Almaric's assumption. Even if it were true.

"Well, good," said Almaric. "That makes us even then."

"Yes," said Posy stubbornly. "I'm a hot super-fox."

"Good," said Almaric. "Can we go to sleep now? Try not to leave me for a famous celebrity before the morning."

Posy bit her lip now, glancing out at the passing countryside on the road. Oh, Almaric. She had loved him. He had loved himself a lot too.

Another time; a beautiful summer's day. They'd had the most gorgeous picnic on Hampstead Heath, and Almaric had lain on her stomach and they'd talked nonsense about clouds passing by and moving into the park, and drank cheap Cava and eaten strawberries and chocolate and crisps and laughed about absolutely nothing. Then she'd started on about how he must come and meet her mother, she was only down the road, and he really hadn't wanted to and she'd turned it into a big fight about how he didn't want to meet her family, and anyway, why should he have to? Almaric, she was fast discovering, didn't really like doing anything he didn't want to. He was creative and a free spirit, Posy told herself. They were renowned for being just a teensy tiny bit . . . well, she would never say it out loud. Of course he couldn't wash up his own coffee cups or take her out to dinner or spend time with her family; he had to follow his muse and in any case, the less they went out the more time they had to stay in and make love and she could gaze at him when he was sleeping. She was absolutely sure, had never been surer of anything in her life. So what if he didn't want to meet her mum? He was the man for her. She was twenty-eight, and it was time. Now she just had to wait for him to propose.

He'd gone to meet her mum finally, of course, after they'd been together for several months, but he had been sulky and awkward when he got there. Of course her mother was delighted to meet someone who had no interest in sucking up to her—and, even better, had a creative job—and he proved the only boyfriend Posy ever had that she liked. Why, Posy wondered, did that rile her so? That they had really liked one another?

Was it that just after Adam, who had given her so little attention, and Chris, who, after they'd been together for such a long time, they'd just fitted each other like old socks and old shoes and hardly noticed one another at all, she'd met Almaric, this amazing, wonderful guy, and she wanted to smother him completely in her life; make him share every cell. Because she wanted to share every cell of his.

He was the man who broke her heart. Broke it so completely, so relentlessly she'd felt she could never have it fixed again. That someone else would do, but not in a way she could ever risk being hurt so much. Someone nice. Someone safe. Well, that plan hadn't seemed to be working out so well for her either.

She remembered again Matt's first visit to her mother. Flowers, a nice bottle of wine, the lot. He'd looked so nervous when he asked if what he was wearing was OK. She'd laughed out loud.

"I promise, it really won't matter."

"What, so I could turn up in a boiler suit?"

"If you like."

"Arsenal top?"

Posy had laughed.

"Oh, no, obviously she's a Queen's Park Rovers fan."

"Rangers. They're called Rangers. You really don't know *anything* about sport, do you?" He'd tickled her affectionately under the arms.

"I grew up in a very feminine home. I know a lot about Simone de Beauvoir."

Matt smiled, nervously.

"You're not worried, are you?" said Posy, genuinely dis-believing. Matt was so calm, so sorted, she couldn't imagine him being scared of anyone.

"Posy, I've heard you on the phone to her," said Matt. "She does sound a little . . ."

"Terrifying?"

"Uh huh."

"Oh, that's just her way," said Posy, breezily. "Don't let her rile you up too much."

Matt looked bemused. "Why would she want to rile me up?"

Posy stopped at the door. "You know, that is a good question. Why *does* she do that?"

And sure enough, they'd sat uncomfortably in the messy kitchen, until Posy cracked and got up to make tea for them all, while Matt was left to answer sarcastic questions about why people needed personal trainers—couldn't they control them-selves at all?—and Posy pointing out that actually some people did see eating as a necessary part of their day rather than a hid-eous inconvenience, and her mother sneering and saying, Yes, fat people, and after that she'd had to crow Matt along to family occasions with an iron bar. Almaric, on the other hand, had liked her mother and her forthrightness; they'd got along very well, as long as they only went when he could be bothered.

Great white clouds were massing up behind the cliffs, giving the clear blue sky the look of a line of freshly washed laundry. Posy pulled over the car in a layby and got out. There were new lambs in the fields, she noticed. Yup, much nicer than sheep. It was a fresh day like this that Matt had gone down on one knee.

She sighed. Oh God, she missed him so much. *So* much. Was this what love was, then? Infatuations that came and went?

A door in your heart that opened, then got slammed shut? When Almaric had broken her heart, she'd thought she would never laugh, never smile, never even see anyone ever again. But then he'd been there. Looking so fit in those damn sweatpants; teasing her, laughing with her, turning her misery into a memory. And now she'd lost him too. Because . . . because of this man. She hoped he could help her.

She took out the rest of her service station sandwich and ate it, kicking stones and looking at the grass and the sky. What was she going to say to Almaric? She had tried to find a way to speak to him before she turned up—Margie didn't have a telephone number, but he couldn't have been that impossible to track down—but in the end, she had bottled it. Partly because she didn't want to use the phone in the flat, and partly because she was hoping inspiration would hit her as to what, exactly, she wanted to say. Could I ever have got it right? Will I ever get it right? Do I still love you? She swallowed the rest of her Diet Coke and, taking a deep breath of the clean, sweet chilly air, got back in the car.

Chapter Twenty-one

Llanuwchllyn was a lovely place—beautiful, rustic cottages arranged around a picturesque old stone bridge. It was a perfect setting for Almaric, surrounded by attractive things; living out his life on his own.

Parking at one end of a quaint shopping street, Posy consulted the address, but in fact it wasn't really necessary. Outside one of the old buildings, an old-fashioned plaque swung on metal chains. LLANUWCHLLYN POTTERY, it advertised. In the windows were the familiar shapes of the long, elegant flower pots Posy knew so well, along with squatter teacups and bowls with the name of the town on them, and even a few odd animals scattered about. Posy smiled. She'd redone her makeup in the car, and tried to think about what she wanted to say, but she couldn't—she wouldn't know till she saw him. She hoped she wouldn't cry.

The street was cobbled, and busy with English tourists enjoying the early spring sunshine; couples of a certain age, in slacks and pastels, glasses and tidy hair. Posy wondered if she would ever be one of those. Well, maybe not *those* ones, with the matching Scandic jumpers and comfortably wide-fitting shoes bought out of the back of a Sunday supplement. But these people, pottering about the little Welsh town—had they had the same doubts as her? The same dreams? She looked at the women: they all seemed so complacent and contented, with their bumbags smugly perched on paunches and widened hips; blouses ironed, hair sensibly cut. Had they loved, and agonized, and cried over the bald, portly chaps behind them, stuttering over the maps and carrying flasks over their shoulders? Had they thrilled to the sound of old-fashioned telephone bells, announcing the promise of Phillip, or Stanley, or Peter, or John, with their feathered gray hair, broken veins and downturned mouths? Had their flashes of love lasted all their lives long? Did they live on the memories of afternoons spent lingering on sunny beds, eating grapes, wishing for empty days that would never end, just turn into long evenings of lovemaking and wine until, exhausted, they would fall asleep on one another's damp bodies like babes in the wood?

"Come *on*, Malcolm," one particularly surly woman was growling, as if their day out at a languid Welsh village resort was on an extremely tight schedule. Perhaps it was.

Oh, those arguments. The first time he'd been late.

"Were you at that pub?" she'd demanded, conscious to her own ears that she sounded shrewish. She'd never heard her mother talk to her father like that. But then, see how that had ended up.

"What do you mean, "that pub"?" he'd said, some beer on his breath. "We just went for a drink."

"Who?"

"Me and my class."

"You and your harem went to the pub, did you?"

"What are you talking about? I sometimes go to the pub with the students afterward. So what."

Posy couldn't help her twisting misery. Didn't he realize that every second he spent away from her was torture? That she just wanted him by her side all the time? She sighed.

"Posy, you know I am going to go out now and again."

"Aren't I enough for you?"

"Don't be daft."

"I'm not daft! I've seen those girls! They're absolutely desperate to get their mitts on you!"

"So what?"

He was trying to jolly her out of it, but she wasn't having it.

It hadn't exactly been their last argument, but it was the beginning of the end. She couldn't help it. He was so beautiful, so amazing. She couldn't believe she had him in her life. So she pushed him and pushed him, alternating between sniveling neediness and furious jealousy. Neither of which, unsurprisingly, he found particularly endearing.

She went through his coat and his phone, acts which made her shiver when she thought about them. She called him constantly when he was out. She tried to organize coupley things with other people they knew who were a pair. He hated all of it. Why couldn't she get enough of him? He was everything she'd ever wanted—why wasn't that enough?

But the more she pushed, the further away he went. She knew she was doing it; why couldn't she stop? Why did she insist on putting dinner on the table every night; talk about getting a flat together when it was so obvious he wasn't in the least bit interested. But it didn't matter to him. He didn't see thirty on the horizon (in those days, Posy thought thirty was quite a scary number rather than, as she now knew, *nothing* at all); he saw nothing on the horizon at all. He didn't even bother to sell his pots and he made practically nothing from teaching, enough to fund his beer and fags and that was about enough for him really. But Posy was so sure he was The One that she ignored all this. How could a man who read poetry to her on dazzling London nights underneath the stars at a roof terrace party, who left her a drawing of her asleep tucked under her pillow—how could this man not be perfect?

"Yes, but those things don't cost him any money," Leah had commented, but Posy had ignored her, ignored anything that took away from her beautiful Almaric.

And it had seemed like that that final night—after one in the morning when he got in. He smelled of beer, but something else too. He was so beautiful, Posy remembered, so gorgeous still, even slightly drunk and wearing an old gray shirt. But she still hadn't stopped herself, again.

"Were you drinking with those girls?"

He turned on her. "No, Posy, I wasn't drinking with them. I was snogging them. You've seemed to want me to do it for so long, I thought I might as well give it a shot."

Posy took a step back, suddenly feeling very, very frightened, as if he'd slapped her.

"What do you mean?"

"This is what you wanted, isn't it? Going through my stuff, questioning me every time I leave the house. You wanted me to cheat on you, didn't you?"

"No!"

"I mean, the weird thing is . . ." He was actually very drunk,

Posy realized. "I didn't really want to. But when you became so convinced that I was about to, I thought I'd better oblige. She wasn't all that."

Posy found her hand was clapped over her mouth.

"Almaric" was all she could say.

"Almaric."

A small bell jangled the door as she entered the tiny shop. Through, in the back room, a figure stood silhouetted in the doorway, his head turning as she tentatively stepped in.

There was a huge crash. Posy watched, shocked, as a large gray vase slipped out of his hands and shattered all over the floor. They both stared at it for a moment, transfixed. Then Posy raised her head.

"I should have rung," she said. Almaric was staring at her as if he'd seen a ghost.

He'd hardly changed at all. His long-fringed eyes still looked soulful; his bohemian curls had taken on a tiny strand of pure white that actually looked rather stylish.

"Posy," he said finally. "Is it really you?"

"Well, it would be a terrible waste of a vase if it wasn't," she managed, and took a further step into the shop.

"Shit, yes." He looked down. "Great. Well, it wasn't a classic."

They looked at each other a bit longer.

"I'll . . . I'll just get the broom. No, wait, hang on. Come in. How are you? What . . ."

Neither of them knew what to do. Clumsily, Posy walked over to him, trying not to step on any of the broken shards on the floor, or knock over anything else with her handbag. In such a poky space, it wasn't easy.

"Uh, hi there," she said.

"Uh, hi," he said back, raising his hands, which were covered in clay.

"Uhm."

Posy wasn't sure whether to kiss him and was worried that he might think she was leaning in for a snog, so as Almaric leaned over she ended up blowing him an unfortunate kiss, which caused her hand to hit him on the chin.

"Ooh," said Almaric. "You're not a ghost then."

"No," said Posy. "Uh, sorry."

"Oh no, I'm glad."

"No, I mean, I'm sorry I biffed you on the chin."

Almaric stood back. "Oh yeah. Don't worry about it."

They paused again, both of them standing among the shattered clay.

A small voice came from the back of the shop. "Aren't you closing up then?"

Almaric turned his head. "Yes, yes I am."

Posy glanced at her watch. "You're closing up?"

Almaric looked uncomfortable. "Uh, yeah. I guess it's about time."

The voice came from the back again. "Big day tomorrow."

He looked at her. "What are you doing here?"

Posy winced. "Well . . ." she said.

"Will it take a bit of time to explain?"

"Possibly."

Almaric looked like he was doing long division in his head. "Uhm, hang on . . . I have to make a few calls. Would you like to have dinner?"

Posy blinked. It was such a civilized suggestion—and very

unusual from Almaric, who never normally remembered to eat at all.

"Uh, OK."

Almaric disappeared from view and Posy heard snatches of what sounded like quite awkward phone calls. The girl from the back came through—she was young, gorgeous, and covered in clay dust—and gave Posy a long look.

"Hi," said Posy, unnerved. The girl let out a long sigh and disappeared back into the other room, obviously unimpressed. Posy wondered if she was used to fending off visits from Almaric's exes. Probably.

Almaric steered her now, without a word, out onto the crowded high street and down toward a quaint little coffee shop that was so crowded with chintz, teddy bears, small pottery animals, winsome wall stencils, and wood carvings that it was nearly impossible to sit down at all.

"Nice," said Posy.

"They're all like this," said Almaric, glancing at his watch. "And the pub doesn't open till six."

"No, no, this is much better," said Posy. She looked at his hand. There was only the faintest trace of a pale white line. She imagined women in bed with him asking where he'd got it. Did they laugh at her? she wondered. Or did they understand completely that sometimes, you absolutely and utterly had to throw something at someone? But that had come later.

They were the youngest people in there by about forty years. Posy felt herself wither under the unerring scrutiny of lots of grandmas. This wasn't exactly how it had been in her imagination. They'd been walking—arm in arm, perhaps—along a riverbank, not ordering a pot of tea for two. Although . . .

241

"And can I have an Eccles cake, please?" she added.

The only other youngish person in the place, a sullen plump teenager wearing the fussy black-and-white maid's outfit as scruffily as she could, sniffed. Then she bestowed a radiant smile on Almaric and asked if he'd like any buns. Posy rolled her eyes.

"Actually I don't have an appetite," said Almaric when they sat down.

"No, me neither," said Posy. "I just ordered that cake for something to do."

"Ah. So I suppose I should ask, really," he said. "Why?"

"Why am I here?"

He nodded.

"Well, that's not the worst thing you could have said," mused Posy.

"Oh good," said Almaric. "What would that have been?"

"Hmm. "Who are you?," I suppose. Or you could have yelled."

"Oh Posy," said Almaric. "Why would I have done that?"

"If you'd thought I was a crazy stalker or something."

"I knew you were a crazy stalker the second time I met you," he said. "Didn't worry me."

"Then," said Posy.

Almaric shrugged.

Their tea arrived in a floral pot. The young waitress leaned over and pressed her bosoms close to Almaric as she poured it.

"How's the shop?" she asked.

"Not bad, thanks, Jade," said Almaric, moving backward. Posy shook her head in amazement.

"What?" he said, when the waitress had gone.

"It's you," she said. "You are absolute catnip to girls."

"I'm not," he said. "In the slightest. It's just all the men in this town are about a hundred years old, that's all."

"Uh huh," said Posy. "Right."

"So . . . what are you doing here?"

Posy put her teacup down.

"Well," she began. "It's like this," she went on. "In fact," she said.

She realized she wasn't going to be able to finish the sentence.

"Oh Almaric," she said, as a great big fat tear ran down her face and plopped into her tea. Almaric glanced around nervously, worried she seemed to be making a scene. "I just . . . I'm just making such a mess of my life."

Posy desperately tried to get a grip. This wasn't what she meant to do at all! She didn't want to bubble and moan all over him as if she was trying to get him back! She'd wanted to be cool, calm, collected, and unfazed, and lay things on the line totally.

"What's wrong with me?"

Oh, no, that was even worse. Posy swallowed, trying to get a hold on herself.

"Do you want to go out?" said Almaric. "Of the shop, I mean."

Oh God, he thought she was flinging herself at him again! Oh no! It was impossible. The tears just dropped faster and faster into her tea.

"What's up with her?" asked Jade rudely, as she put down the Eccles cake, which made Posy even worse.

"Uh, have you got any money to pay?" asked Almaric. "I came out without my wallet."

Hysterically sniveling, Posy found her purse.

"Come on, girl, let's get you out of here."

His kind tone didn't help anything. Posy sniffed and winced as she felt the whole cafe go silent as he lifted her elbow.

Posy pushed her hand to her eyes and tried to gulp down the huge lump in her throat that just wouldn't move. Half blinded by tears, she made it through the door, which jangled loudly, just in case a single person had missed her before.

"Come on," said Almaric, and he half led, half pulled her up the street toward the open countryside. The light was fading, but it was still a beautiful evening, with a hint of warmth in the air and crocuses and daffodils infesting the roadside. All round the village stood great green hills, the sun setting behind them. Posy, though choked, could still see their beauty.

"Wow," she said. Not pausing to look, Almaric pushed her on till they were out of the village altogether and found, set back from the road, a park bench. He sat her down there, and wrapped his coat around her.

Posy sobbed and sobbed until the evening started to go dark around them and, finally, she felt emptied out.

"Oh" she said eventually, when she felt slightly more herself. "Oh, I am *so* sorry."

Almaric shrugged. "You'll probably make the local paper. I think you're about the most exciting thing that's happened round here for months."

Posy swallowed hard. "I must look a complete fright."

Almaric shrugged again, which meant, yes, she must. Posy rubbed frantically underneath her eyes to try and get rid of any remnants of mascara. She hiccuped up a smile.

"OK, good to see you, I'm going to go now."

He smiled back. "Well, it was fun."

"It *was*."

She sat up straighter and gave him back his coat. "OK," she said. "OK. I'm ready." She took a deep breath. "I was getting married," she began.

"Oh, lovely," said Almaric. "Of course, so am I, tomorrow."

Chapter Twenty-two

Posy just stared at him.

"You're *what*?!"

He smirked. "I know, I know. Don't tell me."

"You and my mother spent an entire evening once talking about how marriage was the terrible enslavement of the patriarchy and a crime against women!"

"Was that the night you cried all the way home?"

"Yes, because you were never going to get married!"

Posy was so shocked she had almost forgotten to be sad. This wasn't the Almaric she knew, not at all.

"To me, obviously. You were never going to get married to me," she added quietly.

"But now *you* are getting married," said Almaric kindly. "That's fantastic."

Posy felt the tears rising again. "But we're not! He thinks I'm not ready to make a proper commitment."

"Really?" Almaric sounded surprised. "I thought you were desperate for that."

"So did I," confessed Posy. "And I do love him, Almaric, I really do."

"So what are you doing here? Short on pots?" He put his hands in his pockets. "I will say, pudding, I thought you might be here because you wanted to stop the wedding."

"Would I do that?"

Almaric held up his wrist. "I don't know."

"I am sorry about that."

Posy left a pause for Almaric to say that there were a few things he was sorry about too. He didn't.

"Leah thinks . . . she thinks I can't move on because I never got over you."

There. It was out. She had said it.

Almaric sat back on the bench.

"Well," he said, "there are a lot of tears on my jacket."

"I don't think they're all for you," said Posy. "It was just a shock seeing you again."

"But you drove here, right? It wasn't a coincidence."

"Oh, no. Margie gave me your address."

"Who?"

Posy reminded him.

"Oh God, yes, can you ask her to stop sending me pictures of her cats dressed up for Christmas?"

"No, I shan't," said Posy. "In fact you should send her a thank-you card, she's devoted to you."

"Well, I didn't ask for that."

"No, you didn't," said Posy, "but still. It's your own fault for being handsome and nice without being sappy and a good listener. It's a dreadful combination for London women.

They've never seen anything like it before. It's like giving them poison."

"OK," said Almaric.

"You know," said Posy, "I wasn't sure what would happen when I saw you."

"Hysterics," said Almaric.

"Yes," said Posy.

Almaric looked awkward.

"What's she like?" asked Posy. "How old is she?"

"Don't ask me that."

"Really? That young? Or really ancient and minted?"

Almaric smiled. "You don't think much of me."

"I think entirely too much of you," said Posy, realizing as she said it that it were true. She thought entirely too much of him, too often.

"She's twenty-four."

"A child! Child abuse! She's not even old enough to vote!"

"Posy, you can vote at twenty-four."

"Yes, if you've learned to *read*."

Almaric smiled again. "Oh, Posy. You haven't changed."

"You have though," said Posy, feeling weary finally.

"OK. Well." Almaric looked thoughtful. "I'm marrying her because she's right. For me. Not what anyone else thinks is right, not on paper, not following a life plan. Don't start crying again, you were wonderful too, until you tried to kill me, and please don't apologize again. You were wonderful, Posy. She's home. That's all. That's true love. I can't explain it any better than that."

"What was so wrong with me?" said Posy. "Really? What makes me so fundamentally unmarriageable?"

"What do you think it is?" said Almaric, glancing at his watch and leaning back.

"My big hands and feet," said Posy instantly. Almaric's face creased up.

"There's nothing wrong with your feet," he said. "Christ. Is that what you thought?"

"It's definitely noticeable though."

"No, Posy, it's not your feet. Your feet are cute, in fact."

"Cute. That means enormous," said Posy.

Almaric rolled his eyes.

"Well," she went on, "I was hoping it was my feet, then I wouldn't have to find out it was something else really awful about me."

"Like your ears."

"What's wrong with . . . Oh, shut up."

Almaric put his hands on her face and drew it close to his.

"Darling Posy. You weren't looking for me. You were never looking for a life partner. You were always, always looking for a home."

"What do you mean?"

"A home. A mummy who looked after you and a daddy who loved you. A home. It was completely obvious."

"That's ridiculous."

"That's right, that's what all the cooking was for. Who taught you to cook, your mum?"

"Shut up about my mum's cooking."

"What time are you coming home? Who are you with? Where are you going to be? If we don't get married I'm going to throw a crock-pot at you." He paused, gently stroked her cheek. "Did you ever have a man in your life who didn't come home?"

Posy shrugged, feeling one long tear drip down her cheek.

She thought about it. It couldn't be. But then Adam had spotted that vulnerability and taken advantage of it, her very willingness to please. And Chris had just been perfectly happy to play the daddy, until she had realized how very unsexy it was. Which made sense, she supposed. And what about Matt? Was he a man on his own terms? Who didn't want to be put in a box, or made to fit something she needed? The thoughts raced through her head.

Almaric sat up.

"So you see, sweetheart—it was never me you needed to find."

Almaric walked her up the street.

"You're not driving back to London?"

Posy shrugged.

"No, don't. I know a good B&B."

"Is it full of your wedding guests?"

Almaric was surprised. "Oh, yes. I suppose it is." He looked at her. "You'll get over me, won't you, Pose? I mean, it's been too long, don't you think?"

Posy looked at him. He was pushing back his black curls with a long hand. He was ridiculously gorgeous—and getting married. It hurt, of course it did. But on the other hand, she had been slightly worried she would end up prostrate on the floor in front of him, and yet here he was—beautiful, heartbreaking, kind, but . . .

"I couldn't say your name," she said suddenly, shaking her head. "I found it so hard to get over you . . . I couldn't even say your name."

"It's a stupid name," said Almaric.

"I know. Steve would have been better."

"It would."

Their last fight. Over what, she just couldn't remember. It had blown up out of nowhere, it seemed, until Posy felt herself shouting like an old shrew.

"Why are you never here when I need you?" she found herself yelling.

"Why do you need me?" Almaric had shot back defiantly. "You're a grown-up woman who's perfectly capable of looking after herself."

"I just . . . I just want you to come home when you say you'll be home, that's all. Is that too much to ask?"

"It's too weird to ask," Almaric had said. "What are you, eight? Are you sure you're talking to me?"

"What do you mean?"

Almaric shrugged. "Well, it just doesn't sound like you're talking to me, that's all."

"Tell me what you mean by that." Posy started banging the chili stew into the sink and running it away.

"Well, it sounds like you're trying to replicate some damn family life you've never even had. I mean, look at that. Why are you cooking me dinner? Some days I don't even eat dinner. You're not my wife."

Posy bit her lip. Almaric caught her expression.

"Oh Posy," he said. "Is this what all this shit has been about?"

"No," said Posy. "I'd just like to know where we're going."

"Well, I don't know," said Almaric. "I don't know what's going to happen in my life, do you?"

Posy shrugged her shoulders.

"I mean it. I don't want it. I don't want to know. I don't want to get married, I don't want babies on the rug, I don't want any of that. Any of it."

And before she knew what was happening, she'd hurled it. The cooking pot. The noise was unbelievable, it smashed off the back of the kitchen wall, chili and vegetables exploding everywhere. As Posy stared in horror, Almaric dropped to the floor, clutching his right hand.

Posy had felt as if she'd boarded a holiday plane full of hope and expectation, only now to find it plummeting to the ground. And she didn't know what to do; didn't know how to make him look at her the way he had looked at her the night they ran away and went to the bar, or the music festival where they forgot to see any bands, so happily ensconced they were in love and cider and wellingtons. The secret jokes, the midnight feasts, the pillow fights; the plans, the travel, the future she had always had in her heart.

And here it had ended, in a dank Accident and Emergency, where they had sat for four hours barely speaking, waiting for a grumpy nurse to get him stitched up. The nurse asked him pointedly if he'd like to see a policeman to file a complaint. He'd shaken his head briskly. Posy would have almost welcomed it, just to get him to engage with her. As it was, she sobbed and apologized, but he just stared at her like she was an alien species. There was no getting through to him. She had crossed a line, done something unforgivable. To the man she loved.

"I didn't mean it," she'd said. "I didn't mean to hurt you."

But he had smiled wanly and stared out of the window. They took one cab back from the hospital. It made two stops. And she was at home, by herself—her stew, her heart, her guts, her life, all in pieces on the kitchen floor.

"I was going to say, if you wanted . . . I mean, I'm sure you don't, but, if you like, you could come to the wedding tomorrow."

"And torture myself some more? I don't think so."

"Fine," said Almaric. "It's at ten at the chapel though."

"I think I'll just turn in," said Posy. "It's been a long day."

Almaric nodded. "I'll show you the B&B."

Posy wearily followed him up the road.

"Shouldn't you be somewhere else?" she asked.

Almaric shrugged. "Oh, just the wedding dinner with Sukie's family. I don't care, they'll be fine. Don't give me that look."

"What look?"

"That look. That "Almaric doesn't visit my family enough" look."

Posy dropped her gaze. "Did I really do that?"

"Totally."

Posy shook her head. Had she really given him such a hard time? Without even realizing she was doing it?

"OK, here you are." It was dark as they came to a small half-timbered inn with a welcoming glow of light coming from inside.

Almaric looked at her. "Please. Tell me. You are over me now, aren't you? Please say yes."

Posy looked at him. "I may not ever be fully over you. But I think . . . it's OK."

Almaric took her face in his hands.

"It's not me, Posy. Remember that. It's not me."

Posy lay on a comfortable single bed wide awake and staring at the ceiling. From downstairs came the noise of carousing—Almaric's friends, no doubt. It wasn't annoying, she found it comforting if anything. Proof that somewhere, somehow, in the world it was possible to be having a good time.

Falling in love with Almaric had been so dramatic, so sudden. One day she was walking along with nothing in her life, and the next day he *was* her life. It had knocked her for six, taken her completely by surprise. She realized now, of course, that, in fact, it was first love. A very late first love. Chris had been sweet and comfortable, but it hadn't been love. Adam had been fun and adventurous, but that wasn't love either. With Almaric it had hit her hard and fast, and she'd been genuinely surprised by it; it had blinded her to everything.

Then when Matt had come along it hadn't been fireworks, passion, and fights and drama. It had been low-key, sweet, lovely. But that didn't mean it wasn't the real thing. It never had done. Just because it wasn't surprising hadn't meant it wasn't right.

Posy let out a low groan. Oh God. She had really stuffed this up. Really, really, really. Those other men: they were ciphers from her past. If anything they were reflections of her—who she'd been then; timid, anxious. Looking for something, someone else. What had Almaric said? Looking for her father. Matt had hinted as much too, many times—oh Christ, why hadn't she listened to him? Why had it taken her ex to even make it obvious? She hadn't been ready before. She wasn't ready now, maybe, until she'd found a way to sort herself out. But she'd had the best possible thing right in front of her eyes.

And she'd stuffed it up. Stifling a howl, Posy bit the pillow. Oh God. *Oh God*.

Chapter Twenty-three

Posy thought she would never get to sleep, but the drive and the tears got to her in the end. And, oddly, when she woke up the next morning, she felt a little better. In fact, she felt well enough to eat a large, delicious Welsh breakfast. OK, so her life wasn't sorted, but somehow, the shadow of Lord Voldemort, her life-defining love . . . it was receding. It wasn't gone—perhaps she would always have a tiny corner of her heart reserved for the first man who inadvertently stole it—but maybe she could be fine with that. Maybe a lot of people had somebody like that. Maybe that was what Facebook was for. To see them as a person; someone real, not a specter or a ghost.

The breakfast room was full of jolly young people all dolled up—very young, in fact. Posy was used to going to weddings with anxious-looking brides in their thirties, but these people were clear-eyed and bushy-tailed and probably on the bride's side (Almaric was always a bit shifty about his family—they were all accountants and it harmed his cool maverick artist image).

As she paid up her bill and left, feeling, at least, a slightly older, wiser Posy, a huge group of them pressed through the lobby, bouncing with excitement.

"It's just over there," said one of them in a thick Welsh accent, pointing to the beautiful old chapel, which was festooned with flowers outside and thronged with happy people. This was obviously a big wedding.

Posy rolled her eyes. She supposed she could just pop in for a second. Just to have a look.

"Bride or groom?" asked a friendly looking chap handing out hymnals at the church door.

"Groom," said Posy firmly. She would slip in at the back and pop out again after the vows. It would hurt, of course it would. But she had an inkling that, one day, she'd be glad she did.

Almaric was down at the front, eyes straight ahead. He looked gorgeous in his tailcoat—well, he couldn't be anything else, thought Posy. It was odd, like being in someone else's fantasy. Should it have been her? Living on thin air in the Welsh countryside? She supposed it wasn't really worth speculating about.

She hoped Almaric didn't see her. She didn't want him worrying that she was going to leap up at the bit about there being any just cause. And she wasn't going to do that. Of course not.

Suddenly the organ struck up. It was "Angels" by Robbie Williams. Well, I wouldn't have chosen that, Posy found herself thinking, and gave herself a strict talking to.

At the door of the church, silhouetted in the morning light, was a ravishingly pretty blonde girl in a hugely wide tulle gown with layer upon layer of netting. The congregation burst into spontaneous applause. It was the kind of dress a four-year-old would draw. Posy smiled. The girl was gorgeous. She was nothing like Posy. And maybe that was OK.

The girl started to walk down the aisle, nodding and winking to friends in the pews and making an "Ohmygod' face. She was carrying a huge shepherdess basket of flowers and was followed by nine bridesmaids from small to enormous, in striped pink and silver, each carrying a parasol. It was full on. Posy, used to discreet and tasteful town weddings, enjoyed it immensely.

Sukie—that was her name—was progressing slowly to the front when suddenly there was a bit of a flurry and commotion. It was hard to hear what was going on when the organ stopped, and all that could be heard was a loud BANG, the bride shrieking, *"What the fuck?,"* a huge basket of flowers being thrown everywhere and Almaric's voice shouting, "Posy, is that you?"

Posy dashed forward at the sound of her name being called. Almaric looked furious. Sukie was in a gigantic frothy heap on the floor. And, climbing on top of her, fingers flailing as if trying to claw the dress off her shoulders, was Margie.

"Margie!" shouted Posy, as the bridesmaids descended on her and started hitting her with their parasols. Margie yelped, but did not give up the struggle.

"You can't have him!" she was shrieking.

"Who the hell are you?" Sukie yelled back. "Get the *fuck* off my Swarovski crystals, there's five thousand of them *handstitched.*"

Posy started to struggle through the throng at the back of the church, who looked just as delighted as if the service had gone on as planned. She'd got a picture in her mind of Sukie being a sweet gentle individual. This girl looked terrifying. She glanced at Almaric who was looking at Sukie with moist-eyed pride. Then he turned to Margie.

"Yes," said Almaric, "who the fuck are you?"

"I'm *Margie*," said Margie, her glasses caught up in her perm as she looked up from where she was prostrate on the floor. "Almaric, I love you."

He shook his head.

"Sorry . . ."

Posy struggled to the front of the crowd. She glanced at Almaric. He looked confused.

"It's Margie," she hissed. "The cat lady?"

Almaric finally recognized her.

"Oh my God, the cat lady! Did you put her up to this?"

"NO!"

"Who the fuck are *you*?!" said the bride, squaring up to Posy.

"Nobody! No one! An old friend of Almaric's."

Sukie turned on her husband-to-be.

"Not again."

"Not that kind of friend," said Almaric, looking uncomfortable. "I promise, sweetie-pants. It was ages ago."

"That's what you said about the hotel receptionist," spat Sukie.

Posy bent down and beat off the parasols. "Margie! What the hell?"

"I knew there was a reason you must be coming this weekend," said Margie.

"There wasn't, truly." Posy gathered her up in her arms.

"So I checked the banns."

Posy sighed. "Did you really?"

Margie nodded. "I thought . . . I thought there might be a last chance."

Posy realized Margie was wearing a too-tight-round-the-bust embroidered purple dress that clashed with her hair.

Almaric was looking at Posy.

"It had *nothing* to do with me, you have to believe me," said Posy. She knew he would. Almaric's charming, arty free-and-easy effects on women was just something he lived with and Sukie would have to learn to.

"Come on, Margie," said Posy, helping her to her feet. "Let's go."

"Yes, you'd *better* go," shouted Sukie.

"I'm really sorry," said Posy. "You look absolutely gorgeous by the way."

In an instant Sukie changed.

"Oh, do you think so? I thought the dress might be, like, too much, but then Jade said don't be daft, how can it be too much, you're getting married and I thought, yeah, might as well, but then we couldn't get it delivered from Hong Kong in time, and then, I thought, maybe I should make it myself, but Lorraine McConnachie said it would be shit and I thought I'll show her, but then—"

"Sukie," said Almaric with a slight edge in his voice. "Do you want to do this or not?"

"We'll be . . . in another country," said Posy, half dragging Margie up the aisle. Almaric nodded, barely noticing, and as they got to the doors, Posy heard "Angels' start up once more.

"I think that went well," she said to Margie as they emerged. Suddenly a flash went off, blinding them in the morning light.

"Argh, Christ, what was that?" said Posy.

"Sorry, love," came a voice. "Wedding photographer. Thought you was the happy couple."

Posy went up to him, smiling. "Promise me," she said. "Promise me you'll put that one in the album."

"Sure," said the photographer, and took another couple for good luck, as Posy and Margie staggered up the street back to the car.

Chapter Twenty-four

Posy is bone-bloody-knackered.

It was very late and very dark by the time Posy and Margie made it back to London. Margie had sobbed much of the afternoon. Posy had let her. She had understood. Occasionally she leaned over and patted her hand. Until Margie perked up a bit just past Bristol and said, "Well, I guess it's just you and me together in all this, spinsters for life," whereupon Posy had wanted to smack her hard.

Once they got out of the countryside her cheap city package mobile signal came back. But there was nothing on it. One odd message from Fleur saying she was off to visit Dad and did she want to come, at which Posy had rolled her eyes, but apart from that, nothing. Nothing from Matt at all, not even inquiring after Pepe.

She was so agitated by this that, at a service station, she jumped back into the car and backed it out slowly. Into a bollard.

Posy dropped her head into her hands.

*

She dropped Margie off in Croydon, which was miles out of her way and kind of her. Margie didn't thank her. Matt was home and watching TV when she got back and jumped up guiltily.

"Hey," she said. Not a phone call. Nothing, nothing at all. Even now, when she was done with it all. It wouldn't matter to him.

"Hey," he said. He looked guilty and upset too. They were making each other so miserable.

Matt was biting his lip. "Here's the thing," he said. "I was thinking, while you were away."

"Yes?" said Posy, wondering if it would be possible. To explain that she'd sorted things out with Almaric, that she thought it might be fine, that she was wondering if there might be the tiniest, most minute possibility of a second chance.

"And, well, I got an estate agent in to value the place."

Posy was so shocked she felt like he'd slapped her across the face. Obviously the setup now wasn't exactly perfect, but still, selling up? Moving out, moving on? Surely not.

"I crashed Pepe," she found herself saying, chin in the air.

"What?" Matt went white.

It didn't sound as good in Posy's head as she'd been thinking, defiantly, walking in the room.

"Well, you're breaking my heart, so I, er, dinged your car."

But Matt didn't hear: he had already jumped up and was heading for the door.

"It's just a scratchy dent kind of a thing," said Posy. "He'll be fine. I patted his boot and everything."

Matt shook his head. "Don't you want to know what the estate agent said?"

Posy gulped. "Uh. Whatever."

"She said, forget it, it's worth about five quid now."

"Oh," said Posy. "Well, that's good."

There was a silence.

"What do you mean, "That's good"?" said Matt suspiciously. "Why is it good that the biggest investment of our lives is now worth less than, and I quote, "The car parking space outside it"?"

Posy realized she just couldn't fight it anymore. It was pointless. It was done.

"I'm very tired," she said. "I think I have to go to bed."

Matt sighed. "And I have to go see to Pepe. Is there any point in being cross with you about it?"

"Do you mean, could you make me feel worse than I actually do at the moment?" said Posy. "Not really."

"Thought not," said Matt, pulling on his coat.

"Matt," said Posy as he stood at the door. He turned expectantly.

"Do you think I was looking for a father figure in my life?"

Matt screwed up his face. "You want me to spank your bum for breaking the car?"

Posy stared at him pitifully.

"Posy, I . . . what did you *do* in Wales?"

"Figured out some things," said Posy meekly, hoping this would stop him from going to see the car.

"You shouldn't try and figure things out while you're reversing," said Matt.

"I know that now," said Posy.

Matt headed for the door again. Then he popped his head back in.

"Did I think you missed your dad? Yes. Of course I did. I do. I said it several times. I also suggested you go visit him. So does Fleur. You just never listen to me."

"But I never mention him," said Posy.

"Yeah, well, that's obviously why, you idiot. You never say his name, not on Father's Day, not at Christmas, not when you're talking to my dad. I was surprised when I met him and found out he wasn't dead or a Tory politician or something."

"Oh," said Posy.

"So it's obviously *something*," said Matt. "Something huge."

Posy stared at him.

"You did ask," said Matt.

"I know."

"Meanwhile, however, my baby is lying out on the pavement wounded and alone."

"Go to him," said Posy, flapping her hands. "Go."

"Don't be stupid, you were both absolutely fine!"

Jonquil banged the Battenburg cake on the kitchen counter and Posy winced. Battenburg meant that her mum had gone to a special effort to make everything nice for her visiting. Battenburg was special. Posy fiddled with the plastic corner of the wrapper. She hated marzipan. Her mother had never known that.

"The best psychoanalytical minds of the day said that the best thing to do was total honesty, total freedom. You weren't children, you were smaller adults."

"Except that we *were* children," said Posy softly, taking the scum off her cup of tea.

"So, I told you straight up, didn't I?"

"That our father was worthless and didn't care enough about his family to live with them?" said Posy.

"Wasn't that true?" shot back her mother. "That sounds like exactly what happened to me."

Posy shrugged.

"And then, I was quite surprised by this, you and Fleur didn't seem to want to engage with it quite as much as I'd expected," said Jonquil. "Why was that?"

How could Posy explain? The tears, the horrible unnameable emotions that were going on in the house. They couldn't ask about that; it just wasn't information they were qualified to know. It had seemed like they would hurt their mother less if they didn't ask; if they didn't pester her as to the whereabouts of Daddy. Suddenly Posy was hit with an image of the two of them, her and Fleur, coming home from school and perching themselves on the bottom of the stairs, so that if their father came home that day he would see them immediately. They carried two pieces of string with Blu-Tack fixed to the ends as camouflage. When their mother asked them what they were doing they said "Stair fishing," and dangled the strings off the banisters. Had she really not known? Had she really not seen?

"Because it was your job to *protect* us from the horrible stuff!" burst out Posy, savagely squeezing the pink and yellow crumbs between her fingers. "It was your job *not* to tell us everything about him and everything he'd done wrong."

"But it was the truth," said Jonquil, appalled. "You should always tell children the truth."

"No, you shouldn't," said Posy stubbornly. "You should have told us he was a pirate captain in the Far Eastern islands!"

"You wouldn't have thanked me."

"I'm not thanking you now."

"Oh Posy," said Jonquil. "It was just a divorce. People have them all the time."

"*Oh Posy,*" mimicked Posy. "*It was just a terrible betrayal, upset, and destruction of all the security you'd ever known. People have them all the time.*"

"Don't get hysterical."

"You mean it's never crossed your mind? All those failed relationships, all those times you made remarks about my "not being the settling down kind"? You never ever ever thought to connect the two things?"

Jonquil shrugged.

"I don't want you to get tied to a man. Or any human being, for that matter. I just want you to be your own woman."

"Why can't I be my own woman while I love another man?"

"I haven't seen much evidence of it in my life."

"That's because you spend all day dealing with over-pampered self-obsessed north London nut-jobs," spat Posy viciously.

Jonquil rolled her eyes. "Hostility, darling. It's a defense mechanism, you know."

"Yes. Against you."

"Well, I'm not going to fight with you."

"You *shouldn't* be fighting with me!" said Posy. "Don't flatter yourself! You should be apologizing and explaining things to me."

"Never apologize, never explain," mused her mother. "Who was it who said that again?"

"A sociopath," said Posy. "I just need to know. Did my father love me?"

"What can I say?" said Jonquil, stirring her long-cold, long-dead tea. "He loved you both very much. He didn't change nappies . . . men didn't then. But he threw you up and down in the air, took you swimming, tickled you, tucked you in at night."

"They tuck you up, your mum and dad," said Posy, sadly.

"Can't you see what I'm trying to say?" said Jonquil. "He did everything that people call love. He did everything that looked like love; he provided for you, cared for you."

Posy's eyes were wide and she was trying not to cry.

"But don't you see? In the end, it wasn't enough. His love wasn't enough to stay."

Jonquil's face turned hard. "I know you find me difficult, Posy."

"Uh huh."

"I know you think I'm hard work, and annoying."

"I'm sure you think the same about me."

"No, I think you're self-obsessed and a touch pathetic."

"MUM! *Stop* with the honesty!"

"But do you know what it would have taken me to walk out and close the door on my own children?"

Posy looked at her; her eyes were fierce and intense.

"They would have had to set me on fire, Posy. They would have had to set me on fire to separate me from you and Fleur. And he gave barely a backward glance. And I could never, *ever* forgive him for that."

"How's Mum?" said Fleur on the phone.

"Stop it," said Posy.

"What?"

"Stop knowing exactly what I'm calling about."

"It's because I have a special psychic aura thing," said Fleur.

"It's because you're a total flake and you've probably just spoken to Mum."

"Yeah," said Fleur. "So?"

"Go round and see her," said Posy. "I think sometimes we forget how much she loves us."

"What, just because she says really mean things to our faces and never cooks for us or says anything nice or buys us anything or is happy for anything that happens in our lives and keeps trying to diagnose us with weird psychological illnesses?"

"Yeah. Because of that."

"Can you lend me the bus fare?"

Posy sighed.

"And by the way," said Fleur. "While you're bossing me about to go see Mum, why won't you go see Dad?"

"You don't even remember," said Posy. "You don't even remember how sad Mum was. You were too small. You don't even know."

"Well, why don't you go see him and ask him why?"

"Actually, I'm fine," said Posy. "And, really, one problem at a time. Which at the moment is trying to stop the love of my life from hating me."

"Oh my God, why does Lord Voldemort hate you?"

"What makes you think that's him?" said Posy, hanging up.

Chapter Twenty-five

Posy is looking for someone who can do cheap car
re-sprays.

"Come on," said Leah. "Drink will cheer you up."

"I still blame you for *everything*."

"Yes. Me. Not the wine."

"No."

They'd come out to Express 34, a new bar that had opened
in full-on hope despite the recession. There were about six
people in it, all of them looking like they were glumly spending
their redundancy checks on blue drinks.

"So, did it help?"

Posy took a deep breath. "No. And, maybe, yes."

Leah raised her eyebrows.

"Almaric—"

"Ooh! You said his name!"

"I know. I suppose it's progress."

"It definitely is! And you haven't immediately thrown up on

the floor! And you've regained all that weight you lost after you and Matt broke up— I've gone too far, haven't I?"

Posy shrugged her shoulders. "He did say something interesting though."

"Oh yes?"

"He said . . . he said he thought I was looking for my dad."

"Your *dad*?"

"Uh huh."

"Oh. Mine's usually in the shed."

"Thanks. That's helpful."

"Sorry. So, is he right?"

"I don't know. What do you think?"

"What do you think about your compulsion to cook all your boyfriends dinner at six o'clock every night?"

Posy put four olives in her mouth thoughtfully. "I don't! I don't cook for Matt!"

"That's because he only eats mung beans and leaves."

"Yes, OK, that too. And I didn't cook for Adam."

"You didn't love Adam."

"Neh," said Posy. "I guess not."

"What about Almaric? Did you . . . How did you feel?"

"Well," said Posy, "apart from the carnation in his buttonhole, and the girl in the big white dress—"

"No way!" said Leah, as Posy filled her in with all the details. "But I thought he absolutely definitely emphatically wasn't the marrying kind."

"Yuh," said Posy, "it turned out he was just absolutely definitely emphatically not the marrying-to-*me* kind."

"Harsh," said Leah.

"But funnily enough," said Posy, "once it was pointed out to me that he wasn't ever really going to get back together with me . . ."

"By getting married to someone else."

"Do you think it could possibly have been a cry for help? Like those fake suicide attempts people make?"

"No," said Leah.

"Okay. Well, once I realized that, I could kind of look at it objectively for what it was, do you know what I mean?"

Leah nodded. "Like, how am I objectively the most single person on earth?"

"Yes, like that."

Leah picked up her blue cocktail and sipped it mournfully.

"Anyway, I realized . . . I mean, he was a lovely bloke, but just obviously having a bit of a laugh and so on, in London. What he *really* wanted to do was come back to Wales and make pots with a fat Welsh lass."

"Was she fat?"

"No."

"Oh."

"Not yet."

"Oh."

"I'm just . . ."

"I understand."

They sat there in silence, nursing their drinks, until Posy—who'd been trying to restrain herself on the grounds that it was a bit cruel—decided instead to spill all the beans about Margie.

"And how's Matt?" Leah asked finally.

"He wants us to sell the flat."

"No way!" said Leah. "You'll get about five pence for it!"

"Thanks."

Posy looked up miserably. "I've ballsed it all up, haven't I? I've ruined everything. Tearing about the country while all the time Matt was here waiting for me to sort things out and I just completely ignored it."

"It seems very sudden, this flat thing," mused Leah. "I wonder why now and not before when he was cross? I always just thought he'd come round."

"Me too," said Posy. "It's just I could never get him on his mobile, then I went away, so I suppose he must have been doing all his thinking without me, and I guess he just came to all his conclusions on his own."

"Men never come to conclusions on their own."

"Oh no, they don't, do they?" Posy bit her lip. "So what do you think?"

Leah shrugged. "You don't suppose Matt would have . . ."

"What?"

"Well, while you were out and about . . . did he think he was single then, do you think?"

Posy sat for a second, staring at her drink.

"I'm sure that's impossible," said Leah. "I'm sure just because you were going to see all your exes to blubber on about where it all went wrong, he still felt totally secure in himself and like he had nothing to prove."

"Oh, no, it can't be," said Posy, thinking about his being out all the time. And had that been a new yellow shirt? She felt like someone had just stabbed her in the heart.

"I'm sure it's not," said Leah. "And the fact that you couldn't raise him on his mobile and that he wants to sell the flat are just kind of coincidence."

"Oh fuck," said Posy. "No. Don't be stupid. Don't be daft. He won't be doing anything, he'll just be at work."

"And you know that for certain, do you? You're totally sure?"

Posy shrugged.

A memory crossed her mind. Her and Matt, in a cinema somewhere. Watching a movie where the hero was leaving his safe girlfriend to kiss the beautiful rebel. Matt had exhaled strongly. Posy glanced at him.

"What?" she'd whispered.

"Well, look," he'd said. "He's just going to get himself into stupid trouble for no reason. What a total waste of time. If he wants to bang that one, he really ought to tell the other one."

Posy had smiled inside, suddenly feeling very safe. She slipped her hand into his.

"Hey," he'd said. "Forget it."

"What?"

"You're going for my popcorn."

"I am not . . . just a bit."

"No!"

"Give me some!"

"I said before do you want popcorn and you said no!"

"Which meant, I will share your popcorn."

"Which means, No. It's not good for you anyway."

"GIVE ME SOME!"

The person sitting two rows in front of them turned round, giving them a stern look.

"Now ssh," Matt had said, cramming her mouth with popcorn. She had chewed happily and nuzzled into him in the dark, feeling safe and protected and happy, the film washing right over them.

Back in the bright bar, a very drunk man lurched up to her and Leah.

"G'day, ladies, fancy a go? Just one careful owner . . . No, actually, she was a bitch, my ex-wife. Still. Buy you a drink?"

"GAVIN?" said Posy in horror, coming back to earth with a bump. What was she thinking, letting Matt slip through her fingers? What on earth was going on in her head?

"Oh God, Leah, I have to leave."

"Don't go!" said Gavin. "Uh, I'm your boss!"

"No, Gavin, it's not that."

"I am your boss though."

"Shut up! No, Leah. I've just realized."

"What?"

"I LOVE HIM! I LOVE HIM! I LOVE HIM!"

"You really do?"

"I really do." Posy's eyes were shining and her face was sure.

"You know," said Leah, smiling. "That's kind of the reaction we were looking for when you got engaged."

"Just one drink," slurred Gavin. But Posy was gone.

She ran out of the bar as fast as she could manage, pulling her phone from her bag. She tried Matt. No answer. Again. Nothing. The flat. It rang out. Oh, why wasn't she a more suspicious character? After all, it's not like anyone would blame him.

Maybe he *was* working late. Yes, that would be it. Working late with some over-stressed executive desperate to look younger than he was and keep his job. She'd go to the gym, it wasn't far from here. See him working out with someone and set her mind at rest.

The panic, though, gripped her as she walked through the

darkening March streets. Not Matt. He couldn't. He wouldn't do this to her. He wouldn't. He was her man, her boy, her Matt.

And, she realized suddenly, racing across the Euston Road as a taxi beeped at her, she knew. It started to rain. She couldn't stop, because she knew. Suddenly, in the rain, haring up the Euston Road through all the traffic, pushing past people trying to get home, trying to catch trains at the station and all of them, it seemed, going the opposite way to her, she knew. As she pounded the pavement—she hadn't had this much exercise, she realized, in months, maybe she should do some more of Matt's workouts—she knew, she just *knew*, suddenly, that she loved him. Why, though, had it taken so long? Why couldn't she find it in the countryside, among other people, other men? Because she was looking in the wrong places.

Matt's gym was on the north side of the Euston Road, on the ground floor of a glass skyscraper, set up so that passers-by could peer in and see people jogging or generally preening. It had never made the least bit of sense to Posy—why would people want to run on the spot next door to Regent's Park, one of the loveliest places on earth? And, given that they did, how did they then want everyone walking past them to see them bouncing up and down with a sweaty crotch?

But this was Matt's world. And she had never really taken it seriously. And perhaps it was time to.

The gym glowed blue with fancy lighting. Posy realized as she drew closer that she wasn't a member, had never even bothered to take up the free family pass Matt had offered. Had she really been so disinterested in his life? Bitterly ashamed, she caught sight, in the car park, of Pepe. The car had already been fixed, its scratches removed. Matt had just quietly gone and sorted it out. He hadn't made a song and dance about it, hadn't made a fuss. Just because he wasn't a drama queen, like Adam, or liked to be mysterious, like Almaric, didn't mean he wasn't loving; just because he treated her well didn't mean he was weak.

Well, she was going to show him. She was going to throw herself at his feet. Apologize over and over again; beg for a second chance. He had loved her enough once, hadn't he? He had to give her another chance. He had to. And she would be the most faithful, loving, listening, caring girlfriend in the history of the world. This break had to be over. It had to be. She couldn't live without him anymore.

Staring through the heavy, blue-tinged glass, sure enough, she could see him. There he was now, helping out a blonde girl on some thigh exerciser thing . . . he must be bending down to make sure she was doing it right. He must just be checking on her breathing, that must be why his face was so close to hers. And she was beckoning him closer, pulling down the side of her leotard . . .

Matt backed away, but he was laughing. He held up his hands. He was clearly saying, "Not here." Not here, that was all. And the beautiful blonde was laughing too. She was gorgeous. Irresistible. They looked so happy.

Oh fuck. Oh fuck.

Posy slumped down with her back against the glass, and, very slowly, let herself slide all the way down to the dirty grimy rain-sodden Euston Road.

Chapter Twenty-six

Posy Fairweather relationship status: Single.

Pepe the sports car flew past Posy sitting on the pavement, without noticing her huddled there. Posy caught a glimpse of a head of long, artifically yellow hair tossed back in laughter. It was Matt and the blonde. Together. Happy. Laughing. In love. He was funny, Matt. Not enough people gave him credit for this. He was brilliant. Nobody paid enough attention to that when they were teasing him about being a P.E. teacher. Oh, crap.

Where could she go? Now she'd found out her suspicions were right—she could probably have come here any night since they'd broken up and seen exactly the same thing—then there was nothing else to do except go home and think. But what next? Hadn't she learned anything?

Of course she didn't sleep. She was waiting, constantly, to hear Matt's key in the lock. Would he make excuses? Pretend he'd been out with the boys? Or start a fight? Which?

But it didn't matter in the end, because he didn't come home at all.

*

Dragging herself into work the next morning felt hideously cruel and torturous. If Mums got maternity leave, Posy thought ruefully, the terminally single ought to get heartbreak leave. It was just as painful, and you didn't even get presents.

Only twenty minutes late, with an extra shot of caffeine in her coffee, Posy could barely stand up in the lift. Margie glanced up, sniffing, and went to make a mark in her book. Posy gave her a look that said, "Don't you dare." Gradually and carefully, Margie put the pen down.

"How are you feeling?" Posy asked kindly. Margie looked like she'd hardly slept.

"You look absolutely terrible too," said Margie. "Have you slept a wink?"

"Wotcha?" a voice interrupted.

At first Posy didn't recognize him. Her chubby, genial Aussie boss Gavin was standing there. His suit, which had some stains down it, was hanging off him. She squinted up at him.

"How are you doing?"

"Yeah, not so good, not so good . . . I'm out of the house now."

Posy noticed he was wearing odd socks. "So, where are you living?"

Gavin shrugged. "Uh, over in Earl's Court. With a few chums, you know. Single life again. It's a full laugh, mate."

"Is it?" said Posy. Gavin's shoulders slumped.

"I'm sleeping on the sofa. I'm sleeping on the bloody sofa, Posy. I'm forty-two years old, I've got two kids and I'm sleeping on a sofa. That smells of spew."

"Oh Gavin," said Posy. "I'm so sorry."

"Aw, she-et, it was nice to meet your friend the other night. She seems sweet."

"Cool. Listen, I think I might know a small flat for sale, if you're interested."

Posy sleepwalked through the day. Gavin had agreed to come and look at the flat on the weekend so that, she supposed, could be that sorted. Then she could start looking around for something to start her life over again. Or what was left of her life. Or Gavin's.

Before she got to the front door, she sensed Matt was there. Swallowing hard, she put her key in the lock.

Matt was standing in the kitchen, looking nervous. Posy stared at him, her heart brimming over. Neither of them spoke.

"So how was she?" said Posy finally.

"How was he?" said Matt furiously. "Because, of course, when we accuse each other, it's always true."

Posy shrugged, heading not for the kettle as she normally did, but for the fridge. She poured herself a large glass of wine and tossed it down her throat.

"OK," she said, "I'm going to bed."

"It's six o'clock," said Matt.

Posy turned to face him. "I'm surprised you're not tired too."

Matt bit his lip. "What do you mean?"

"Oh, nothing! Of course you're allowed to go out and have fun, don't mind me."

"A friend wants to work with me on developing the business, that's all."

"Sure it is," said Posy scornfully. She'd seen that blonde's face. Matt wasn't stupid. "That's why it's perfectly fine. It's your life. You have to do whatever you want."

Matt looked down. "But Posy, it's you who keeps fannying off with all those blokes—"

"So that makes it all right for you to do it too. It's fine. I understand."

"But I *didn't*!"

"That's right. You slept in the gym."

"Posy," he started, "maybe she does want to chat me up a bit. But she's got lots of ideas—"

Posy cut him off. She couldn't bear to hear it, not after she'd seen the evidence. "I've got someone to come and look at the flat at the weekend. I think it would be a good fit, he wants somewhere small."

"Well, *that's* handy." Matt had gone puce with anger.

"And he wants to move, like, really really fast."

He would move in with the tall blonde bird, she expected. They always did. Plus his gym was so bloody hoity-toity, she'd probably have tons of money and he'd be a kept man and become personal trainer to the stars and release his own fitness video and become a millionaire and they'd have incredibly gorgeous blonde kids and be in *OK!* and live happily ever after. He wouldn't want to stay in Elephant and Castle, that was for sure.

"So that's it?" he said. "That's it?"

Posy was so numb and choked. Her ideas from the night before, of begging him to take her back, of throwing herself on his mercy . . . how could she have been so stupid?

Later, she lay in the big bed and missed him more than ever, missed the shape of him, the smell. But she couldn't. He was someone else's now. And, like with everything else, she had only herself to blame. She sobbed quietly into her pillow, so as not to wake him.

Posy fell asleep eventually and woke late morning, the sun already high in the sky. It was Saturday morning. No sound of Matt—he had probably gone to her house, she reflected miserably. They would have leggy blonde highly aerobicized sex with lots of screaming and wailing and then they would go to some glamorous outdoor cafe and drink lattes and have scintillating conversations . . . She was probably a huge sports fan and knew all about teams and how long games take and things. And she would toss back her long blonde hair with her taut arms without a hint of wobble, and . . .

This was useless. This wasn't helping her at all. She had to get up. Posy threw back the covers and opened her curtains. It was a gorgeous day outside. It was Saturday. She had absolutely nothing planned; Leah had mentioned a fashion party that she could get her into, but the idea of being surrounded by dozens of nine-foot Eastern European teenagers while she reflected on her lost love just didn't appeal.

Apart from that, the day was a gaping hole. Everywhere couples would be sitting outside, going to art galleries, shopping, having lunch, enjoying one another. She and Matt used to like wandering up to the South Bank. He would browse the music shop in the Royal Festival Hall for obscure bands and orchestrations, she would rummage through the second-hand books outside. They would go and eat and have an ice cream and . . . what would they talk about? She couldn't even remember. She just remembered that it was easygoing and completely relaxed, and she didn't have to pretend to be impressive, like she did with Adam, or exciting, like with Almaric, or attentive, like with Chris. It was just a flow, an easy, likable time spent with your best friend. Who happened to be really fit.

Posy let out a loud groan. Oh God. How could she have cocked this up so badly? She had thought it would work; a real voyage of discovery into herself, which would allow her to know herself better and be able to come back to Matt a real and rounded person, so they could step into the future together. Not hurling herself off the abyss.

There was one thing left to try, she realized, boiling up the kettle for instant coffee. Just one thing . . . Obviously nothing could be changed with Matt now, she'd accepted that. But to help her move forward . . . Well, it wasn't like she had anything else on today.

The train took forever to limp its way out to Manningtree, the small Essex town where Ray and Marian lived. Posy had been driven there before by Ray, long ago, but couldn't remember the way and hopped in a cab. She knew she should have called before just turning up—as far as she knew, they could all be on holiday in New Zealand or something—but she couldn't face it; knew if she tried to talk on the telephone, her voice would stick in her throat and she would stumble to get the words out and probably cry. Best to just turn up. Although that hadn't worked so well the last time she'd tried it, she thought, remembering ruefully Almaric's wedding. Had that only been a week ago?

She smiled to herself. How could she have carried a torch for him for so long? He was just a bloke, after all. A bit of a daft one, if his new wife was anything to go by. No, that wasn't fair.

He was terribly handsome and sexy and sweet. But she could appreciate that without wanting to throw herself on his funeral pyre anymore, so it had to be a good thing.

Ray's house was just as she remembered it, having spent so many sullen hours there in the past; a scrupulously tidy semi-detached in a cul-de-sac, with a crazy paving drive and a wishing well in the front garden. Her mother had always been preposterously snotty about the very concept of a cul-de-sac. Posy looked around at the children playing on their bicycles in the sunshine and thought it might not be the worst place she could imagine to grow up.

Taking a deep breath, she rang the little doorbell, which chimed perkily. Glancing around, Posy could hear garden sprinklers and kids laughing. Not the police sirens and helicopters you heard round her mother's house.

"Yes?" said a woman's voice impatiently. She had half her bright yellow hair smoothed out carefully and half in a frizz; she was obviously at it with the GHDs and the effect was so odd that Posy couldn't speak for a moment or two.

"Posy?" said the woman. "Posy, is that you? What's up, love, is anything the matter?"

Posy had never really got to know Marian. She had dismissed her—like her mother had, she realized now, God, was she *really* so like her?—as a brassy, sharky husband-stealing hussy with no education. But looking into her face, it seemed kind, and, at the moment, concerned.

"What is it? Tell me, quickly," said Marian. "Before my hair gets totally ruined."

"No, no, everything's fine," said Posy hastily. Then, seeing Marian's face, she said, "Well. Apart from . . . *some stuff.*"

"Come in, come in."

Marian ushered her over the threshold and into the immaculate sitting room. The chairs looked like they'd just had the plastic taken off them. The ornaments—all of horses and frogs for some reason—had a highly polished sheen. The carpet had deep Hoover lines grooved into it. The whole place smelled of perfumed air freshener, and slightly singed hair.

Marian guided her toward the cream leather sofa and glanced down at her shoes on the cream carpet. Posy slipped off her Converse automatically and lined them up in the hallway. Marian flashed her a grateful look.

"I'll just get my GHDs," she said. "Won't be a sec. Can't live without 'em."

Posy sat with her hands clenched together in case she accidentally got fingerprints on something. This was, hands down, the cleanest place she'd ever been. She listened out, but it didn't sound like there was anyone else in the house. On the other hand, it was quite possible that Marian took the topic of noise as seriously as she took that of dust, and sought to eradicate it at all times.

After ten minutes Marian reappeared with her hair perfectly straight, like great layers of straw on a face too old for it. She was also carrying a tray with freshly brewed coffee and some freshly baked biscuits. Posy eyed the biscuits.

"Did you just make those? On the off-chance?"

Marian laughed. "Oh no, the boys like them when they get back from the footie. Don't want to deny my little Jasie."

Given that little Jasie was at least three stone overweight, was still living at home at twenty-two, and had never held a job for more than a fortnight, Posy thought that it was a bit more than biscuits he needed, but she didn't want to mention it. She helped herself to one. It was delicious.

"Won't Jason mind me eating his biscuits?" she asked mischievously.

"He'll do his nut," confided Marian. "We just ignore his little tantrums."

"Yum," said Posy, taking another bite. She hadn't eaten properly in days.

"So, darling, what's the matter? It's the wedding, isn't it? Your mum doesn't want me there." Marian laid a hand on Posy's arm and stared directly into her face. "Darling, I totally understand. I wouldn't step on your big day for an instant. Don't worry about it for a tiny second. Although if you could find it in your heart to ask Jason I'd be so delighted." She lowered her voice. "I'd so love him to meet a *nice girl*."

Posy bit her lip. "Actually," she said, quietly, hating to say it out loud, "the wedding's off."

Marian's eyes popped out. "Oh, sweetheart," she said, "my darling. I'm *so* sorry."

It was such a kind, maternal thing to say—something her own mother would never have dreamed of saying—that Posy thought she was going to cry again.

"It's OK," she said. "I'm going to be fine."

"Well, of *course* you are," said Marian, putting her arm around her. "Doesn't mean it's not right difficult now, does it?"

"No," said Posy. "No, it doesn't."

"So, tell me everything," said Marian, in a comforting tone. "I was going to clean the house—it's *such* a tip—but why don't you tell me what happened instead. Sometimes it helps, you know."

Of all the people in the world Posy might previously have

considered pouring out her troubles to, Marian—the brassy, tarty, forward husband-stealer—was the very last person she'd have thought of. She'd imagined treating her with her usual polite and icy silence while trying to get her dad out for a walk.

But now she was here, in the enemy's house, drinking her very good coffee and eating her delicious biscuits, it suddenly didn't seem the worst idea in the world to get someone else's perspective; someone who might even understand too.

"Well . . ." she began.

Half an hour later, they both sat there in silence. Marian was twisting her hair anxiously, so that all the hard smoothing work of the GHDs appeared to be in vain. Her perfectly made-up eyes had smudged, and her fingers wrung together. Posy finished and looked around.

"Well," said Marian, "I don't half regret giving up the fags. Could do with one right now."

Posy smiled sympathetically.

"Well," said Marian again. Then she leaned forward.

"Posy, darling, I know you think I nicked your dad, I know that's what your mum always told you. And I wasn't going to get dragged into a slanging match—especially not with your mum and all those long words she uses."

Posy smiled weakly.

"But, honestly, truth is, by the time I met your dad he was living on his own—hand on heart, I swear to God, and you know why? Because I was the barmaid in his new local. He used to come in every night—not to drink, just because he had nowhere else to go. Remember that flat?"

Posy did. Her father had moved into a tiny bedsit that

smelled of mold and had scary loud people next door who made tons of noise. It frightened her. They used to refuse to go.

"I could see he was still wearing his wedding ring, I wasn't stupid. Stayed well clear. Well, I was *quite* stupid. Been burned before, oh yes. Anyway, never mind about that. Quiet nights, we'd chat. He hated that bedsit, hated being apart from you. He just felt he'd been such a failure. It's a hard thing for a man, feeling like a failure."

"I never feel like anything else," said Posy.

"Oh, don't talk like that," said Marian. "Don't be ridiculous. My dad died when I was eight. Asbestosis, because the boss of his factory couldn't be bothered to strip it out, even when they knew it was dangerous."

"I'm sorry," said Posy.

"OK," said Marian. "But everyone has their troubles, you know? It's how you deal with them that counts."

Posy nodded.

"Anyway, your mother, she was tough, eh? Wouldn't let him back in the house. Blocked access, messed him about."

"She said it was all he deserved," remembered Posy. "For what he'd done to us."

"Well, we'll never know the truth of that," said Marian. "But the way I hear it, she'd driven him half crazy with her moods and demands and psychology and fighting."

Posy would have liked to deny that her mother was capable of those things. But she couldn't.

"I mean, Posy, he was the saddest man I'd ever met."

"So why didn't you tell him to go home?" said Posy. "Why didn't you send him back to us?"

"I tried," said Marian. "You won't believe me, but I told him what I told all my sad male clients, and you got a lot of them in *that* pub. I said, "Go home, love the one you're with and look after your kiddies.'"

"But he couldn't."

"He couldn't. She wouldn't hear of it."

Posy swallowed. "So . . ."

Marian looked dreamy. "Oh, Posy, I was madly in love with him. He's a helluva man, your dad."

Posy looked at Marian. How old was she back then? Late thirties? It must have been her last chance, or near it. And he'd been a handsome man, her dad, she knew that much, she'd seen the photos. She must have been overcome.

Marian leaned over. "Don't . . . don't think he didn't try, Posy. He really did. Your mum made it so so difficult for him. And she told him that psychologically it was best for you and Fleur if he kept his distance."

"She didn't," said Posy, white with anger. "She would never have said that."

"Tensions were running so high, Posy. It was a really tough time . . ." She caught sight of Posy's face. "Well, of course I don't have to tell you that."

"No," said Posy.

"He may find it hard to say," said Marian. "But he means well, truly. So do I."

"It seemed so quick," said Posy. "You, after Mum."

"I was thirty-seven, darling," said Marian. "I pushed like crazy for it. All my fault, I'm sorry. I should have been more sensitive."

Posy nodded. She understood.

"I was . . . I was desperate for a baby of my own. Especially since it didn't look like I was going to get a look-in with you girls." She smiled. "You little mites, clinging to the banisters. I just wanted to take you home, give you some oven chips, and sit you in front of the TV."

"We weren't allowed TV," murmured Posy automatically.

"Mmhmm," said Marian. "Or oven chips, I suppose."

"We lived off hummus mostly," said Posy.

"Never tried it," said Marian.

"Oh," said Posy. She sighed. It made sense.

"Did you badger the hell out of him?" she asked, suddenly.

"No!" said Marian in surprise. "I just said, Look, if you're about it, get a ring on my finger and I want to get up the duff. But otherwise just leave."

"Like that?" said Posy.

Marian shrugged. "Well, why not? What's the point in not being straight about what you want?"

"Because it scares men off?" said Posy.

"No, it scares wankers off," said Marian. "The decent ones, they know the score. Marriage, Posy. It ain't a trick, or a con, or a trade-off of sex, or a guarantee . . . it's an understanding that two people are going to share their lives. And that ain't easy, so if you can't be upfront right from the start, I don't know how much hope there is for you . . . well, that's what I think, anyway. And Ray and me have been together for twenty-three years, so I think there's something in it."

"Straight-up honesty?"

"Well, he thinks I have blonde hair," said Marian. "But apart from that, yeah."

"Yeah," said Posy. He probably knows about the hair too, she thought, but didn't mention it.

Suddenly there was a key in the lock. All of a sudden Marian's confiding mood changed.

"Ooh, my boys are home and I haven't even got my face on!" said Marian, jumping up and grabbing the plates and cups. "Or dinner or nothing!"

"Can I help?" said Posy. Marian looked at her doubtfully.

"Go give your dad a cuddle," she said.

Posy stood up nervously, as the sound of blokes talking and removing their boots filled the house.

"Great bloody scoring from Rooney," said the younger voice.

"Bloody right," came her dad. "Top bloody buy too. Christ, I'm starving."

"Mum!" came the younger voice. "We're hungry!"

"All right, darlings!"

Posy wondered if her dad had always spoken that way. She didn't think so. Had he had to pretend with her mother? To the point of putting on a different voice?

"Oh, and we've got company," shouted Marian.

Ray put his head round the sitting room door, then did a double take.

"Oh!" he said. "Uhm. Err. Posy. Hello! Uh, make yourself at home. Sit down! Sit down! MARIAN! Can you make Posy a cup of coffee . . . or something else?"

"I'm fine, thanks," said Posy. "Marian and I were just having a chat."

Ray's brow furrowed. "About what? Is it the wedding? Oh, don't tell me Jonquil's gone off on one about the wedding. Are we all banned?"

"Uh, no," said Posy, wondering if it would ever get easier to explain. "Actually, there's not going to be a wedding."

291

Posy was gratified by how sad he looked. He didn't look slightly satisfied, like her mother had, or completely unsurprised, like Leah, or totally disinterested, like Fleur, or relieved, like Gavin. He looked sad.

"Oh, Posy, darling," he said. "I'm so sorry. He seemed such a lovely chap. We were so sorry you didn't want us at your engagement."

"I did!" said Posy. "I was really upset when you didn't make it . . . did Jonquil call?"

Ray looked embarrassed. "She said you'd rather we didn't."

"Oh *God*. Anyway. He was . . . is a nice man," said Posy.

"And it's not something you can sort out?"

Posy shrugged. "I don't think so." She thought of that girl's long, tossy hair. "No. Definitely not."

"Oh, love. If there's anything we can do—anything at all—just let me know, OK?"

Marian appeared in the doorway with a fresh pot of coffee and a large sponge cake she appeared to have magicked out of thin air. It had a slice missing. Jason followed her in, licking his fingers.

"'Ello, Posy."

"Hello, Jason."

Jason threw himself down on the sofa and switched on the television to the football highlights.

"*Jason*," said Marian. "We've got company."

"It's only her," grunted Jason.

"*JASON!*"

Jason tsked, and headed upstairs, where the football could soon be heard blaring out of his room.

"He does love his football," said Marian fondly.

"Dad?" said Posy.

"Yes?"

"Can I ask you something?"

Ray looked a bit worried, but rallied fast. "Course, darling."

"Why did you and Mum get married?"

Marian and Ray looked at each other in disbelief.

"What?" said Ray.

"You and Mum. Why did you tie the knot? I mean, you just seem so badly suited."

Marian heaved a sigh. "Honestly, I know she's your mum and all that, Posy, but she's a right crazy daisy sometimes."

"What do you mean?"

"Posy," said Ray. "Me and your mother were never married."

Posy clutched the arms of her chair.

"*What?*" she said, slowly.

"We were never . . . your mother had kind of said something about being against marriage . . . and I thought that meant she didn't want me to ask her, and then she got pregnant with you—I was *delighted*, by the way—and so it didn't seem to be that important to her and it just never came up again."

"But she said . . . she said marriage was terrible and she should know, she'd been through it." Posy was completely, totally, and utterly aghast.

Ray winced. "Well, not with me," he said. "That's a joke."

But Posy was shaking her head. "She said . . . she said she burned all her wedding photos. And her dress. When you left."

Ray raised his eyebrows. "Posy, I'm so . . . I mean, your mum . . . she's always been a bit different."

"But she uses your name!"

"She always thought it was a pretty name. She hates her maiden name."

"McGillyunddy?"

"Bless you," said Marian, then put her hand to her mouth. "Sorry. Bad joke. Bad timing."

"So you're saying the reason she hates marriage is because you wouldn't marry her? She's a lying witch."

"She's your mum," said Marian. "She loves you."

"I wish she wouldn't show it by trying to completely screw everything up," mumbled Posy. "I can't believe . . . all this psychological advice, all the sniffing and disapproval, all of this *crap*."

Marian looked at her sadly.

"I doubted every relationship I ever had . . . I listened to what she was telling me." Posy looked up, her eyes stinging. "Sorry . . . I'm sorry, I shouldn't have come here."

Ray's voice was kind.

"Darling . . . darling Posy, you're my daughter. I know I've been a crap dad, I know that. I never tried hard enough. That's why we've tried again with Jason . . ."

"MUM!" came a bellow from upstairs. "Where's my tea? I want sausage and mash, but no lumpy bits in the mash this time."

Marian beamed as if he'd said something really clever. "Jason's such a stickler about his food!" she said.

"But I found it so hard to get through to you," said her dad, his eyes damp. "And if we could try again, Posy . . . if I could be a proper dad to you."

Posy thought about what Almaric had said; that she'd been

chasing her father. Yet here he was, all the time, just an hour away. And, it turned out, he hadn't even been the problem.

"That would be nice, wouldn't it, love?" said Marian. Posy nodded, blindly, her mind reeling.

"And maybe," said Marian shyly, looking nervous. "When I come up West, we could go shopping together, maybe. I mean, Jason's great and everything but he's not much use for girly shopping."

"Maybe we could," said Posy. "Look. I have to go. I have a lot to think about."

"Of course," said Ray. "I understand. Can I run you to the station?"

"Yes, please . . . Dad," said Posy.

Posy got the text on the train. It just said: I'm going to stay at Roddy's for a bit.

Posy was so furious she didn't even stop to think. She just caught a cab straight to her mother's house.

Her mother often saw clients on weekends and was upstairs, with her DO NOT DISTURB sign on the door. That sign was sacrosanct. Posy pushed open the door with a loud bang.

"What . . . Posy, what the hell—? Excuse me, Duncan."

Jonquil rounded on her. "I'm sorry, Posy, I have a client right now."

A balding, sad-looking middle-aged man sat on her couch.

"I don't give a fuck," said Posy. She turned to the man. "Don't listen to a thing she tells you."

"Actually she doesn't really tell me anything," said the man. "She mostly just says "Hmm" and "Tell me more.'"

Posy ignored him.

"Why the *fuck* didn't you tell me you and Dad weren't married? Why didn't you invite him to my engagement party?"

Jonquil looked flustered and taken aback.

"What other lies have you told me about him?"

Duncan was sitting up on the couch now, watching with interest.

"Darling, this is not the time nor the place."

"No, it never bloody is. It's never the time to tell me the truth, is it, Mum? All these years you paint yourself the bloody victim. While trying to make victims out of us."

"Well, Fleur seems to manage."

"Fleur has never had a boyfriend or a job! Because you've terrified the fucking life out of her! How is that managing?"

Jonquil pursed her lips.

"And I have bollocksed up everything I've ever done because . . . because you told me. You told me settling down is wrong and marriage is wrong and you've never even been married and know nothing about it. You think just because no one wanted to marry you that no one should get married." Posy felt herself choking, and desperately tried to pull back on her hurt and anger.

"That's my fault for trying to get her a good education instead of throwing herself at men all the time," said Jonquil to Duncan.

"You're never going to change, are you, Mum? You always want to control me."

"Maybe you guys should try therapy," said Duncan helpfully.

"My daughter would have to learn to listen," said Jonquil.

"*No*," said Posy, suddenly, uncharacteristically, righteously furious. "*You* listen. I have a lovely dad and I had a lovely boy-friend and you poisoned me against them both, and I am *never*, ever listening to you ever again. I don't even want to see you."

Jonquil tried to look unconcerned, but Posy could see some-how the hint of panic in her eyes and, for once, felt powerful.

"Goodbye. And just in case you ever get access to your family ever again in your life through Fleur or whatever . . . why don't you learn to make them a fucking sandwich?" Posy marched out and slammed the door with such force the entire house shook.

Chapter Twenty-seven

Chris is pregnant.

Comment: Like.

Comment, Posy: Hurrah hurrah hurrah for finally some good news! Are you going to move? Where will you put it?

Comment, Chris: Posy, babies are only small.

"Leah? Where have you been? I really really really *really* need someone to go out and get drunk with."

"Eer? Uh. Mm. Hang on. *Stop* that!"

"Leah! Is someone else there?"

"Mmm."

"What? Who?"

"Ehm, well . . ."

"TELL ME!"

"Who's that?" came an off-phone voice. A familiar off-phone voice.

"Ssh! It's Posy! I mean, it's, uhm, my friend Posy, nobody you know."

Posy held the phone away from her head, then brought it back.

"*Gavin?* Is that you?! Leah, is *Gavin* there?"

"Uhm . . . no?"

"Tell her I'm not here," came the voice. Posy rolled her eyes.

"Well done, Gavin. What's he doing there? What what what?"

Leah giggled. "Uh, Posy, is this urgent?"

"It might be."

Posy heard nuzzling noises on the phone and sighed.

"No. No, Leah, it's not urgent."

"OK then," said Leah. Posy hung up, shaking her head.

"Fleur?"

Fleur tsked. "Oh, there you are. What is it? Are you still moping around?"

"I have . . . uh, yes, I am. Anyway, I have something to tell you. It's quite big news, though—we should probably meet."

"Neh, I'm busy."

"*How* are you busy?"

"OK, I'm not busy. But if you're just about to say, blah blah I love Matt I love Almaric blah blah blah I'm so sad, you can probably just do it over the phone and I can just say Mmhmm and do other stuff."

"That's . . . is that what you do?"

"And Leah."

"It's *not* what Leah does."

"Mmhmm, you know she's designed pretty much her entire first collection while on the phone to you?"

"She has *not*."

"So does she always put you on speakerphone or not?"

"Fine, world's most annoying sister," said Posy. "Fine. Did you know *this*, then? Mum and Dad weren't married."

There was a pause.

"Oh, yeah, that," said Fleur.

"What do you mean, "Oh, yeah, that"?" said Posy in consternation. "What do you mean? You *knew*?!"

"Uh, well . . . Mum told me not to tell you."

"She did what? How did this happen?"

"Well, every time I've tried to tell you, you've been haring off on some stupid boy goose chase and it's been impossible to talk."

"Oh really?" said Posy. "Well, that is a good reason. If only modern science would invent some kind of technology that allowed people to communicate even while they weren't face-to-face."

"You should go see him, you know. They're all right, Marian and Ray."

"Have you been seeing them a lot?"

"On and off. They help with money from time to time."

"They would. Oh, Fleur, I wish you'd told me."

"Well, I was hardly thinking about it every single day, was I? I don't spend every hour of every day going, Oh dear, I wonder how this might affect Posy."

"You don't spend a single second of any year thinking of how things might affect me!"

"Well, get over it," said Fleur. "Does it matter?"

"When Mum kept going on about how crap marriage was and how it was pointless and how I shouldn't get married . . . yes, it matters *a bit*."

Fleur sighed. "OK. I'm sorry. Can I still be your brides-maid?"

"Are you even listening? Matt's moved out! I'm never get-ting married! She's won!"

"OK."

There was a pause. "You know," said Fleur, "I wish you'd answer Mum's calls and emails. She really misses you. I think she's . . ."

"What?"

"Sorry."

"Don't be stupid, Mum is never sorry about anything. Ever. She never does anything wrong."

"I'm just saying," said Fleur. "I'm just saying, I think she's sorry."

Posy wandered round the flat. It seemed bigger without all the size-eleven trainers cluttering it up. Bigger, not better. Empty. Like her. Cut off and adrift. Alone. She had to get out. She had to.

Chapter Twenty-eight

Posy is _____.

"Fleur, have you heard from Posy?"

"Who is this? Why are you calling me so early?"

"Fleur: one, it's Leah, whom you've seen twice a week since you were nine; and two, it's quarter past eleven in the morning."

"Fascist," said Fleur.

"Anyway, forget about that now. Have you heard from Posy?"

"Yes," sniffed Fleur. "Can you *imagine* anyone more self-absorbed?"

Leah could, but she didn't mention it. "Oh, that's a relief," she said. "Only Gav mentioned she hasn't been into work for a couple of days and was a bit worried about her."

"Who's Gav?" said Fleur. Then it struck her. "Her boss? You call her boss "Gav"? How? Why?"

"It doesn't matter," said Leah, cursing herself.

"Are you sleeping with him?"

"So when did you hear from her?"

"I don't know," said Fleur sleepily. "A few days ago, I suppose. She was, like, totally upset when she found out Mum and Dad weren't married."

"Your parents weren't married?"

"Hey, big furry deal, OK?"

"No, I know, but your mum goes on about marriage to Posy all the time. She took it really seriously."

"Hmm," said Fleur.

"When you say a few days, what do you mean? Tuesday?"

"Uh . . . no, it was the weekend."

"How would you know?" said Leah sarcastically, then realized it was pointless. Fleur never got sarcasm. "So it was five days ago? And you haven't seen her since?"

"I'm not her babysitter," said Fleur sulkily. "Anyway, I was going to call her. I've had *the* most unfair electricity bill—"

Leah hung up, starting to get worried. It wasn't at all like Posy not to turn up to work. Gav had been very sweet about it—but then he *was* very sweet, she couldn't believe how lovely he was. She was trying not to think about it, but she loved his hunky Australian shoulders and his funny accent and . . . well, no, she had to focus. She'd called Posy's number over and over again, to absolutely no avail. Posy hadn't updated her Facebook page for ages, which was very very unlike her.

Leah took a deep breath. Oh God, *Posy*. She was the worst person for getting into scrapes. On the other hand, if it hadn't been for her, she'd never have met . . . She thought back fondly to the previous evening. Gavin had admired her hat without even asking why it was made of twigs, then, as they'd got into bed, held her head in his hands, kissed her softly on the forehead, and said, "Leah, you are healing me." The thought was keeping her warm, even as she started to worry.

"Hello? Dr. Fairweather?"

Posy's mum sounded brusque and distracted. "Yes?"

"It's Leah, Posy's friend."

"Ah. Have you seen her? She called, had the most ridiculous hysterics then wouldn't pick up the phone to me. It's the most absurdly passive-aggressive behavior. So of course I've stopped ringing."

"Of course," said Leah. Her own mum was a midwife—sweet, kind, and capable and they liked to go to antiques shops together on her days off. Sure, they'd had their run-ins when Leah had first started wearing ripped tights as trousers, but now they spoke to each other most days. She would never understand Posy and Dr. Fairweather, had spent her childhood terrified of the woman.

"So you have no idea where she is?"

"Sulking somewhere, I expect. If you have children, Leah—and it's not for everyone—"

"Thanks," said Leah.

"Remember, they can be absolutely thankless. Utterly so."

"OK," said Leah. "I'd better go."

"Wait," said Jonquil, a tremble appearing in her voice. "Wait. Call me the second you know where she is, OK? And tell her . . . tell her . . ." Her voice cracked. "Just tell her to call me, will you, Leah, darling? Will you do that?"

"Yes," said Leah, grudgingly.

Right, thought Leah. Desperate times called for desperate measures. She was going to have to hack Posy's Facebook account. See if there was anything in her mailbox that could give a clue as to what was up. This was where she had met all these men, she must be able to find them from here.

She fired up her computer. Posy's login was her name, she knew that. But her password? Posy was such a doofus, it was probaby just "Password." She tried that. No. Password1? No.

OK. So maybe she wasn't such a doofus as all that. Leah looked at it again.

Posy. No. Almaric. No. InsuranceHoldings. No. What was Matt's car called again? Hmm. Matt. No. Pepe. No.

Aha! Posy's favorite band of all time? MortenHarket. No. Hmm, they'd never had a dog. She tried the names of everyone they knew, everything Posy had done. Pottery. Sports. Shetland. Wales. Elephant.

What *was* it? Leah thought again and again through Posy's life. Indecision? Saab? SevenForAllMankind? FacebookFriend? Daffodils? Grazia? Fishfingers? SexandtheCity? DirtyDancing? Robertdowneyjr? RobertDowneyJr? RobertDowneyJunior?

What did Posy have? What did she like? What did she want? LotteryWin? Bentley? HollandPark? Size10? Mummy? Hampstead? Watermelon? Bananarama? Spa? Chips? SpaChips?

SpaChips? Leah sighed. She'd tried calling Matt, of course, but she couldn't get hold of him either. Their house phone was ringing off the hook and their message box was full, which implied that neither of them were there. She hadn't been down to see; Matt would have answered if he'd been there in case she was a client. It was very mysterious.

ProtectandPerfect? Gap? Marketing? ILoveMarketing? IHateMarketing? ThirtyTwo? Babies? Timewasting? SesameStreet?

Posy loved *Sesame Street*. Oh, this just wasn't working at all. But if she could get in, Leah thought, she would surely find a clue as to where Posy had gone.

Twiglets. Sanddunes. Yellow. Christmas. Kosher. Kosher-Christmas.

Oh, Posy, thought Leah. What do you care about? Really? Truly? What do you want?

She typed it in very slowly.

T-R-U-E-L-O-V-E.

Ping.

You have fourteen new messages.

Leah scanned through the emails—most of them circulars, nonsense, or from her. The unopened messages went back three days. *Three days??* How could that be? For the first time, Leah started to feel worried. Posy was *always* on top of her email; she was a total addict. She'd even checked it up on the Shetlands. And it had been three days since she'd been in to work . . . where *was* she? Where could she be? She glanced at Posy's status update. It simply said: Posy Fairweather is_____. Normally this was the kind of thing people stuck in when they couldn't be bothered. But in Posy's case, did it mean something else? Something subliminal, a clue?

Leah sat back, not sure what to think. She should start opening the mail, she supposed. Suddenly the computer made a little purring noise and she jumped. A small box opened in the lower right-hand side of the page. It was the instant messaging box jumping up.

"Posy?" it said. "Are you there?"

It was Matt. He must have seen she was online. Oh my God, he thought she was Posy.

– Hello? she typed tentatively.

– Posy, thank God, where u been? Been worried sick.

Leah couldn't help herself. Just this once. Just so she knew, so Posy knew. Once and for all. With a horrible sense of foreboding she typed:

– Did you miss me?

Then she sat back, heart pounding.

The reply was a little while in coming.

– Uh, yeah. Where have you been?

– Thinking. Where you?

Leah wondered if Posy would already know where he was.

– Look, it's just . . . I'm staying with a friend.

Leah's eyes blinked in fury. He couldn't have. How *dare* he? Didn't he know how shattered she was?

– YOU MOVED IN WITH THAT FLOOZY from the GYM???!

– No, Roddy.

– Well, sod that, it's Leah, not Posy.

– What???

Leah shook her head and rang him on his mobile. He didn't pick up.

– Answer your phone!

– I can't, I'm in some kind of sugar warehouse, there's no reception. Who is this?

– It's Leah. I'm looking for Posy.

– Is she hiding in her computer?

– This isn't funny. Nobody's seen her. Or heard from her.

– That's impossible. Posy never shuts up.

– Not this time.

There was a long break. Then Leah's phone rang.

"I'm hanging over the balcony."

"Of your luxury love pad?"

Matt sighed. "No, in fact. Melissa asked me to move in with her and offered to back starting my own business."

"*Did* she now?" said Leah.

"I said no, Leah. For Christ's sake. This is me."

"Oh," said Leah.

"So . . . what about Posy?"

Leah paused. "I think she was missing you so much," she said quietly.

"She kept leaving," said Matt, his voice showing his pain.

"Matt," she said. "Remember how you two met?"

Matt didn't even like using the computer much. Sitting down in front of a screen all day was a mugs' game that made your thighs spread, in his experience. But he'd signed up to Facebook so he could see his friend's wedding photos and had found it quite useful to keep abreast of his chums, though he certainly wasn't going to spend his life thinking up witty status updates or quippy comments; he had far too much to do. So he was surprised one day, two years ago, when a message popped into his inbox from out of the blue.

"*Hello*!" it said. "Are you the Matt Farmer I know? Because I realized that a) I never returned that blue shirt you lent me and, b) I let a dog sleep on it once. However I was just cleaning out my wardrobes after a horrible break-up and considering setting everything on fire, so I thought I'd give you a chance to reclaim it. If you would like it. Posy. P.S.: if you are not the Matt Farmer I know I think you should have a lovely day."

It had made him smile and, for want of something better to do, he had clicked through onto her profile. A laughing girl with bouncing hair and dark eyes was grinning at the camera. She was single . . . in London . . . two years younger than him . . . had loads of friends on her profile.

> Posy Fairweather is wondering where she can get hold
>   of a flame thrower.

He had smiled and typed back:

"Hello there. No, I'm not the one you know, I think it's quite a common name. Are you sure you need to burn everything? Oxfam are quite helpful."

The reply shot back.

"Have you never broken up with anyone? I don't want happy reminders of him being spread to all corners of the world. Nope. Sorry. I promise you I am not normally a crazy person but I am making an exception for one day only and cathartically setting it all on fire."

"Has he got any cool stuff I could rescue first?"

"Just me."

And, amazingly, they had started chatting. After a month or so, mention of the other chap (Posy had never ever mentioned his name) had died down, and he'd started to look forward to hearing what she was up to every day. Inevitably, it was soon mooted that they meet.

"What would be worse?" Posy had mused (he had kept all of

her emails, reread them endlessly). "Meeting alone in a pub and then both of us having to run to the bathroom to be instantly sick, or meeting with lots of people and then have them staring at us all night and making unkind remarks behind our backs."

"That depends," he'd said, "on whether you think I'm a rapist—dodgy to be on my own with—or a con man—dodgy to be around lots of your friends with."

"What about a rapey con man?"

"They only like to meet in City bars."

He'd always been puzzled by the size of Posy's LOL after that.

It was summertime, gorgeous. They'd decided to meet on the South Bank in the end—"There are so many people," said Posy, "that when I see you and have to spew and vomit I can quickly hide behind a tree."

"Yes," Matt had agreed. "And when I find you really tedious and boring I can do free running to get me out of there."

"And if it's really terrible I can just throw myself into the river."

"Or in front of a train."

"Are you crazy?" Leah had said to Posy. "The last nine people I met through online dating were awful. Don't go."

"You're just grumpy because they were all five-foot-four. You didn't give them a chance."

"I couldn't bend down low enough to hear them!"

"Well, he's a personal trainer. At least he's going to be fit."

"Very small men can be fit!"

"Stop being heightist."

"You say that when you get home tonight with a crook in

your neck and you've had to take off your shoes and he's spent all night telling you that good things come in small packages."

"You're meant to be calming me down, not totally freaking me out."

"You've been talking to this guy online for two months."

"Uh huh?"

"So when you find out he's a tiny little small person, you're going to be so super-disappointed."

But from the moment Posy had tentatively come down the steps off Waterloo Bridge, to see what she instantly knew was him (although he had hardly any pics on his page and a horribly cheesy one his gym had taken to put on their site), she hadn't felt nervous at all. Or disappointed. He was standing there, in jeans and a stripy polo shirt. He looked completely normal. He didn't look dark and dangerous, or big and hippy-ish, or passionately poetic. He just looked . . .

She wrinkled up her nose.

"Uhm, hello? I've got a message from Posy Fairweather, she says she's terribly sorry, but she can't make it."

He had grinned, a lovely white-toothed grin.

"Oh, that's a terrible shame. Although frankly, between you and me, she was a shocking bore and looked like she probably smelled. Do you fancy going for a walk instead?"

And they took a walk, but it was so noisy and busy on the South Bank, and suddenly Matt had said, "This sounds crazy, but do you fancy getting out of here? I mean, out of town? Unless you've got lots on this afternoon."

"I do," said Posy. "I have to call off Special Branch."

Matt nodded. "We could buy a picnic?"

"Could we have crisps? Or are you the kind of personal trainer that says no crisps?"

Matt had looked at her with intent in his eyes. "I might *suggest* no cheese and onion."

And Posy's heart had done a little skip, even as she was telling herself sternly that she would love Almaric forever and could never be happy again.

They had taken the train out of Waterloo Station and got out at Edenbridge.

"Have you got walking shoes on?" asked Matt.

Posy had dressed down for a daytime date, she didn't want to look too available, and she associated her daft dresses and high heels with Adam, which made her feel stupid and tarty. She was wearing her favorite soft faded jeans, a floral shirt, and Converse low tops.

"Will these do?" she asked.

"We won't go far."

"Are you going to make me climb a mountain, Matt Farmer?"

"Wouldn't dream of it, mysleazyinternetdate.com . . . uh, sorry, I mean Posy Fairweather."

"Matt?" said Leah on the phone. "Are you still there?"

Where had it gone? thought Matt. Their easy laughs, how relaxed they had felt with each other from the get-go. From the start. When did all that crumble into suspicion, fear, worry? They hadn't been worried then. That day, they hadn't a care in the world.

"Leah," said Matt. "I think I know where she is."

"Oh, great, I'm glad I wasted all this time committing fraud," said Leah.

"Sorry," said Matt.

Leah paused. "She really loved you, you know," she said. "You fixed her. Mostly. It was just a wobble."

"Oh, fuck it," said Matt.

Posy Fairweather is a total idiot with bad hair who
   doesn't contact her friends enough or know when
   she has a good thing and ruins everything and . . .

Chapter Twenty-nine

Posy Fairweather knew exactly why she was at the top of a mountain. She just wasn't entirely sure when she was going to come down. An old university friend had invited her to stay for a few days in Margate, where she'd moved with her new husband, and she had thought, sod it, and agreed. She needed to get away and it didn't really matter where. But then, on the train she'd seen the station sign, *their* station, in front of her eyes and suddenly, without thinking about it, just as the doors were about to close, she'd leaped up and jumped off the carriage. Without, she realized ten seconds later, her phone, which had been lying on the table in front of her.

After the first bubble of panic had passed, she relaxed. So what, it was only her phone. It was never going to ring and if it did it would just be someone annoying, pestering her. OK, she'd miss a few days of work—it hardly mattered, seeing as she'd introduced Gavin and Leah, apparently. Hopefully they'd be so wrapped up in one another they'd hardly notice. Her mum would be glad of the break and Fleur wouldn't care. And Matt

314

wasn't there. He wasn't there, and he wasn't here, on top of their mountain.

"It's not a mountain," he'd announced, as Posy had started complaining, before they'd even got halfway up. "It's a gentle hilly incline."

"And my arse is a banjo," panted Posy. "Can't we catch a cab up?"

"No!" said Matt as she collapsed on a grassy indent, and he sat down beside her. "Look around. Isn't it beautiful?"

Posy looked around. The gentle undulating hills of Kent could be seen for miles; the clouds providing light and shade over the stone-walled fields and dotted farms. Not a single person could be seen, on a warm afternoon in early spring.

Matt waited for the quip. It didn't come. Posy stared and stared, drinking it all in. She filled herself up with it; quite an unusual feeling. She felt peaceful, and happy, and home. Not anxious, or desperate to be someone else, or nervous, or rejected, or strange.

"Yes," she said finally, in a more serious tone. "Yes, it is."

"Good," said Matt, rifling in his rucksack. "You'll be glad I brought this then."

Posy looked around curiously. "Is it crisps?"

"No," said Matt, drawing out the bottle of champagne and packet of plastic cups.

"What! When?"

"I popped into Threshers while you were in the loo."

Matt popped the cork calmly and firmly. Posy looked at him, then they shared a long glance and laughed at the stupid, easy, obviousness of it all.

*

Posy wished she had something to drink now, other than the warm, slightly stale water she'd hauled up the hill, and the dusty flapjacks. She hated flapjacks, why had she even bought them? She looked out over the peaceful fields, a noiseless tractor far far below; little white specks of sheep and the sun filtering here and there through the clouds, throwing one field of yellow rape into shining relief. She closed her eyes. She could almost feel it, a peace, a calm flowing through her once again; her chattering mind—"Does he like me? Do I like him? What's she doing? What's my mum up to? Where's Dad?"—finally shutting up for once. What was it? What was this constant barrage, this constant commentary on her life from her brain, yapping on and on, telling her to compare herself to X, or finish Y, or to look at this guy, or that guy, or this flat, or that job, or that mad twenty-first-century London life. She breathed in, and out again. Calmly.

Back in London, Matt was charging around Roddy's very chic, very minimalist East End flat, trying to grab what he thought he might need. He changed into his hiking boots then remembered how much Posy hated those boots ("When you put on those scary hooves I know I'm going to finish this day under canvas and it makes me *very* unhappy'), and put his trainers on, then he thought he was being silly and he didn't even know where she really was and put his boots back on. Then off again. Maybe shoes? Now he was just being stupid. He grabbed his rucksack and was marching out the door in trainers when the home phone rang. He glanced at it. It didn't even look like a phone, it looked like a weird piece of carved bone. It probably cost hundreds of pounds and he probably shouldn't get his greasy fingerprints on it. It bleeped at him insistently, Melissa's name flashing up on the fancy display. He sighed and tentatively picked it up.

"Hello? Darling? Is that you?"

"Melissa," he said, grudgingly. He glanced at his rucksack. Time was of the essence. If she was there. And she'd probably be elsewhere by now anyway, it was a pointless, stupid exercise. So a few seconds wasn't going to make any difference. Nonetheless, as he sat on the four-thousand-euro couch imported from Italy, he could feel his foot jiggling with tension. She'd offered to help him, but it didn't feel right.

"Are you missing me?" she asked gaily. "New York is super-tedious. I wish you were in my flat. We have so much to discuss."

"Mmmhmm," he said noncommittedly.

"What's up, darling?" Melissa was used to getting her own way. She'd been extremely surprised when this lowly personal trainer hadn't taken her up on her offer to move in and back him, but that only made him more attractive in her eyes. It wouldn't take long.

"I tell you what, when I get back tomorrow night, why don't I sashay over to wherever you're staying and you can give me a long bath and soothe my jet lag away . . . maybe a touch of firm massage?" She gave a low laugh into the phone.

Matt glanced in panic round the flat. Melissa would probably like it here. It was huge and immaculate and posh.

"Uhm, Melissa, I was just leaving—"

"Did you get my email? I know it was a bit . . . saucy."

Matt mumbled an apology. In fact, unusually for him he'd been checking his email every half an hour. But every time

Posy's name hadn't appeared in his inbox, he'd closed it down again without even glancing at anything else.

"So?" she said. She sounded like she was impatiently drumming her fingers on a countertop.

Matt knew he was throwing away a chance at his own business; a hot, sexy affair and even a possible whole new life.

"Can I call you back in ten minutes?" he said.

"Sure, lover," said Melissa languidly. "Ten minutes."

Ten minutes later, Matt had already jogged half the distance to Waterloo Station.

Posy woke up. It had been the calmest, deepest, and most dreamless sleep she'd had in . . . she could hardly remember. She felt wonderfully rested, and although she normally told the time off her watch, she could see by the position of the sun that she'd been out for a couple of hours.

It was funny—although she hadn't done anything except jump off a train and climb a hill, she felt completely different in a way she couldn't put her finger on. Maybe it was just getting away from people for a bit, but she felt changed. Cleansed. Calm. She was going to make her way on to Margate, have fun for a few days and catch up with some people from university—about ninety percent of them had moved to London, had children, then moved down there—relax, take things easy for a little, and if she ever, ever in her life again was lucky enough to meet someone who was funny and sweet and kind, she wouldn't care one whit about his job or his clothes or her mother or her past or her friends. If she ever met another Matt . . . She wouldn't. She knew that much.

She must phone Leah when she got there, let her know what

was up. Mind you, she didn't have her number. She didn't have anyone's number, they were all on her phone. The only number she had in her head was her mother's and, somehow, she didn't feel like calling that right now. She might be healing, but not *that* fast.

No, she would wander down the hill, catch a cab from Tourist Information to the station, and head for Margate. Hang out with Carla for a few days, get her head back together, then she was going to ask Leah if she could move into her flat for a bit. With luck, if Gavin was installed in Elephant and Castle, Leah would spend all her time there and she could enjoy Leah's art books and exotic teas and cute little roof terrace all on her own. Yes, that was definitely a very good idea. And then she could look to the rest of her life—there were plenty of bold, happy women in their thirties without men. Yeah.

Matt jumped off the train at Crockham Hill, glad he'd plumped for the trainers in the end; they gave him added speed over the terrain. The champagne he'd bought chinked in his rucksack. She had to be here, he thought fiercely. She had to be, as if he could make it so by force of will. But where else could she be? If she wasn't at her mum's, and she wasn't with her friends . . . OK, there were maybe a thousand or so places she could be. But if there was to be any hope for them, if what Leah had said were true; if, as he could just about get his head round, she really had tracked down her exes simply to clarify her true faith in him . . . *if* any of that were the case, there was only one place to be. He hoped she was wearing sensible shoes.

Posy headed down to the little pay phone situated at the bottom of the hill, clutching the card for the local cab firm in her pocket. She could head straight back to the train station. And while she was waiting she could take one last look around, drink in the scenery. This place wouldn't hold sad memories, she decided. Just happy ones, hopefully.

"Forty minutes for a cab? Really?" said Posy. She was disappointed, which she realized on some level must be her non-Zen self coming back; she was impatient to move on and keep going. She turned and glanced for the last time at Crockham Hill. She didn't think she'd be coming here again.

"Forty minutes? *Fuck*," said Matt, listening to the tannoy announcement about the expected delay to the train, as it sat, hardly any distance from Crockham Hill station. If he could have jumped out of the window he would have, but it was a new train and everything was sealed shut. He sat there, drumming his fingers with frustration. Would she still be there? What would he do if she wasn't? No, she would be. She would be. He had to believe that.

Posy sat with her head against the window of the cab, dreamily looking out at nothing. The weather had come in again, the clouds turning gray in moments and now fat droplets of spring rain were hitting the windows. It gave her a sweet sense of melancholy that didn't make her feel unhappy. A crazy jogger was going the other way—what on earth was he thinking of in this weather? Who went for a run when it started to rain? She closed her eyes. maybe she could sleep on the train.

*

Matt tore along past the few cars that dotted the road—there was even a cab, he wouldn't have thought there would be cabs out here—as the rain came down heavier and heavier. Oh, this was terrible, there would never be anyone on the hill, especially not someone as weather-phobic as Posy. He was going to get cold and wet and . . . hang on, why *was* there a cab out here?

Who did that jogger remind her of? It was funny, really.

What way had it gone? There was only one road, wasn't there?

"STOP THE CAB!" screamed Posy.

"You what?" said the cabbie, who was crawling through the driving rain. "We're in the middle of bloody nowhere."

"That's *exactly* where I want to be," said Posy.

The mud churned over Matt's trainers. He was being an idiot. This was even stupider than the last stupid thing he'd done, which was get on the train, probably. She wasn't in that cab. He stood, undecided, on the road. To go back or not to go back? The lights were vanishing over a lift in the road. When, suddenly, he saw the brake lights go on, and the cab slow to a halt.

He stayed where he was, let her walk to him. She was wearing the same Converse shoes, damned useless for climbing a hill, and even worse for climbing a hill in the wet. The rain was tearing down now, they were both absolutely plastered in water. The cab sat for a second, then took off, obviously dismissing them both as lunatics.

Posy pushed back her sodden hair from her face and peered

through the downpour. There he was. Holding out his hand. His big, strong hand. Everything, really, when it came down to it. Everything she needed. A hand when she was stuck; a smile when she came home sad. Compatibility, suitability, some stupid checklist that she'd been carrying around in her head, as if by ticking off a load of boxes she would find the man who wouldn't make her feel the way her father did—had done, for that was in the past now too. Someone who wasn't about fixing her past; someone who was there to go forward into the future. Someone who was right there in front of her. Who wasn't X or Y, who didn't contain certain qualities that she'd made up out of her head and decided were necessary. Someone who wasn't perfect—of course he wasn't. Thank God, she certainly wasn't. She glanced down. Why wasn't she moving? Then she realized that her shoes were piled high with mud and she was stuck firmly to the ground. Matt was staring at her incredulously.

"Are you stuck?" he asked, a smile twitching his lips. In fact, he was so hopelessly, totally relieved it was all he could do not to cry.

Posy, lip wobbling, did her best to grin at him.

"I think," she said, her voice trembling, "I think that I am stuck. That without you . . . I can't get anywhere."

Then she dissolved into tears.

"Hang on, girl, hang on," said Matt, jogging lightly over to her.

Ankle-deep in mud, Matt was even taller over her; somehow even stronger and more masculine-feeling than before. Posy felt a huge wave crashing over her, a relief and joy so incredibly strong it was entirely overwhelming. She collapsed, weeping on his chest.

"No!" said Matt. "Please! Be happy, not sad! Please . . ." He took a breath. "All I want, Posy, all I've ever wanted—it's not a model, or a fitness freak, or anybody else . . . I just wanted you to be happy."

Posy sniffled loudly and messily. She'd never quite got the hang of pretty crying.

"Because, for some reason, whenever you are happy, I'm happy too. I don't know why. So don't bring me down."

"I'm . . . not . . . sad," choked out Posy.

"You could have fooled me," said Matt, wishing he'd thought to put a tissue in his bag. Although it was so wet.

"Do you want to wipe your nose on my fleece?"

"Uhm, not really."

"Well, the thing is, if you don't wipe your nose somewhere, I don't know how I'm going to kiss you."

"If you really loved me you'd manage it, snot and all."

"You think?" said Matt, dropping his head.

"No! NO! Leave me alone—hang on, I'll sort it out." Posy turned round and frantically rubbed her face in the rain.

"Are you still having a blub?"

"Don't you *ever* cry?"

"Never."

She tilted her face up to his.

"De-snotted?" he asked.

"I think so. There might just be a little bit . . ."

But he was already kissing her, hard, and full-on, through the mud and the cascading rain.

They stopped when the rain did. Matt glanced down. Posy's shoes had set solid. Matt shook his head.

"What are you like?" he said.

"Ecstatic."

"Come on, take them off."

And he lifted her back on to a verge, then threw down the waterproof cover he'd had in his backpack.

"Dib dib dib," said Posy.

"Shut up, you," warned Matt, as he deposited her on it.

Then he withdrew the chilled bottle of champagne. Posy had a sharp intake of breath.

"Ooh," she said. "How did you know I was here?"

"I didn't," said Matt simply. "I just really really hoped you were. Then I figured that if you weren't, there'd be some girl that would be happy to see a bottle of champagne, and she'd do."

Posy smiled, then waited. Patiently, without worry, without doubts, or second thoughts, or thinking more about anyone else in the world, as Matt looked back, rummaging awkwardly in the bottom of his rucksack. Then he found what he was looking for and knelt down, carefully making sure his knee was on the edge of the waterproof and not the grass.

"Posy," he said, again. She held her breath, not wanting to ruin the moment by making smart remarks or, in fact, saying anything at all.

"Posy. *Please please please, let me, let me, let me, let me get what I want this time.*"

She looked him straight in the eye and without a doubt in her mind, or a thought in her head beyond happiness, acceptance, joy, and relief, she said: "YES!"

Posy is unutterably overjoyed.
Matt is glad to be back in his own bed.

Chapter Thirty

"Are you totally, absolutely sure?" asked Posy. "Because I'm definitely having my doubts."

"Shut up," said Leah. "It'll be gorgeous. Trust me."

"I don't trust anyone who wears as many ostrich feathers as you do."

"That's because you don't understand fashion."

"I'm anti-fashion. I'm going to do what Matt does and live in trackie bottoms for the rest of my life."

"Not if you want to see me again, you aren't. And I'm your head bridesmaid, so I get to choose."

"That's not how it works!"

"Yes, it is. That is exactly how it works."

"I'm sure it's not."

"Ssh," said Leah, her mouth full of pins.

"Well, when I am *your* head bridesmaid, I am putting you in such a great big white meringue that you'll need someone to help you get to the toilet."

"Be quiet."

"And the top will be a strapless bodice completely encrusted with Swarovski crystals."

"Shut up."

"And a huge pointy tiara . . . OWW!"

"Don't argue with the person with the pins."

Posy examined herself in the mirror. In fact, although it was a bit avant-garde, her Leah-designed wedding dress—a starkly simple, boat-necked square top in cream jersey, which hugged her waist then became a deconstructed knot of ruffles and ribbon in the skirt—made her look slender and elegant, somehow untouchable and, well, she had to admit it, it was lovely. She adored it.

"It won't be long anyway," she said.

"Woan be long what?" mumbled Leah through the pins.

"Till it's you and Gavin."

Leah straightened up. "Well, for starters we'd have to wait for his divorce to come through, and there's his kids to think of, and he'd have to want to get married and ask me and every-thing . . ."

"Neh, it'll happen," said Posy.

"You reckon?" said Leah, smiling.

"Yes. Work is totally brilliant, he just swans around in a daze grinning all the time and singing happy songs. Me and Margie just take huge lunches."

"Does she still talk about Almaric all the time?"

"Yes. I see it as doing community service. But I'm signing her up for some online dating."

"You're kidding."

"No, I'm not. Through Facebook. There's a group called 'Ifancywomenwithcats.'"

Leah shook her head. "Gosh."

The door of the hotel room banged open and Fleur entered.

"What's going on? Can I get drunk yet?" She flumped down on the bed. "Sis, I've decided. I don't want to wear that bridesmaid's dress."

Leah sniffed pointedly.

"Fleur, could you not have let us know more than an hour in advance?" said Posy. She wasn't going to get upset with her sister. She wasn't going to get upset with anyone, not even her mother.

It had been a very quiet chat, in the end. Posy had explained, without losing her rag, for once, that she and Matt were getting married regardless of what anyone thought; that her father, Marian, and Jason would certainly be there (subject to Jason being arsed, of course—he was delicate), and she was welcome to attend or not depending on her personal beliefs.

And she and her mother had met, again, formally and cordially for lunch, and there had been no shouting, but her mother had, looking her straight in the eye, apologized. Explained she had meant well but that she had let her personal disappointments creep in and that she hoped Posy understood. And Posy was so happy and delighted with everything in the world, she'd said that she did indeed understand and that in fact if her mother hadn't told her all those mad lies she might not be as happy now, which they both realized was a bit of a stretch, but was going to have to do. For now. She'd worry about the grandkids later.

Jonquil was currently sitting in the hotel lobby, sipping tea and looking so frightening that none of Matt's friendly relations dared to approach her.

"See, that's the thing, sis," Fleur was explaining, "I *loved* the dress. It's totally amazing and everything."

Leah stopped bristling.

"So I thought I'd wear it out on the town, yeah? So I wore it last night. And, anyway, to cut a very very long story short, it slightly, like, got taken off with someone's teeth."

Leah and Posy rolled their eyes.

"Well, thanks, Fleur," said Posy.

"I'll pay you back," said Fleur.

"With what?" said Leah and Posy in unison.

"Aha!" said Fleur. "Mum's agreed to take me on in partnership. I'm going to be a psychotherapist too!"

Both the girls stared at her. Fleur stared back complacently.

"What?"

"Spell it," growled Posy.

"What?"

"Can you spell psychotherapy?"

"While you're getting into this," said Leah, "the sample I brought in case you did exactly what you did actually do . . ."

Fleur tutted as she wrestled herself into it. "It's crap being sample size."

Posy and Leah exchanged glances.

"Maybe it was just me doing the learning this year," mused Posy.

"What? What are you all talking about? You're all *so* boring," said Fleur, stomping off.

It was only a short aisle down Marylebone Registry Office, even though the room itself was very beautiful, and Posy was determined to savor it for as long as she could.

"I may have been engaged twice," she'd said the week before, "but I'm only getting married once."

"I am *incredibly* glad to hear it," Matt had said, pulling her back to his warm, muscled body. He had called Melissa, who hadn't taken it personally, but had moved gyms. After he'd explained to Posy his plan to finance his business ("In sex?" she'd asked, and he'd reassured her for the final time, no), they had started looking for financiers together and it looked like they'd found someone. It was very exciting.

"It is nice—horrible, but a bit nice," Posy had mused, thinking about Melissa. "To have the chance to feel sorry for someone for once, rather than everyone feeling totally sorry for me all the time."

"I wouldn't feel sorry for Melissa," Matt had said. "She makes more in a year than we will probably make in our entire lives."

"Yes, but I'm sure she's terrible in bed."

"I wouldn't know."

"I'm kidding! Hilariously! Kidding! Too soon?"

"Too soon," Matt had agreed, taking her in his arms.

And now here was the room, packed with people. Her father looked absolutely fit to burst with pride as he proffered her his arm.

"I dreamed one day of doing this," he'd told her that morning, as he'd put a new chunky gold necklace round her neck, which had made Leah blanch with horror but didn't bother Posy because of what it meant. "Your mum told me over her dead body it would ever happen with either of you."

They peered through the doors to the front row where her mother was standing, looking chic, tall, and cross.

"I'm not married yet," whispered Posy. "Look out for concealed weapons." Her father squeezed her arm.

"You look beautiful. Weird, but beautiful."

"I will take that as my motto."

The music struck up, the swooning opening chords to "How Soon Is Now?" Posy, having not been quite sure exactly how she would feel at this moment, suddenly found her mouth cracking open in a huge, daft smile. It didn't go with the wonderful, austere frock, but it was completely genuine and utterly uncontrollable and she didn't even try to stop it.

The room was pink and green and beautifully decorated—Paul McCartney had got married here, and Liam Gallagher. And her. She glanced around. There were Chris and Elspeth, Elspeth's belly taking up a seat and a half—she must be ready to pop at any moment. Chris seemed to have got larger too, as if in sympathy. How on earth they got onto that barge she had no idea.

And was that Adam wearing sunglasses *indoors*? In *August*? He was sitting next to a very young blonde in a cerise minidress whose mouth was hanging open. She looked incredibly bored already, just wait till she got to the speeches. Almaric and his bride had sent apologies, which was a huge relief to Posy. She didn't think it was entirely beyond Sukie to body-charge her up the aisle, just so she could know what it felt like. Almaric, though, had sent her the most beautiful vase—twisted and fragile like the stem of a rosebush with, carefully inscribed on the bottom, *For posies for Posy, with my greatest esteem and regard, Almaric Grunt.*

"His surname is GRUNT?" Matt had asked in consternation.

"Uh, yeah. That's why he had such a pretty first name, I think," said Posy.

"You wanted to be Mrs. Grunt?!"

"Only when I was an idiot. Can I be Mrs. Farmer, please?"

"Well, you'd never have accidentally picked him up on the internet."

"No. Please can I be Mrs. Farmer?"

"Maybe. Except when you're misbehaving, in which case I reserve the right to call you Mrs. Grunt."

Gavin was near the front with the youngest of his children, who was wearing a princess fairy dress and looking delighted, and sitting next to Margie, as Leah was on bridesmaiding duties.

"You're going to do it, after all," he'd said, when she'd gone to explain to him, at some length, why even though she'd used up every drop of her annual leave, and then some, haring up and down the country that year, could she please have some more to do what she had originally planned to do in the first place and get married and go on honeymoon?

"I know," she'd said. "Are you going to try and dissuade me as well?"

"Actually," Gavin had said, "funnily enough, I don't feel so bad about marriage anymore."

"Is that so?" Posy has asked mischievously. "Well, I am *so* happy that you're happy."

"Hmm. Is this some terrible thieving annual-leave flattery?"

"Yes," Posy had said. "But I *am* happy that you're happy."

Marian and Jason were on the end of the front row, waving furiously. Marian was wreathed in smiles. Jason had some ketchup on his top lip. And there, at the end, was her mother, turning round with a fixed, bright red-lipsticked smile on her face.

Matt stood, with his brother next to him, smart in a gray suit at the end of the aisle (she'd managed to talk him out of his "dress trainers'). He wasn't crying, or joking, or looking nervous. He looked completely and utterly confident, capable, strong—her man. Posy hadn't thought her smile could get any wider, but it did. He grinned at her, and gave her a single wink. Posy advanced toward him, the registrar smiling patiently. Just as she got up there, though, she felt compelled to move. Just for a second, she slipped out of her father's arm and moved to the right, toward the front of the pew. She kissed her mother full on the cheek.

"I love you," she said. Her mother bit her lip, hard, and brought up her long thin hand to cup Posy's chin.

"I love you too," she whispered, the words unusual in her mouth. "I love you too. And I wish you so much happiness."

Posy blinked once or twice then turned back again, toward Matt, who was patiently and calmly holding out his arm.

Posy Farmer has changed her status.
Comment: Like.
172 people like this.

Epilogue

Scotland, 2015

Posy sat fiddling with the damn fire again. Aelthred, whose bright red hair echoed her father's so much, sat next to her.

"It's very cold, Mummy," she said.

"It is, my sweet," said Posy, pulling her up into her warm jumper. "That's because your father is out chopping down the wood, then he will come back and build up the fire and our cottage will be all warm and cozy."

"Goody! Goody! Goody!" shouted Aelthred. "It's the coziest place in the whole world!"

Posy hugged her knees. She'd put on so much weight, but at least it kept her warm. If only Chris would let her get a television. Or go to the cinema. Or take her out. Or let her buy cloth instead of suggesting she spin it.

"Mummy?" said Aelthred sleepily as she cozied up in her mother's comfortable folds. "Can we go to the manure heap tomorrow?"

"Hmm, a special treat, eh?" said Posy, sighing.

"It's nice to feel cozy and safe, isn't it?" said Aelthred.

"Is it?" said Posy. "I suppose."

Monaco, 2015

"Well, would you like that new express tummy tuck or not?"

"Yes. Why not?" said Posy. "After six kids, it's probably worth getting some work done."

"And so worth having the kids, don't you think?"

"Oh yes," said Posy dreamily, staring into Adam's eyes. "You know, darling, I never ever thought us getting married and becoming super-rich could possibly have worked out so well."

"You never know how people change," said Adam. "Although obviously it's great that I've still stayed in shape and everything and am such a reformed character."

"It *is*," said Posy. "Shall we take the yacht out after lunch?"

"Let's."

Wales, 2015
Extract from the *Welsh Daily Argus*:

Posy Grunt, 38, widow of the famous potter Almaric Grunt, today faced up to reports of the potter's womanizing ways as the dispute over his inheritance hit Cardiff County court.

The couple, who had no children, endured a famously boozy and tempestuous marriage before Grunt, 38, drove his car off a cliff following a night-time binge.

"I loved my husband very much," the widow—Grunt's second wife, after his first, Sukie Grunt, had run away to join the circus—said, leaving court. "The fact that he was followed everywhere by a bunch of floozies wasn't really his fault. He was terribly attractive."

Felicia Thomas, 24, who was with Grunt the night he died, vigorously denied the allegation. "Almaric understood the real me," she insisted. "He could look into your soul."

"He could look into your knickers!" Mrs. Grunt shouted on the courtroom steps, before being led away by her best friends, Gavin and Leah O'Hanrahan, 38.

London, 2015

"It's your turn. You bred a hyperactive climbing monkey, you get up for him."

"You do it, though."

"No, you do it."

"Please. I will love you forever and make you some banana bread."

"Banana bread? What about real cake?"

"There's fiber in banana bread, Posy."

"Yes, that will persuade me to get up at five-thirty. Fiber."

"He's crying very loudly."

"I know. Does it appeal to your paternal instincts?"

"OK, let's say one-two-three and we'll both get up."

"I love your motivational attitude."

"One, two, three . . ."

"You didn't get up!"

"Neither did you!"

"Mamma? Dadda?"

"Come in, sweetheart. Into the bed?"

"Dus."

"Now, Rory, let me teach you some exercises."

"Now, Rory, would you like to cuddle up and have some extra sleep and relaxation?"

"Then we'll get up and have some muesli?"

"With Coco Pops sprinkled on the top. And we'll read maga-zines."

"Then you can come help Daddy train for his triathalon."

"Then come back and watch telly."

Matt looked across the pillow and smiled. "It'll be a lovely day."

"Oh yes," said Posy. "I think it will."

ALSO BY JENNY COLGAN

THE GOOD, THE BAD, AND THE DUMPED

WEST END GIRLS

CHRISTMAS AT THE ISLAND HOTEL

500 MILES FROM YOU

WHERE HAVE ALL THE BOYS GONE?

DIAMONDS ARE A GIRL'S BEST FRIEND

AMANDA'S WEDDING

MY VERY '90S ROMANCE

THE BOOKSHOP ON THE SHORE

CHRISTMAS ON THE ISLAND

THE ENDLESS BEACH

CHRISTMAS AT LITTLE
BEACH STREET BAKERY

THE CAFÉ BY THE SEA

THE BOOKSHOP ON THE CORNER

SUMMER AT LITTLE BEACH
STREET BAKERY

LITTLE BEACH STREET BAKERY

THE CHRISTMAS SURPRISE

CHRISTMAS AT ROSIE HOPKINS'
SWEETSHOP

CHRISTMAS AT THE CUPCAKE CAFÉ

WWW.JENNYCOLGAN.COM